BENT WINGED ANGEL

HANNAH SHIELD

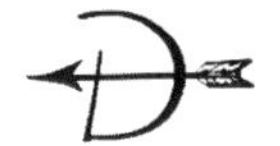

BENT WINGED ANGEL (Last Refuge Protectors Book 2)

Cover Photography: Wander Aguiar

Cover Design: Angela Haddon

Produced by Diana Road Books

BENT WINGED ANGEL

Last Refuge #2

Prologue

Scarlett
Thirteen Years Ago

"SERENITY, your first mother is calling for you."

Ugh, I thought. *Why?*

"Coming."

I wiped the nose of the toddler I was holding, a two-year-old named Virtue. "They mean *Mercy* is calling," I whispered in her tiny ear. "But Mercy's not my mother. And she's not merciful, either." I grinned at my stupid joke, and Virtue grinned back. She was always smiling. Except when she was tired. Then she was a terror.

"Serenity," an impatient voice said, and I sighed.

"I'll see you later, sugar." I set Virtue in front of a toy train and got up, rushing to the door before the little girl started to whine. A few other kids looked up from playing. I patted their heads as I left. "Be back soon."

Outside, I walked across the grass to my father's house. Mercy was waiting for me in the living room. Mercy never smiled, at least not at me. Her eye roved critically over my dress, probably picking out flaws as she went. I stood up straight and proud. She didn't like that either.

"I have news," Mercy said without preamble. Blunt as always. "Dawson Witkins has chosen you."

I started coughing. Choking on nothing but air. "What? *Why?*"

"I've asked myself the same. The first son of an elder? For the likes of *you*? You should be a fourth wife, like your mother. Not a wife to someone like Dawson. Certainly not his second."

"But—"

"Quiet, Serenity. Hold your tongue." Her nose wrinkled as her critical gaze moved over me. "It's that red hair of yours. That figure. It's not proper."

How could I help my figure? I held back my eye roll. That would've earned me a slap.

"Tomorrow, we'll start on your wedding clothes. Dawson will want to see you in the morning to confirm your betrothal. So make sure you're ready."

Tomorrow morning.

My plan of escape wasn't nearly finished. But I couldn't meet with Dawson tomorrow. He was awful. Everyone knew that. He was the kind of man who took liberties. And *marry him*? Heck no. Not in a trillion years.

That meant I had to run. And it had to be tonight.

I snuck out of my window and climbed down the uneven bricks. I had them memorized by now. My home-sewn bag was strapped across my torso over my dress. It held my father's compass. A water bottle. An old map of Hartley County I'd found in the trash. Food, clothes, other things I might need.

I didn't know much of the world outside Paradise Ranch. Not firsthand. But the boys were allowed into Creekview, and they brought things back. I'd seen books and magazines. Most people didn't live like we did.

The elders' sermons told us we were blessed to be separated from the sinful outside world. But I refused to believe it. Was it a blessing for my mother to have no choice about her life? Or for me to have no choice in mine? Outside Paradise Ranch, girls my age went to school in big buildings with computers. They went to dances. They played sports. They could talk to boys freely. Have boys as friends.

They didn't have to marry gross men like Dawson Witkins. Much less do what it took to carry their children.

I reached the lake and went to our spot. Kenny was already there. He was usually the first there on the nights we met. "I heard," he said, not smiling. "Everyone was talking about it at the bachelor house. My brother…"

"Mercy told me." I sat on a rock beside him. The lake reflected the moon, breaking it up into pieces. "Dawson wants to see me in the morning."

"It's not *fucking fair*."

Kenny was my closest friend. He had been since we were little, back when we'd played together. But even though we weren't allowed to see each other anymore, we'd found ways to get around that rule. Like meeting here by Paradise Lake a few times a week.

Kenny was also Dawson's younger brother. He knew what Dawson was like.

"You brought your bag," he said. "Does that mean…"

"It has to be tonight."

"Shit. You're right. But I'm not ready. I thought we'd have more time. And if they'd have let me choose you instead…"

"I know." Then maybe we wouldn't have needed to leave at all. The idea of marrying Kenny wasn't horrible. But I didn't want to marry *anyone*. I wanted school and books. I wanted a life that belonged only to me.

My friend looked at me, seeming to gather himself up. Kenny was two years older than me, but I'd never felt it until now. "Then we'll leave. I'm going to take care of you. I promise."

I hugged him. "Thank you for coming with me."

"If we get separated for any reason, meet me in Creekview. There's a cafe with a blue door."

I thought we should just leave now with what I had. But Kenny insisted on going back for his things. I waited there by the lake. The night was quiet except for insects. The faint splash of something in the water. Ripples in the moonlight.

More than anything, I wished I could've said goodbye to my mom. My *real* mom. But she would understand why I'd left.

I had so many plans for our new life. Kenny and I would have to find a place to live. Maybe work to pay our way first, and then go back to school for diplomas later. I'd read a book where someone did that. But I wanted a new name for myself. I hated the named Serenity. I never felt serene.

I liked Scarlett. It was a color, but it also felt like an emotion. Something bold and loud and unafraid.

Kenny was taking a long time. What was he doing? *He'd better not be bringing his rock collection,* I thought. For seventeen, he could be such a little boy sometimes.

Finally, I heard his footsteps on the path. But I didn't suspect anything was wrong until I heard his voice.

"Serenity? Hey, where are you?"

That didn't make any sense. He knew exactly where I was. In our usual meeting place. And his voice had wavered on my name.

I started backing away.

Then he shouted, "They're coming. *Run*."

I ran.

Voices followed me into the woods. Harsh yells. Brush being trampled. *Gunshots.* I ran so hard that tears burned in my eyes and my lungs ached. Branches scraped my arms and face. I tripped again and again. My heart felt like it would burst. But even then, I didn't stop.

Another gunshot rang out far behind me, echoing across the valley.

CHAPTER ONE
Scarlett

IT WAS one of those days that the sun seemed to shine a little brighter. No clouds dared to block the light, and Main Street's windows sparkled. Days like this, I couldn't believe how lucky I was to live in Hartley.

This date, especially.

Thirteen years, I thought, marveling at the number. Sure, it went up every year. Like clockwork, right? But I always had to stop and give this anniversary the respect it was due.

Thirteen years since I'd arrived in this town. Since I had escaped.

I filled my lungs with warm summer air and smiled to myself as I walked toward Jessi's Diner. Through the big glass windows, it looked like the booths were packed. The bar counter only had a couple of stools open, and I recognized less than half the people here. Last winter, this place had been deserted except for my best friend, laboring in the kitchen all by herself. Incredible how much could change in so little time. A truth I knew well.

The bell on the door jingled as the door opened. "Going in, Miss Scarlett?" asked the woman who owned the local grocery. She was on her way out.

I lifted my chin and smiled. "Thank you, hon. Beautiful day, isn't it?"

Humming "Independence Day" by Martina McBride, I made my way to an empty stool and sat, dropping my backpack at my feet. Jessi was helping another customer, but she nodded hello at me, and I waved back. Her boyfriend, Aiden, was in the open kitchen cooking something in a pan, tossing its contents up and down like a fancy chef from TV. He gave me a quick salute.

Jessi put in the orders she had been taking, and Aiden's face lit up as they spoke quietly together.

Those two. Ugh, they were too cute.

I couldn't be happier for Jessi that she had found the right guy. Not just someone to look out for her, but to make her happier than I'd ever seen her before. Back in January, Aiden had gotten stuck in Hartley during a snowstorm. He'd promptly fallen for Jessi and uprooted his entire life to be with her. They had the kind of sweet love story that I'd thought was only real in books and movies. Just recently, they'd moved in together and were renovating their apartment. They worked every day side by side.

If you asked me, that was a *lot* of togetherness.

I would've settled for a sexy fling. It had been a while for me. A long while. A few months back, a certain someone had caught my eye. Tall, tan, mysterious… But Trace Novo didn't seem to have the slightest interest in me.

Not like I was pining over the man or anything.

All the same, I glanced around the diner quickly, just in case Jessi's brother was here. There was no sign of Trace. I couldn't decide whether to be disappointed or relieved.

Jessi plunked a coffee mug in front of me and filled it to the brim. "Here for lunch?" she asked, adding a hefty dose of sugar from the dispenser. My best friend knew what I liked.

"Nah, just the coffee is perfect." I wrapped my hands around the mug and inhaled the scent.

"What are you up to today?" Jessi asked casually. "Work?"

"I took the day off." I'd told her that already, but I couldn't blame her for forgetting. The woman had enough projects. From the circles under Jessi's eyes, I guessed that she could use a day off of work, too. Unless Aiden had just been keeping her up late with all that lovin'.

Jessi tapped her chin. "Oh wait. *Now* I remember." Smiling, she reached beneath the counter and produced a gift bag with a flourish. "Happy Independence Day."

A couple of people glanced over, probably confused because this was August, not July. My chest was warm as I looked inside the bag. There was a paperback novel and a gift card for the new bookstore that had opened down the street. "You sneaky minx. This is so sweet. You shouldn't have."

"It's a big day for you," she said softly, so nobody else would hear.

"It is." I looked down at the paperback. It was a small-town romance from an author I'd been eying the last time Jessi and I were at the bookstore. A lump bunched in my throat. "Thank you."

"What are best friends for? It's the least I can do, considering all you've done for me."

I didn't talk about my childhood much. I preferred to focus on the here and now. But in the last seven or so months since we'd become closer, it had been amazing to watch Jessi heal from her past. Both of us had escaped from men who'd wanted to control us, to destroy every ounce of our free will and independent spirit. I'd never had a friend like her before. Someone who could understand those things about my past, even if she didn't know the worst details.

Today, I was finally ready to share my own story.

"I was hoping we could talk," I said.

Jessi reached across the counter for my hand. "I can take a break soon and have Aiden cover for me, if you can wait?"

"Of course I can."

"Hold that thought. I'll be back in a bit."

While I waited, I snapped a quick photo of the diner and posted it to my Instagram page. I liked to cross-promote with Jessi's place on my social media. Jessi and I were both well known in Hartley for our sweet creations. I ran Scarlett's Sweet Shop further down Main Street.

Our little town had been getting more media attention lately because of the scandals and upheavals that had taken place last winter. It wasn't an ideal way to gain foot traffic, but thankfully, the worst of that mess had died down. The increase in tourism had been great, despite the weekend crowds that had the old-timers complaining.

If only I could find a new handsome face to overshadow someone else in my mind. No such luck yet.

After the lunch rush, Jessi took off her apron, nodding at me. "Come around back."

We went into her minuscule office. It didn't fit much except a small desk and her cash safe. I perched on the desktop, and Jessi closed the door, sagging against it. She gave me a tired smile.

"Has Aiden been keeping you up late?" I asked.

She waved a hand. "Oh, I'm just stressed. We had a little hitch in our financing for Last Refuge." The concern in her eyes told me it wasn't such a *little* hitch. No wonder she was stressed. They were supposed to break ground in a few weeks.

The Last Refuge Inn & Tavern was Jessi's dream. She and Aiden wanted to convert an old ranch into a hotel and restaurant. And she would devote some of the lodging to a shelter for anyone who needed help and had nowhere else to turn.

Aiden was planning something else for Last Refuge, too.

A team of ex-military guys called the Last Refuge Protectors. But Jessi had asked me to keep it quiet because Aiden hadn't told Trace yet. As if *I* would tell Trace. The man had barely spoken to me in months.

"What's the financing hitch?" I asked.

"It's not important right now. Today is about *you*. You wanted to talk?"

I nodded. "I was hoping you'd be up for a hike. I brought snacks. Both salty and sweet, of course. I've even got a playlist cued up on my phone. Cheesy love songs to hike to. We could hang out." And I could tell her my story, because it was a long one.

"A hike would be great. Let me just—" Then her face fell. "Dammit, Aiden and I have a call with the bank in half an hour."

"That *little* financing hitch?"

She groaned. "This sucks. I hate financing."

It did suck. But I hid my disappointment. This wasn't Jessi's fault. And besides, she was so cute when she pouted, especially because she didn't do it often. How could I possibly be mad at her? "We'll hike another time, sugar. It's not a big deal."

"It *is* a big deal. You wanted to talk. We could do that now, even without the hike."

"Another time," I said again. This story would need more than half an hour.

"What about tonight? I want to celebrate your day with you."

"Tonight, I want you to rest. You're working yourself too hard. You and I will celebrate later. How about in three weeks, after the ground-breaking on Last Refuge? The financing will work out. I have faith in you."

"Now you're comforting me! Today is supposed to be about you." She stood up straighter, looking determined.

"You should still have your hike. Trace could go with you. He was around here somewhere just this morning."

My skin tingled at the thought of her older brother.

I'd had a little *something* for Trace when he'd first shown up in town. From the moment I'd seen him, I'd wanted to know his story. Trace had been running from something. I knew what that looked like. He had strolled into Hartley with a limp in his gait. A ratty backpack, apparently the sum total of all his possessions, having left everything else behind. His unruly hair, lean muscles, and most of all, those piercing dark blue eyes. Same shade as Jessi's, yet Trace had a thousand-yard stare that said he'd seen more than anybody should in one lifetime.

And the way he'd stepped in when Aiden and Jessi needed backup? He was the perfect mixture of sexy, mysterious, and dangerous. What girl could resist? I would've been up for a casual arrangement. That was the only kind of relationship I ever had. The only kind my heart would allow after my history.

Trace had stayed at my place one night just after he'd arrived in January, and I'd behaved myself. Nothing spicy had happened. In fact, Trace hadn't said much to me that evening at all. He'd been all dour and inscrutable. But I'd thought we had a decent start at a friendship. We'd made a great team, too. Helping Jessi and Aiden to save the day.

But since then, he'd distanced himself. It was clear that he wanted nothing more to do with me, not even being friends. I'd tried not to take it personally. But Trace's indifference still felt like a rejection.

Get over it, girl, I told myself. Not my job to figure that man out.

"I don't need a pity playmate. I can hike on my own." I picked up my backpack. Jessi frowned at me, so I insisted again, "I will be *fine*."

"At least tell me where you're hiking. And text me when you're home."

"Yes, ma'am. I'm just taking the trail up to Painter's Peak."

"What if a bear eats you?"

I laughed and patted my backpack. "I'm well prepared. I've got bear spray and everything." The can hung from a carabiner on my pack.

"Just be careful." She pulled me into a hug. "Love you."

"I know, hon. Love you too."

As I left the diner, my phone chimed with a new notification from Instagram. I tugged out my device and thumbed to the app. There was a new comment on my Insta account. The post I'd made earlier.

But as I read the comment, the contents of my stomach reared into my throat, and the rest of me went ice cold.

Thirteen years, Serenity. Do you think about the promises you broke? The people you betrayed and left behind? Women like you should be PUNISHED. Someday soon, you will be.

"What the hell?" I murmured aloud.

I clicked to the sender's account. It was anonymous. No followers or posts.

But the sender had called me Serenity.

My chest tightened, and I couldn't fill my lungs all the way. My eyes moved to the south, toward the mountain pass that led to where I'd grown up. The pass wasn't visible from here. Yet that part of the sky seemed to have a permanent shadow hanging over it.

Or maybe that was just me. My past weighing over my mind. Today especially.

I'd always known someone from the compound might

find me. Those first few years, I'd been terrified of it. After all, I hadn't gone very far. I was almost hiding in plain view. But with each passing year, it had seemed less and less likely. Why would they care about me any more? I'd assumed they had forgotten about me a long time ago.

But this person knew I was Serenity. Would see from my Instagram page that I lived in Hartley. And they wanted me to be afraid.

Was it just meant to freak me out? Was it an actual threat?

I moved around the side of the building to the alley, just to catch my breath. I was a grown woman now. Not a teen runaway who was terrified of the outside world, yet even more terrified of the home she'd left behind.

Then I *felt* someone else there. A shadow loomed behind me. The hairs on my arms rose.

I spun around, grabbing for my bear spray as a tall form stepped out into the open. Lightning fast, he lunged at me. Plucked the can from my grip. Pinned me up against the side of the building.

I opened my mouth, dragging in another breath to scream.

"*Scarlett*, it's just me."

I saw dark blue. The piercing gaze that I hadn't been able to get out of my mind for months now.

Jessi's brother.

Trace Novo.

CHAPTER TWO

Trace

"SCARLETT," I said. "It's just me."

I'd pinned her up against the wall of the diner. She was struggling, pupils blown wide with panic. Nearly got me with that bear spray, too. She wasn't seeing me. But finally, recognition seemed to dawn. Good thing, because the last thing I'd wanted to do was hurt her.

"Trace?"

"Are you calm now?" I asked.

Scarlett's eyes narrowed. Then she flattened her palms on my chest and pushed. She didn't have a prayer in the world of moving me if I chose not to move, but I took mercy on her and stepped back.

"What're you thinking, sneaking up on me?" she demanded. "I could've maced you!"

"I'm all in favor of you defending yourself. But if you mace random people in the diner parking lot at ten in the morning, Sheriff Owen might have questions."

Plus, if I'd been sneaking up on her, I would've been more strategic than that.

I held out the can of spray, and she snatched it. I bent to

pick up the phone she'd dropped, and she grabbed that from my hand too.

"What's got you so upset?" I asked.

Her cheeks colored. "You just surprised me."

"You were looking at your phone. Whatever you saw got you riled up."

There was that flash of fear again. Then her chin lifted defiantly. "You're really something, Novo. You've avoided me for months. And now you suddenly want to talk?"

"I prefer to keep to myself. It's nothing personal." Even so, a sliver of guilt cut through me. Small but sharp. I had avoided her, but not because I didn't want to be around her.

"It *felt* personal." She sighed. "But if you say it wasn't, I accept that. I know what it's like to...go through something. Want to talk about it?"

"No."

"How did I know that's what you'd say?"

I shrugged. "I guess I'm predictable. You sure you're all right?"

She shuffled her feet on the gravel, undecided about something. But then she spoke. "I'm going for a hike. Would you...maybe...like to come with me?"

Huh. She hadn't liked the idea of hiking with me when Jessi had suggested it.

I'd overheard Scarlett talking to Jessi in my sister's office. Jessi had been a tense ball of stress for weeks over her project on Refuge Mountain. The restaurant and hotel thing. It meant a lot to her, so I'd offered to manage the site. Construction wouldn't start for three weeks, but there had been contractors coming by and giving estimates. Jessi couldn't run the diner and handle the Last Refuge site at the same time, no matter how much Aiden tried to be everywhere for her.

This morning, I'd come to town to load up on supplies,

and I'd stopped by the diner to lend a hand with some chores. I'd heard my sister and Scarlett talking. They might say it was rude to listen to their private conversation, but that was naive. Any decent operative gathered intel however he could find it.

As it happened, Scarlett was someone I tended to pay attention to. That rosy hue in her pale skin did things to me. And that, *right there,* was the truth I would never admit.

I worried that if I got too close to her, she'd be too hard to resist.

But then I'd noticed her up against the side of the diner, expression stricken as she stared at her phone. She'd been terrified. A look I'd never seen on her face before. How could I have walked away after seeing that look?

"I'll hike with you," I said. "But I'm not good company. I can't promise you'll enjoy it."

Scarlett shook her head, making her long ponytail wag. "How do you know? You're not me. Maybe I like brooding, hairy mountain men who never say anything." With a scowl, she walked away from me, hiking boots thudding against the sidewalk. Then she looked back. "Just hurry up already."

I smiled faintly at her curvy backside.

I followed her at a leisurely pace. My knee twinged, but it wasn't bad today. Her stride was far shorter than mine, despite her shapely legs, so I caught up fast. Then I had to slow my pace to stay at her speed. Scarlett hadn't spoken again, but that was okay. We had time. I wasn't the type to fill silences with meaningless banter.

Plus, it gave me a chance to admire the view.

Early in the year, I had shown up in Hartley because Jessi asked me for help with some assholes who were harassing her. When I'd met Jessi's best friend, I'd seen her interest in me. And I'd been interested right back.

Scarlett was a sexy woman. She had T and A for days.

That round ass was currently swaying in her hiking shorts in front of me. But not only that, I actually liked her, and I barely tolerated *anyone* these days.

There was something about her that made me curious. She was always smiling and happy, which would've annoyed me if not for the hardened edge to her personality, like she'd been through enough shit to appreciate the good times. Plus, when bad stuff had gone down right after I'd arrived in Hartley, Scarlett had been there in the thick of it. She'd insisted on defending Jessi and Aiden. Scarlett had even helped save *me*. She was daring, and that made her damn near irresistible.

In my old life, I'd been an intelligence case officer. CIA. Reading people and moving discreetly were second nature to me, and yeah, I'd followed Scarlett a time or two without her knowing. I liked to make sure she got home safe after a night out. If that was offensive to some people's sensibilities, so be it.

But I had resisted the urge to get closer than that because I *had* to resist. She was my sister's best friend. Scarlett didn't need a man like me in her life. In her bed.

That didn't mean I didn't care about her, though.

If she was in trouble, I intended to do something about it. Protect her from it, if I could. Maybe that made me a hypocrite. Hiding so much of my own shit, while asking Scarlett to confess hers.

But she wanted someone to listen, and that was the difference.

Once we reached the Painter's Peak trail, we scrambled up some rocks. I held out my hand to Scarlett. She didn't take it, climbing on her hands and feet instead.

"Ready to tell me what upset you earlier? If you explain what's going on with you, I could help."

She stayed quiet. Thinking. I watched Scarlett's curves as

I waited for her to speak. I could look all I wanted as long as I didn't touch.

The gears in her mind were grinding, and she was almost there.

"I saw a comment on my social," she said. "It freaked me out."

"From who?"

"Anonymous."

"But it wasn't just a random internet troll."

"Exactly." She stopped, hooking her thumbs in the straps of her backpack. "I'll have to explain some things for it to make sense. Kind of a long story."

"We can sit while you tell me, or we can keep walking. Whichever you prefer."

Tendrils of Scarlett's dark auburn hair hung free around her pretty face. She studied me another long moment with her hazel eyes. Then she turned and resumed the hike.

Made sense. It was easier to talk about difficult things when you weren't facing the other person. But Scarlett didn't usually have trouble facing people. She didn't want to look at *me* while she said this. I wasn't sure why yet. But I was about to find out.

"I grew up on a ranch outside Creekview. The town is about twenty miles from Hartley, but that mountain pass makes it hard to access in the winter." She pointed at some distant peaks, still showing snow even in August. "The compound was like another world compared to here. Tucked into a narrow valley beyond rolling hills and miles of woods. We had a very different way of life."

She didn't say anything for a couple of minutes, seeming to retreat inside herself.

"Your family lived there?" I prompted. "At this compound?"

Scarlett nodded. "There were ten families led by the ten elders. One was my father."

She hadn't told me much yet, but her choice of words suggested a cult. I knew there were some out in the wild parts of the Mountain West. But I never would've guessed Scarlett had grown up in one.

Scarlett had stopped walking. Her hand briefly touched her lips. "I haven't spoken to anyone about this in a long time." She forced a smile. "I usually keep things upbeat on this anniversary. I don't like to wallow in the past. I'd planned to tell Jessi about it today, but now I'm not sure I want to dredge this up."

"Because you're telling *me* instead of Jessi?"

She glanced away. "That's part of it."

"Let's go back to the comment you got on social media. Tell me about that."

Her chest moved as she exhaled. She took off her pack and sipped some water from the tube of her Camelback. Her hands were shaking as she took out her phone, unlocked the screen, and thumbed to the Instagram account. She pulled up the comment and handed it to me.

Thirteen years, Serenity. Do you think about the promises you broke? The people you left behind? Women like you should be PUNISHED. Someday soon, you will be.

Anger flooded my veins. Whoever had sent this, I wanted to take them aside for a quick lesson on how women like Scarlett should be treated.

"No wonder you were scared."

"My name was Serenity," Scarlett said. "I changed it after I escaped. Whoever left that comment knows my new identity. Hartley is close to the compound, relatively speaking, but it was never an issue before. I keep my picture off the internet, and aside from that, I just live my life. I didn't think someone would ever…" She waved at the phone, which I still held in my hand.

"It could be a threat."

"It was probably nothing. Just someone wanting me to feel guilty."

"Have you had any indication before that people from the compound knew where to find you?"

"No. Never. I did find some other survivors who'd escaped, both before me and after. We keep in touch, but they would never reveal my new identity. None of them live in this county anymore. They went as far away as they could, but I refused. This is my home too. I won't be scared away."

"You're like Jessi that way. Stubborn."

A smile teased her lips. "I always liked that about her."

"Anyone strange coming by the sweet shop? Hanging around your house?"

"Never. Thank goodness." She shuddered. "I'm going to delete the comment. I want it gone."

"I'm taking a screenshot first. You need a record of it." I captured images of the post and comment, as well as the sender's account.

"I'd rather just forget about it."

"It's not wise to ignore a potential threat."

Shrugging, she took her phone back and stuck it in her pocket. Scarlett swung her pack onto her shoulders and started up the trail.

I wasn't done with this conversation. But apparently, she wanted to move on. I'd oblige her. For now.

A while later, we stopped again, and Scarlett pulled a small bundle from her pack and handed it to me. "I brought snacks."

I opened the wax paper. Dark chocolate nut clusters. "Thanks." I bit into one. "They're good." I liked milk chocolate better, but didn't mention that.

"I should hope so. I make candy for a living, after all."

I wrapped up the rest of the nut clusters. "You do have other talents."

"Like what?"

"Singing."

Her side-eye turned into a glare. "When did you hear me sing?"

"Outside the diner."

Scarlett snorted a little laugh. "Sorry you heard that."

"I'm not. You have a beautiful voice. You should sing more."

She bowed her head. But I could tell she was pleased. "I don't like singing around other people. Just by myself."

"Too bad for everyone else, then. I would offer to sing for you to make it even, but that would really be a punishment."

We were both quiet as we hiked for a good ten more minutes. Just working our muscles, breathing the clean air.

"You moved up to Refuge Mountain?" Scarlett asked.

"I did. I've been staying in one of the cabins at the old ranch." They had no electricity or plumbing. Every couple days, I went to Jessi's to borrow her shower so I could be seen in polite society. Not that I was very civilized regardless.

"It'll be beautiful once the inn and tavern are done," Scarlett said. "All the trails around there. Guests will be able to get out and enjoy the quiet. I love when I can't hear another human for miles and miles."

I paused before responding. "I like that, too."

"Jessi said you sometimes disappear into the mountains for days."

I grunted, not wanting to get into it. My sister didn't appreciate when I took off. Those trips were less a whim than a necessity. When the stuff in my head got too messy to keep ignoring.

"I like going out in the wilderness," Scarlett went on.

"Things don't feel so heavy when I'm outside. Is that how it is for you?"

"It is." She was fishing pretty hard. But two could play at that game. "What else has you feeling heavy? Something more about your childhood?"

"Not going to let that go, huh?"

"I don't think you want me to."

Her eyes rolled. "You know me so well?"

"Just a guess." But I knew it was a solid one.

We hiked a while longer. And finally, she started talking again.

"The compound where I grew up was called Paradise Ranch. It was anything but paradise for me. We had a lot of strict rules we had to follow. But I'm *me,* so I found ways to rebel. When I was a teenager, my best friend was a boy named Kenny, and we used to sneak out at night to see each other. His mom was a fourth wife, like mine, and I assumed I'd be given to him as his wife someday. I didn't feel anything romantic for him. But I didn't think it would be so bad."

My jaw tightened at the way she'd spoken so matter-of-factly about being *given* to a man. But I stayed silent as she kept going.

"When I was fifteen, Kenny's eldest brother decided he wanted me, and he had a lot of status. Our wedding date was set."

Anger burned under my skin. "You were fifteen?"

"Yes. My father's other wives said I should be honored. That I was marrying above my station because I was… because of how I looked."

"That's bullshit."

She looked at me sharply, step faltering.

"I mean, you do look…" I gestured at her, trying to keep my eyes on her face instead of her curves. "You're an attractive woman." *Not the point, Novo.* "But you're more than that."

She cleared her throat and kept talking. "Kenny's brother was awful. We all heard stories about the things he did. Kenny hated him, and he didn't want that for me. So we planned to escape together. But on the night we were supposed to leave, we got caught. Kenny told me to run. I hoped he'd get away somehow and catch up to me. But he never did."

"Did you find out what happened to him?"

She wrapped her arms around her middle. "He's dead." Her gaze was averted, carefully avoiding mine. But I could see the anguish inside Scarlett like it was bleeding out of her pores. "We were supposed to escape together, and I left him. Thirteen years ago today. I call this my Independence Day, but shouldn't I feel guilty instead of celebrating?"

I walked closer until I was in front of her. She looked up at me with more distress than I'd ever seen in those brave hazel eyes. I was shit at comforting people. But I did know more than a thing or two about blame. And Scarlett? She didn't deserve it. It disgusted me to think that the actions of others kept following her, affecting her happiness.

Especially that anonymous comment. *Do you think about the promises you broke? The people you left behind?*

"Whatever happened to Kenny, it wasn't your fault."

She swallowed, blinking like she only just now remembered where she was. "Thanks. I needed to hear that."

"Want to keep hiking?" I asked. "Or head back?"

A mischievous smile teased her lips. "Head back. But I'll race you."

She took off.

As we made our way down the mountainside, I realized I'd enjoyed today more than anything else in recent memory. I didn't like that Scarlett was still torn up about her past.

But I had liked being the one she'd opened up to.

CHAPTER THREE

Trace

"YOUR LITTLE LEGS are fast when you get going. You almost beat me."

She swatted my hip with the back of her hand. "Rude. I'm not that short. No need to sound patronizing."

"You *are* short compared to some people." I pointedly looked down at her. At six-three, I had nearly a foot on her. But when it came to Scarlett, I had no complaints.

Beads of perspiration dripped from my hair down the back of my neck. I was sweaty and winded from sprinting down the mountainside, and Scarlett had nearly kicked my ass. Would've worn shorts instead of pants, except I hadn't had time to change. Also, I didn't like to show the scars on my knee.

I took off my T-shirt and stuck it into the back of my waistband as we walked. I kept my steps even to cover my limp.

Scarlett was ahead of me, but when she glanced back at one point, she did a double take. A choked cough came out of her throat. "You should warn a girl if you're going to do something like that."

"Just trying to cool down." Though the way she was looking at me wasn't helping my effort to be good.

Scarlett wasn't as sweaty as me, but her thin tank top clung to her narrow waist, and a droplet of sweat hovered at the bow of her upper lip. Another at the top of her spine. I could bend down. Lick it off...

Shit. Nope. We weren't going there.

I was pleased to see her relaxed after our tense conversation and all that she'd confessed. But Scarlett usually seemed easygoing, didn't she? Until today, she'd put on a smile, playing the part of Jessi's cheerful best friend. And that had made it easier for me to stay away. Because I hadn't wanted to dim Scarlett's happiness with the shadows that followed me.

Had she needed someone all this time?

"How did you make it to Hartley after you escaped?" I asked.

"Walked here."

My eyebrows raised. "You made it over that mountain pass on foot at fifteen?"

"Took me almost two days. I didn't have much choice. I'd packed up my bag ahead of time, though. Food, water, compass. An extra blanket and hat. That helped a lot."

I was impressed all over again at the resiliency she'd shown at fifteen. But I shouldn't have been surprised. Scarlett was the same way now. At that age, I'd been safe at home with my dad in North Carolina, my plans to join the Army just vague ideas. And the Agency? I hadn't even known that career path existed.

"Once I reached the main road that leads to Hartley, a Good Samaritan picked me up. She drove me to the sheriff's office here in town, and I told the sheriff everything."

"Owen Douglas's predecessor?"

"Yep. The sheriff was shocked by my story, but he didn't

doubt me. He took me and a bunch of deputies out to Paradise Ranch. Marched right up to the gate of the compound and demanded to know what was going on. If they were forcing underage girls into polygamous marriages." She swiped a stray lock of hair from her forehead.

"What happened?" I asked.

"My family looked those sheriff's officers in the eyes and denied everything. I'd expected the adult men to lie. I guess everyone else was too scared to speak up. My sisters, brothers, friends. Even my mother, though I could see in her eyes that it broke her heart. They said…" Her voice hitched. "They said I'd tried to seduce Kenny's brother, and that I chose to run away when he rejected me. That I was shameful and impure."

I shook my head, chewing at the inside of my lip.

"But my mother stopped the sheriff before he could leave, and she begged him to take me away from the compound. To not make me stay. She wouldn't say anything against my father or the others, but she did that much for me."

"She didn't want to come with you?"

"She was too scared," Scarlett whispered. "But the sheriff was a good man, and I think she must've seen that in him. He protected me." Scarlett's eyes sank closed, and a tear slid down her cheek. I brushed it away with my thumb, feeling that brief contact jolt through me.

"I asked about Kenny. Nobody would say outright where he was. But my sisters whispered enough for me to know what had happened. Kenny's brother had shot him the night I'd escaped. I'd heard the gunshot. I told the sheriff, but I had no proof, and my sisters weren't going to talk. I couldn't even prove what the elders had done to *me*. I was tired of looking back. I just wanted to live. After that, the sheriff and his wife took me in like I was their own daughter."

"What's the name of Kenny's brother?"

"Dawson Witkins."

I burned it into my memory. Somehow, Dawson Witkins was going to be very sorry I'd ever learned that name.

We were walking side-by-side on the asphalt back toward town. "I want to look into that Instagram comment further," I said. "I could touch base with some of my contacts. See if they can unmask the account."

"Really? You could do that?"

In my old line of work, it wouldn't have been a question. Now, I wasn't completely sure. Depended on whether or not those former contacts were willing to do me a favor. "I'll try. I'll need your login info for your Instagram account. But we should consider the comment a real threat until proven otherwise. You need to tell Sheriff Douglas about it. Do you have a security system? Cameras?"

She smirked. "This is Hartley. Almost no one has security. A lot of people don't even lock their doors, though after what happened with Jessi last winter, I know better than that."

I grunted at the very idea that she would ever fail to lock her door. "Just be aware of what's around you. Don't go out alone at night. Bring someone with you when you're on a hike. Or at the bar."

"Are you volunteering?"

"Give me the time and place."

Her grin reappeared. "We could mountain bike next time. If you're up for it. Would that be too hard on your knee?"

I didn't want to discuss my injury. Like most of my problems, I preferred to act like it didn't exist. "Mountain biking sounds fine."

There was no sign of Scarlett's earlier distress as we turned onto her street. Her two-story, clapboard house was up ahead. It was painted a cheerful yellow with white trim. Window flower boxes were lush with blooms. Her green Jeep Wrangler was parked under a carport, but as far as I knew,

Scarlett walked places unless she had more than a few miles to go.

"Thanks for listening," she said when we reached her front porch. "It meant a lot."

"No problem." The wooden boards creaked beneath my boots.

Her eyes flicked again over my bare torso. I'd dried off on the walk back, but hadn't put my shirt on.

Scarlett shifted so she was closer to me, angling her body toward mine. "Did you need a ride back to Refuge Mountain?" she asked.

"No, my car's at the diner." I'd bought an old beater not long after getting to town. "I'm not in a rush to head back, anyway. No plans."

Then she looked up at me, and her teeth sank into her lower lip. "Do you want to come in? For a drink?"

Shit.

It had sounded like an innocent invitation. Yet Scarlett wasn't innocent, and neither was I.

"You think that's a good idea?" Because I knew for sure it wasn't.

"It's just a glass of tea. Or ice water. I might even have a light beer stashed somewhere. We can just sit and have a drink."

"We both know that's not all that will happen if I go inside with you."

She gaped at me, though she was laughing. "Your confidence borders on arrogance."

"Never claimed to be otherwise."

Scarlett took a step closer. "I don't know what'll happen. But this day has been full of surprises. Some of them pretty great."

"Your Independence Day does call for a celebration."

"True. I haven't celebrated much yet. You want to help

me?" She shivered as she said it.

Fuck, I did. I really did.

Scarlett needed real tenderness, and I didn't know how to give that to her. But for all my efforts to reign in my attraction, I was struggling to remember why I kept fighting it. I wouldn't be good for her in the end...

But couldn't I be good to her for an evening?

I leaned over her. Scarlett craned her neck. My lips barely brushed hers.

A car drove past, its worn-out engine growling, and backfired. The sound was deafening. I flinched. Grabbed Scarlett around the waist and flattened her body against me.

Danger, my instincts commanded. My vision tunneled, and I reached for the weapon at my lower back. It wasn't there.

"Trace? Are you okay?" Scarlett's big eyes blinked at me. I let go of her fast. Then she reached for me like she wanted to keep me there.

"*Don't*," I said sharply.

I regretted it the moment the word left my lips. But I couldn't take it back either. I stepped away, my knee suddenly throbbing so badly I worried it would give out.

"It's okay. You don't have to talk about it if you don't want, but please come in. You helped me earlier, and I could—"

"You can't," I choked out. I should never have been tempted. Never allowed her to get that close and let down my guard. "I need to go."

Hurt spread across her features.

"It's better for you," I added, and the hurt on her face turned to anger.

"Don't tell me what's good for me. We just spent hours together where I told you some of the worst things that ever happened to me. You won't trust me enough to come inside?"

Scarlett wasn't the problem. She wasn't the one I didn't trust.

"Trace!" Scarlett called out. But I was already limping out of there as fast as my aching leg would carry me. Back to the diner so I could drive to the cabin.

Alone, where I belonged.

I sat on the dusty floor of the cabin on Refuge Mountain, head in my hands.

I hated that Scarlett had seen me like that. It didn't happen often, less as the months had passed since I'd returned to the states after my final mission.

The unauthorized mission that had gone so wrong.

For a few seconds, when the car had backfired at her house, I hadn't known where I was. It was the same whenever I woke from a nightmare. A few moments of heart-exploding confusion, and then I could get my head together pretty quick. But the disquiet lingered. A stain that wouldn't go away.

I was equipped for battle, whether it was with guns or more subtle strategies. My brain was primed for it. It was the calm that could be worse, when a loud but innocuous noise could confuse my senses. I felt more at home surrounded by danger. Living as a civilian, without a target? Without a mission? That was the problem.

My sister suspected, though she didn't know the full extent. When I'd been staying with her, Jessi had asked what had happened. How I'd been injured. Why I'd left my old life. Why I needed to escape into the mountains for days at a time. Why I couldn't tell her even in vague terms why I was fucked up.

When I'd moved to Hartley, I had been hoping for a clean

slate. It had been months since then, yet I wasn't doing all that much better. I'd tried talking about it at the mandatory therapy when I'd been in the hospital. The only things that seemed to work were isolation and distraction.

I was just...tired of myself. Of this darkness I couldn't shake.

But I had to figure this out on my own. And I had to go back to keeping my distance from Scarlett Weston.

Another notification came in on my satellite phone. Scarlett had been texting since I'd left her on her front porch. She'd asked if I was all right, if I needed her to call Jessi or Aiden. I hadn't responded. Scarlett didn't know anything about me. She might've thought she wanted to know. But she didn't. She really didn't.

Yet she kept on texting. If I didn't answer, she was going to keep at it all night. That woman was stubborn enough to do it.

Trace? are you going to answer me?

I'm fine. Could you send your login credentials for the Instagram account where you received the threatening comment? Plus the screenshots I took. I'll get started on finding the person who left it.

you don't have to

Send the credentials.

Please.

even in a text, that "please" sounds forced coming from you [eyeroll emoji]

While I waited for her to stop arguing with me, I pulled up another number in my contacts. Someone I hadn't spoken to in almost two years, though I'd once trusted him with everything, including my life. But I had no clue if he still trusted *me*.

The number rang, and he picked up. "Who's this?"

"Hey, River."

"Trace? Is that you? You *asshole*." This wasn't playful ribbing. He really sounded pissed. "Where the hell have you been? You got rid of your old cell number. Trashed your email. Do you have any *idea* how long it's been?"

"I'm in Colorado." If I'd been using my old cell or email, no doubt he'd know my location already. He would've found me long before now.

"You're with your sister?"

"Yeah." I rubbed my hand over my beard. "Sorry. I know it's been a while."

"No kidding. You disappear without any word, nothing? Two *years*? How have you been?"

"Not the best."

"I heard a lot of things. I can't believe they fucking—"

I cut him off. "I didn't call to talk about that."

"I'm not even allowed to speak my opinion? Since when do you order me around?"

"It's not an order. It's a request." I blinked at the wooden walls of the cabin. "Please," I said in Pashto. One of the languages we both spoke. "I can't talk about it."

I already knew what he'd been about to say. That the Agency did me wrong. And honestly, that would've been worse than if he'd told me I was to blame and hung up. I couldn't stand to hear him feeling sorry for me. Because this was my burden to bear. I didn't want anyone's comfort.

He sighed into the silence between us.

River Kwon and I had met at Langley. He was a former Navy SEAL, born into wealth and privilege, but you'd never know it unless he told you. He wore chunky, black-framed glasses, though he had 20/10 vision. The glasses were blue light blockers. River was a computer nerd. A computer nerd who could infiltrate a terrorist-held ship, plant explosives, and escape with his teammates on their SDV before the captain even realized enemies had been aboard.

Yeah. That kind of computer nerd.

Unlike him, I'd been Army, divorced parents, solidly middle class and suburban. After I joined the CIA, I'd been assigned as a case officer, tasked with developing foreign intelligence assets. It was a matter of spotting someone with a weakness, finding out their pressure points. I'd mostly worked alone.

River had been stationed at US embassies in various countries under diplomatic cover. But despite our differences, River had always come through for me, and I'd done the same. I'd dragged him out of the desert when he was bleeding from a knife wound to the belly. He'd carried me through the sewers of Karachi after I'd been drugged out of my mind.

We knew secrets about each other we'd never share. Once, we'd been as close as two brothers ever could be.

"Okay," he finally replied. "Why are you calling then?"

"Are you in the country?"

"Yeah, I'm in DC right now. What's up?"

"I need a favor."

I told him about Scarlett's situation. She hadn't given me permission to share the details, but this was River. I told him enough. I texted him the login info for the Instagram, which Scarlett had sent me.

"Sure, I can handle it. This is for a friend?"

"She's..." Was Scarlett my friend? Could I even call her that? "She's my sister's best friend. A good woman who's been through a lot."

"Then I'll take care of it."

"Thanks."

"Anything else you need from me, let me know." He was making a peace offering. Since I wouldn't accept his condolences for my career, he was giving me a gesture of friendship. To show I was forgiven for shutting him out. It was probably more than I deserved. And after all we'd been through, I owed River more than that.

But I owed a lot of people, didn't I?

"There might be something you could do for my sister," I said.

I told him what else I'd overheard at Jessi's Diner today. My sister's concerns about her financing for Last Refuge.

"I'm intrigued," River said after I'd finished explaining. "But you have to let me come out to Hartley to see you. I want to meet your sister. *And* this Scarlett Weston."

I closed my eyes and gritted my teeth. "I'm not even sure how long I'll stay here."

At the moment I was helping Scarlett. But she didn't really need *me*. The less time she spent around me, the better. No matter how much I wished things could be different.

After I made sure Scarlett was safe, it might be time to call it. Wrap things up in Hartley, then move on and try to fix myself someplace else. Because unlike Scarlett, I hadn't escaped from *anything* when I'd come to this town.

"Well, you'd better stay long enough for me to visit," River said. "Those are my terms."

"Okay. But not yet. Sometime after construction starts."

"Don't sound so excited about it."

"I'm trying here, man."

"Try harder." He laughed ruefully, and I found myself almost smiling too.

Almost.

CHAPTER FOUR

Scarlett

I BENT over the glass case, placing my candy creations in neat little rows while I hummed along with the radio. This was my happy place. Working diligently in my shop, bringing smiles to the people of Hartley with sweet treats.

My mind was not on a certain tall, scruffy man with piercing dark blue eyes. A man I hadn't seen in *three weeks*.

Nope, not thinking about any such thing like that.

Hartley was abuzz because today would be the official ground-breaking on Jessi's Last Refuge Inn and Tavern. Jessi had sorted out her financing issues, thanks to an anonymous donor swooping in with some extra cash. In fact, I was due at Refuge Mountain in less than an hour for the ceremony. Just had to close up the sweet shop for the day.

I snapped a photo for my Instagram page and posted it. I breathed even easier when I saw nothing amiss in the latest comments on my other posts. Nothing strange had appeared in the account in weeks, and I was thankful for it.

A customer came in, and I straightened up. "Welcome to Scarlett's Sweet Shop. Let me know if I can help. I'm afraid we're closing early today, though."

"That's all right. I saw the sign." A young, handsome guy

was walking toward me, thumbs in his jeans pockets. His T-shirt clung to his muscular frame, and he wore a hat that said Mayfield Construction. "I was hoping to pick up a box of candy for the drive later."

"Then you've come to the right place."

He gave me a tentative smile, head tilting shyly. Looked like a sweetheart, and I did know how to spot 'em. A cutie pie for sure.

I turned when another customer opened the door. "Last minute rush today, huh?" I remarked. But my stomach swooped when I saw who it was.

Trace Novo himself.

I arranged my features into a neutral, pleasant expression. "Welcome to Scarlett's Sweet Shop," I repeated, like he was any other customer. "Let me know if I can help."

One of his bushy eyebrows lifted as he sauntered toward me.

After our afternoon of hiking together, of almost being friends, Trace had gone back to avoiding me. I'd received a single additional text message, saying a contact of his was investigating the threatening Instagram comment. Aside from that, it had been silence.

But *now* he decided to show up? Did he expect me to rush over and be happy to see him?

Trace glanced at the guy in the construction hat, nodding like they'd already met. And then Trace put a hand on my counter and just *stood there*. Not saying a word.

On my front porch three weeks ago, I could've sworn he'd been about to kiss me. Then that stupid car had backfired. His whole body had gone stiff, eyes distant, as if he'd transported to some other place. And it had been like a switch flipped. He couldn't stand to be around me anymore.

Trace had his own issues going on in his life, and I didn't blame him for that. If he wanted to keep the details to himself, fine. I wouldn't push. But I wasn't going to treat him like a friend if he refused to do the same for me. So I went back to tidying up my shelves. Going about my business until Trace decided to speak up.

He did look good, though. His beard was trimmed. His hair was still just over chin-length, which I was glad to see. He could do a sexy bedhead like no other. Bleached on top by the sun.

I couldn't help remembering the sweat running down his smooth, tanned chest after we'd raced down the trail. Why did the man have to be so lickable?

I went over to the guy in the construction hat, who was browsing the fudge case. "Are you going to be working on the Last Refuge project?"

He grinned. "Sure am. We've been up there delivering equipment, and we broke for lunch. I hear there's going to be a little ceremony this afternoon? Whole town's invited?"

"Yep, that's right. Including me, so I'll see you there. I'm Scarlett."

"Skyler."

Trace's mouth pressed into a straight line, watching us.

"Nice to meet you, Skyler. Need anything else while you're in Hartley, you just let me know." I'd said this in a friendly tone, but Skyler's face lit up like I'd offered to buy him a drink at last call. And Trace's expression had turned to a glower.

"I sure appreciate it. For now, I'll take some of your peanut butter cup fudge."

"You got it." I measured out the amount he wanted and wrapped it up. After he'd paid, I said, "Thanks for your business, sugar. I'll see you later." It was the same thing I said to everybody. But Trace eyed Skyler like he wanted to murder the poor man. Was I awful for enjoying that, just a little?

"See you up there, Trace?" Skyler asked on his way out.

"Yep." Trace's voice was tight, and he popped the P on the word. Skyler just nodded politely.

"He seems nice," I said once the door had closed. "You two already met?"

"At the Last Refuge site." He braced both palms on my counter and faced me. "I came to give you an update on my investigation into your Instagram stalker."

"So this visit *does* have a purpose. But it's hardly a stalker. It was a single nasty comment, and they've left me alone since."

"More than one comment. I deleted the others."

I gaped at him. "You *what*? You deleted things from my account?"

"It was getting excessive. I blocked him from commenting on your posts, so the guy made up other accounts too."

"I never asked you to do anything like that. What did the comments say?"

He ignored my question entirely. "That contact of mine has been trying to pin down the location of the account. The person used an overseas VPN to hide his location. Virtual private network."

"I know what it is."

"A VPN isn't infallible, given the resources my friend has, but it slows down the process. We believe the account was operating in Colorado."

Chills sheeted my skin. "So they could be close. It could've come from the compound."

"We can't rule it out."

"All right. How worried should I be?"

"You should keep being cautious. The stalker hasn't said anything specific yet. But I do recommend you get some security cameras."

"You haven't already installed them without asking me?" I

was kidding, but Trace just looked back at me. "Oh Lord, you didn't. Did you?"

"I've got a camera on Jessi's Diner. Aiden knows about it." He shrugged. "It has a view of your street as well, since your house isn't far from the diner."

"You didn't think to mention that?"

"Didn't think it was necessary. But you just asked, so I'm telling you now."

The nerve of this guy. "You've been spying on me."

"It's a public street. That's not spying. Plenty of cities have surveillance cameras."

"But this is Hartley. People expect privacy." Except when they shamelessly gossiped about each other, but that was beside the point. "If they knew, they would kick up a fuss."

"Not going to argue with you about it. I haven't seen anyone suspicious going near your house, and that's what matters to me. But closer cameras would be better."

I huffed. "I'll consider it. But..." I threw my hands up in frustration. "I barely heard a word from you the last three weeks. Then you waltz in here, and I find out you've appointed yourself my protector when I never asked you to. You're even worse than Aiden."

Trace rolled his eyes. "I'm far more subtle than Aiden. He's a good guy, but we're barely anything alike."

Right. "You could've come by, talked to me. Responded to the texts I sent after...you know, what happened that day. On my front porch."

When you almost kissed me and then shut me out.

His eyes slid to the side. "That shouldn't have happened."

The rest was implied. He didn't want to talk about it. Whatever chemistry we might've felt that day, those glimpses of the *something* we might have together, it wasn't getting a repeat.

"Fine. Thank you for your help with this social media

nonsense. I'll think about the cameras." I went to the register to clear out the cash. I still had tasks to finish. "I need to get going. We're due up at Last Refuge soon."

"Can I give you a ride there? Since we're going to the same place?"

"No other reason, right?" I snapped. "Not because we're *friends* or anything like that." I slammed the register closed. "No, Trace. I'll catch a ride with some other people who are headed to the ceremony. If you ever want to talk, I'm here for you. I tried to be your friend. I *shared things* with you. But I can't take this warm and cold, back-and-forth from you. Not knowing where I stand."

He stared at me with that inscrutable, deep-sea gaze of his.

There was more beneath his surface if he would just let me see it. Let me in. He wanted to say something more, and I could feel it.

But he didn't. Of course he didn't.

"Understood," he said. He pivoted and walked straight to the door, not sparing me another glance.

"Dammit." I rested against the wall, my head tipping back.

Had I done the right thing? Was I pushing him away when he was hurting and needed someone?

But I had to look out for myself and my feelings, too. I'd told him I was here for him. That was all I could do. I wasn't the type to bend over backwards for a man who wouldn't give me the time of day, especially after I'd thought we were getting to know each other. Getting to *like* each other.

He was willing to look out for me. But he wasn't willing to get close enough to make himself vulnerable with me.

At least I could be grateful that we didn't wind up in bed together. There was enough awkwardness between me and Trace already.

I hurried to close up the rest of the shop. But something else was still itching in my mind. My Instagram account. I couldn't believe Trace had been messing around on there, deleting things he didn't think I should see. As if I was too weak to handle it.

Even though I was running out of time, I took out my phone and opened Insta.

I scrolled through my past posts, reviewing the comments again. All friendly and positive, because Trace had filtered the negative ones. Just how many comments had he deleted? The more I thought about it, the more infuriated I got. I wondered if I should change my password to keep him out. But *that* would be childish. I did want him to find the identity of my so-called "stalker."

But couldn't Trace have asked me? He was so dang heavy-handed. And not in the way I would've welcomed those hands on me.

I went into my direct messages and was surprised to see one waiting in my "requests" section. That meant it had come from somebody I didn't know. I wondered if Trace had seen it. Had he been checking my messages and deleting those too?

I clicked on the DM request.

Then I had to read it three times for the words to sink in.

Dear Scarlett Weston, you don't know me. I was born the same year you left Paradise Ranch. But I've heard about you and I don't know anybody else who might be able to help. My big sister Virtue is due to marry an elder, the same man you were supposed to wed. I think you'll know what that means. She's scared, and as her brother I'm scared for her too. Please tell me how you got away so Virtue can do it too. Thank you.

Oh. My. God.

I forced myself to breathe. If I hadn't been resting against the wall, I probably would've fallen to the floor. Questions ran in a flood through my mind.

I looked at the account who'd sent the DM. It was anonymous, like the stalker one, but it had made a few posts. My breath caught, recognizing the landscapes in those photos. The outlines of craggy mountain peaks that I knew so well.

And the person's account handle? It was *@creekviewkid13*.

The message had come almost a week ago, and I hadn't seen it.

I remembered a little girl named Virtue. She'd been a toddler when I'd left the compound thirteen years ago. That would put her around fifteen years old. The same age I'd been when I'd escaped.

Could I trust the sender's word? Was it a trick?

But what if it wasn't?

I accepted the message and jotted out a quick reply. *This is Scarlett. I'm sorry I didn't see your message before today. I do want to help you if I can. What's your name? Could you give me some more details about yourself and your sister, so I know what you've said is true? Forgive me but I have to be careful. Write back soon. I'll be waiting to hear from you.*

I had no doubt Trace would see the boy's next message come in, because there'd be a notification on my account. I was sure my "protector" would have something to say about it. But I'd deal with him later.

If Virtue really needed me, I wasn't going to turn my back on her.

The first thing I had to do was talk to Jessi. Today was the start of construction on Last Refuge, and it couldn't have come soon enough.

CHAPTER FIVE

Trace

AIDEN LIFTED THE SLEDGEHAMMER. "Do you want to do the honors, Jessi?"

My sister grinned and took the sledge in both hands. She swung and slammed it into the wall.

We were in the old ranch on Refuge Mountain, the future site of Jessi's Last Refuge Inn & Tavern. Today was the big day. The official ground-breaking. Or maybe wall-breaking was a better term?

I was on the edge of the crowd, leaning against a doorframe. Pride in my sister flickered like a small flame inside of me. She'd worked so hard on this. And she deserved it. But my attention quickly slid over to someone else.

Scarlett was up near the front, and she glanced back at me.

There was something off about her. I couldn't put my finger on it.

My visit to the sweet shop that morning hadn't gone well. But staying away from her hadn't gone well, either. I couldn't get that woman out of my head. I didn't care that she was pissed at me for watching over her. That didn't bother me so long as she was safe.

But for the past three weeks, I'd been remembering that

brief brush of our lips. Not just the desire in her eyes, but the vulnerability.

Standing near her in the shop an hour ago, I'd felt that desire tenfold. Hot and demanding in my stomach. I'd been imagining how she'd taste. How her curves would feel underneath me. All those things I shouldn't want with her.

Ungh. I blew out an exhale.

Everyone clapped and cheered, and I wandered off outside to steer clear of the crowd. Aiden caught up to me. "How're you doing?" he asked.

I turned around and gave him a wry look. I had no doubt Aiden would be my brother-in-law someday, once he got around to popping the question. He was a stand-up guy. After seeing his commitment to Jessi, I had no issues with him being with my sister. But that didn't mean I wanted to spill my guts to him, either. No matter how close we otherwise were.

"Fine," I said automatically. "It's commendable, what you and your family have done for Jessi."

"Your benefactor friend helped. Whoever he is."

I nodded. River had come through with a lump sum donation to fix Jessi's bank problem. I'd chipped in a smaller piece, as much as I could from my savings. River and I had both agreed to keep it quiet, but Aiden had asked questions, so I'd had to give him a few details. Said the donor was an old friend of mine. Kept the rest vague.

River was still threatening to visit Hartley, but hadn't set a firm date yet. Maybe he'd get busy, leave the country, and forget about it. I didn't need another person breathing down my neck and demanding that I bare my soul. Especially not the guy who was, technically, my best friend.

"Jessi said you volunteered to help out around here?" Aiden asked.

"As much as I can." I was going to continue living in the

cabins during the work. Mayfield Construction had started bringing up their equipment this morning. A dumpster and lumber had been delivered. The real demo would start Monday, with the first stage of the project hopefully finishing up before the end of the year. A guy named Liam was the foreman, with Skyler as his second in command. I'd met the two of them when they came up about a week ago, and they'd seemed all right.

But then Skyler had been eye-fucking Scarlett at the sweet shop this morning. And when she'd called him sugar? I hadn't appreciated that *at all.*

Wasn't my place not to like it, though. Scarlett wasn't mine.

Aiden tilted his head thoughtfully. "Maybe there's another role you could take on once it's built. Something that would play to your skills."

He told me his idea for a group of ex-military guys, like us. People with nobody to answer to who'd defend anyone who came to Last Refuge for help. Aiden wanted to call us Protectors.

"You can't have a true refuge without someone to defend it," Aiden said.

As Aiden spoke, my eyes went to Scarlett. She and Jessi had their heads together, having an intense conversation by the looks of it.

"I'd like to have something worth defending," I said quietly.

Once, I'd thought I'd found it serving my country. I still believed in those ideals. But it was a problem when the men commanding you didn't actually uphold their principles. At least Aiden was the kind of man who abhorred injustice and preying upon the weak.

"So you're in?" Aiden asked.

I shook Aiden's hand, giving my assent, even though I

wasn't sure how much I could offer. I still had no idea how long I would stay in Hartley.

My attention went back to Scarlett. Whatever she was telling Jessi, her body language suggested she was upset about it. And Jessi listened with a serious face.

What was going on over there? What had gotten Scarlett so riled up?

"You coming to the diner later to celebrate?" Aiden said. "We'll have food. My parents sent fancy champagne. Jessi will want you there." I heard the warning in his tone. *Don't disappoint her.*

"Yeah." I nodded. "I'll be there."

I wanted to raise a toast to my sister. But I also needed to have another conversation with Scarlett. I was trying to protect her. But if I was honest, it was far more than that.

When it came to Scarlett Weston, I couldn't stay away from her, and I couldn't seem to keep my cool when I was near her. So what the hell was I supposed to do?

Unfortunately, Scarlett was set on avoiding me. She was giving me a taste of my own damn medicine, and it did not taste good.

We started out at the diner, eating appetizers while Aiden and a few other people made speeches. Jessi was beaming, while Scarlett squeezed her hand. Made me wonder if Scarlett had confided in my sister about the Instagram stalker. I didn't think she had.

After the toasts were done, I tried to pull Scarlett aside to talk, but she wasn't having it. She pretended not to see me and chatted with other people instead. Like Liam and Skyler, the construction guys, who Jessi had invited to her celebration. Half of Hartley was here.

Then the party moved to a roadhouse in the next town over. A dive the Hartley locals seemed to know well. Loud music blared inside, and the place was all neon and sawdust. Bar and pool tables on one side. Dance floor on the other. Really not my scene.

But was I going to leave Scarlett alone with that Skyler guy salivating over her?

No, I was not. Not without finding out what had upset her. I couldn't stand it when she looked upset like that. And I was sure it wasn't me. Sure, she'd been pissed at me earlier, but not enough to explain that hollow look beneath the cover of her smile.

Scarlett edged up to the bar to order a drink, and I pushed in beside her.

"Got a minute?" I asked.

"Not really. Unless you want to buy the first round."

"Happy to."

That seemed to surprise her. She ordered a pitcher of margaritas, then turned to me. "Did you need something else?"

It was noisy, so I had to lean in. My chest brushed her shoulder. "You seemed upset during the ceremony. And you were having an intense conversation with Jessi after. What's up?"

Scarlett rolled her eyes. "I don't have to tell you everything that happens with me. You're not my keeper."

"Didn't claim to be. I'm just trying to help."

"Like the way you *helped* by deleting comments that were left for me? Hiding things I have every right to know about?"

So we were back to that. "You wanted to see what that asshole said?"

"I wanted the option. I wanted you to check with me first."

The muscle in my jaw clenched. "Then I apologize. I won't delete anything else without asking you."

Her pretty hazel eyes lifted to mine. Her irises picked up the green in the neon beer sign on the wall. "Thank you."

"But I still don't think there's a need for you to read that bullshit. It was more of the same, that you should feel guilty and deserve to be punished. I'd much rather stand as a barrier between you and that asshole's poisonous lies. Because *none* of what he's said is true." Assuming the stalker was a *he,* which we didn't know. But it was a safe assumption.

"Thanks," she said again. Softer this time.

I inched closer, until my lips brushed the top of her ear. She smelled like strawberry shampoo. I ignored the flare of arousal that sped down my spine. "Now will you tell me what's really bothering you?"

The bartender brought the margarita pitcher. I grabbed it along with the glasses. Scarlett and I stepped over to the side. "I thought Jessi might've told you," she said. "And I figured she'd told Aiden."

We were going to need some kind of bat signal for this Protectors gig. "Nobody's filled me in."

Scarlett pulled out her phone and opened her Instagram app. "I got a DM."

Shit. How had I missed that? "Did it come from the same person who commented before? The stalker?"

She shook her head quickly. "No. I don't think so."

Scarlett showed me the message. "His user name is *creekviewkid13*. I think this person is really a thirteen-year-old boy from the compound, like he claims."

"Would he be allowed internet access?"

"Probably not. But boys and men are allowed into town. He found some way to get online."

I studied the message again and noticed her response beneath. "You wrote back?"

She bristled. "You going to tell me I shouldn't have?"

That had gone through my mind. But I chose not to say it. "You asked the right questions. If he is who he says he is, he should understand your need to confirm. But this could be the stalker again. Playing games with your head."

Scarlett grimaced. "That was my first thought, too. Especially because it came so soon after those nasty comments."

"Two different people finding out your new identity in such a short time. I'm not a fan of coincidences."

"I'm not either. I remember a girl at the compound named Virtue, though. I can't ignore it if there's a chance this could be true."

"And if the stalker knows you, he would realize that about you. He could be preying on your kind nature."

"But why? After all this time?"

Scarlett wasn't naive. She'd seen some of the bad things men did to people who were weaker. Yet the vulnerability in her question struck me right in the chest. I didn't want any more *bad* for her. I wanted to stand in the way. Protect her from it. Whatever might be coming.

"I don't know." I touched her cheek with my thumb, just briefly. Then dropped my hand. "We'll wait for this new person to write you back, but don't do anything until I can have my friend check out his account and his story. Would you do that for me?" I didn't like asking permission instead of just telling. But I was trying.

She nodded, then put her phone away. "We should take the margaritas to the others. They're waiting."

"I've got it." But when I picked up the pitcher, she stopped me with a hand on my elbow.

"We can drop off the drinks, but after, would you dance with me?" Scarlett asked.

Her hand on my arm was already doing things to my head. I could imagine us moving together on the dance floor. Hips and hands connecting...

"I shouldn't."

"It's just a dance."

"I don't think it would be."

The hopeful light in her eyes closed off. "Never mind. I knew you were going to say something like that. I don't even know why I asked."

"Scarlett..."

"Don't," she said, and I thought of that moment on the porch. When I'd said that same word to her. *Don't*. Didn't sound any better coming from her mouth than mine.

Dammit, I'd hated telling her no. But it had to be this way. I knew that. I'd told myself a million times. I was still waiting for it to sink in. So I could stop wanting what I couldn't, *shouldn't*, have.

Just about every guy in the bar, except Aiden, had asked Scarlett to dance. She'd said yes to several of them. At the moment, she was dancing with Marco, the bartender from the Hartley Saloon. Just before, it had been Skyler. Mr. Peanut Butter Cup Fudge.

I ground a cube of ice between my teeth.

"You don't look like you're having fun."

I looked over at Owen Douglas. He was leaning up against the wall beside me, eyes shadowed by his off-white cowboy hat. He was out of his sheriff's uniform tonight. In jeans, like me.

"You've been staring at Scarlett," Owen said. "If you want to dance with her, just go ask."

"I don't want to dance." I took a gulp of my soda. I'd only

had a sip of champagne earlier. Too easy to make stupid decisions when you were drinking.

I was really trying not to make a stupid decision tonight.

Owen chuckled. "Yeah, I'm sure dancing isn't exactly what you had in mind. But either way, won't happen unless you go after her."

I frowned. "Don't believe I asked for your advice."

"Lord knows you're not going to take it."

Owen was a hometown golden boy in Hartley. Local hero who'd served as a Marine, then came home and made good as sheriff. I liked him. Owen was genuine. He cared about Hartley, and he'd done a lot for Jessi. He'd overlooked some very illegal things I had done the past winter because it was for the greater good. He'd even deputized me for a short while during an emergency.

But like everyone else in Hartley, he didn't know me.

"How many people in town know that Scarlett changed her name?" I asked, moving the subject away from myself.

I knew that Scarlett had told Owen about the online stalker because I'd spoken to him about it as well. He was aware she'd changed her identity to escape her past. Owen had promised to keep an eye out for anything unusual around her house and Main Street. He'd redirected some of his patrols to drive past Scarlett's place, and I'd appreciated the gesture. But he only had a handful of deputies for a massive county. There was only so much he could do.

Made me wonder if Aiden had told Owen his idea for the Protectors. I doubted the sheriff would be okay with it. Owen had a tendency to get caught up in rules and procedures.

"Let's see." Owen adjusted the brim of his hat. "Who knows about Scarlett's name change. There's you and me. Jessi and Aiden, I assume. Some old-timers who were deputies back when she arrived in town. Gossip spreads here, but some secrets stay quiet when they're important enough."

"Were you around Hartley when she arrived?"

"Nah, I'd left for Camp Pendleton by then. Didn't meet her until I came home on leave. She was always outgoing. A bright spot in town. But at the same time, she was hesitant to talk about her past or appear in pictures. I knew she'd changed her identity, but not the details of why."

But she told me, I thought. For all her protests, she'd let me get close enough for that. She'd wanted my help. She'd put her faith in me.

"You know, now that I think of it..." Owen looked over at me. "Hartley had a lot of publicity recently. All those news articles about what happened in the winter. There's been an investigative journalist calling my office nonstop. What if Scarlett was in the background of a photo online? The wrong person could've recognized her and made the connection to her former identity. Decided to harass her."

"It's possible."

Owen's eyes narrowed as he studied me. "Did something else happen with that stalker of hers? Anything I need to know?"

"Not yet," I said.

It wasn't just an internet stalker anymore. We'd had an actual plea for assistance from someone at the compound, if that message could be believed. But I wasn't ready to share that with Owen. The guy I really needed to talk to about it was Aiden.

"You planning to tell me?" Owen asked. "Or will this fall into the category of things I'd rather remain ignorant about?"

I smirked at him. "Guess we'll have to see how bad it gets."

"That's not what I want to hear."

My eyes returned again to Scarlett. Some guy's hands were a little too low on her hips. Why did this bar play so many slow songs?

I forced my gaze away. "You've known Scarlett a long time. Why isn't a woman like that with anyone?"

"Good question." Owen tipped back the last of his beer and set his glass on a nearby table. "If you're not going to dance with her, I will."

Wait. *What*?

CHAPTER SIX

Scarlett

I'D DANCED with nearly every guy in here but the one I wanted.

I'd danced a few of the fast ones with Jessi, too. She was having a great night, drinking a little more than usual. I'd just stepped off the dance floor when my best friend swung her arms around my neck and gave me a sloppy kiss on the cheek. "You're the best," Jessi said. Aiden was smirking at me over Jessi's shoulder.

"I know. Are you just speaking generally? Or did I do something specific?"

"Just you in general." Jessi gave me a kiss on the other cheek.

Aiden reached for her. "Okay, that's enough. I'm taking you home."

"Don't be jealous, Shelborne," I said. "Can't help it if she loves me more." I helped transfer Jessi into her man's arms. "Get her home safe."

Aiden grunted at me, annoyed I would ever suggest he'd do otherwise. I smiled at them as they left.

Maybe it was time for me to do the same.

I'd been trying to have fun, but it wasn't easy when Trace

kept staring at me like he was angry I existed. I couldn't believe he hadn't danced with me *even once*. He was the only man tonight I had actually asked. And he'd turned me down. Like he couldn't stand being that close to me for even a few minutes. I was going to drive myself crazy obsessing over it, and that was ridiculous. I had plenty of other prospects. Several guys had made their interest known.

So, maybe I would take one of them home to get Trace out of my head entirely.

But I already knew that wouldn't work. Even if I had another man in my bed, I would've been thinking about him.

And that *really* pissed me off.

Someone tapped me on the shoulder, and I spun around. Owen held his hand out to me. "Dance?"

I smiled. "Thought you'd never ask."

Owen laughed and shook his head as he led me to the dance floor. "Don't let Trace hear you say that. He won't know you're joking."

Just hearing Trace's name made heat spread all over my skin. I rested my hands on Owen's shoulders. "Did Trace say something to you?" I'd seen the two men deep in conversation.

"He asked how many people in Hartley know about your name change. I'm sorry you haven't found your internet stalker yet, but it's good Trace is investigating. I get the feeling he has resources my county budget doesn't allow."

"He's investigating alright. Whether I want him to or not. Did you know he's been deleting comments from my social media without asking me? And he's been keeping an eye on me too, again without asking. It's obnoxious." I decided not to mention the camera because that could actually get Trace into trouble.

"Is he bothering you?" Owen asked wryly. "Do you want to file a formal complaint?"

"It isn't like that. He's just driving me nuts. I get that he wants to look out for me, and I appreciate that. If he can figure out who that Instagram creep is, then I'll be grateful. But I don't need a babysitter."

"Seems to me like he's trying to play your guardian angel."

"Trace doesn't seem all that angelic."

"Definitely not." Owen pulled me closer, though the touch was completely platonic. "Look at him. If his eyes could shoot laser beams, I'd be a smoking corpse right now."

We both looked. Trace leaned against a wall, ankles crossed, staring back at us. His stern expression didn't change. He was barely more than a statuesque silhouette in the darkness of the bar. But those eyes.

"I don't see why he's staring," I said. "He doesn't want me."

"He asked why you aren't with anyone. He's trying to hold back because he's got a lot on his mind, as is obvious to anyone who meets the man. But he's only got eyes for you."

I scoffed. *Why wasn't I with anyone?* Trace had all the info he needed to answer that question. My messed-up history. I'd healed, but those pieces hadn't stitched together in the right places. I wasn't cut out for love.

But sex? Bring it on. Not with Owen, because I didn't want to muddy that water, no matter how handsome a cowboy he was. And not with Trace, because he wasn't interested, no matter what Owen claimed.

Why couldn't I just pick up some guy tonight and keep things simple? Trace was beyond complicated.

"What about you?" I asked Owen. "Why aren't you with anyone?" The Hartley sheriff was perpetually single.

"You asking for a friend?" he said with a playful wink.

"Asking because *you're* my friend."

He laughed and twirled me around. I caught Trace watching us again.

"People would be too nosy about who the sheriff's dating," Owen said. "They already say I'm too young for this job. I need their respect. Can't afford any kind of drama."

"Sounds lonely."

"Nah, it's all right. Frees up my attention to focus on my constituents. Like you." Owen tugged me a bit closer again so he could lower his voice. "I know you and Trace are up to something, and it's not just your internet stalker anymore. Wouldn't surprise me if Aiden was involved too."

"What makes you say that?" Had Trace mentioned the latest message about the girl, Virtue?

"Instincts. I'm not demanding that you tell me the details. Just promise you'll be careful. And that you'll let Trace keep you safe."

I didn't want to get into it with Owen, so I nodded. He was right in some ways, wrong in others. But I was surprised how much he'd guessed already. "I'll be careful."

"Come to me if you need me. No matter what it is. Okay?"

"Yes, Sheriff. But it goes the other way, too. I'm here if you need me. I could play your wingwoman and find you a date."

"I'll let you know."

The song ended, and Owen squeezed my shoulder, kissing the top of my head. My eyes went straight to Trace again, and this time I found him glaring with animosity.

What the heck did that look even mean?

As soon as Owen was gone, Skyler appeared in front of me. "Another dance? I love this song."

"Why not?" I circled my arms loosely around his neck as we swayed. Skyler was a nice guy. I hoped he didn't mistake my friendliness for something more. If he wanted to be friends, though, I was down.

That was more than *some* people wanted from me.

Skyler smiled shyly. "You don't recognize me, do you?"

"Recognize you?" I leaned back in surprise. "Have we met before today?"

His fingers moved on my hips. "It was a couple times last year. I was in Hartley for a few days. Came into your shop." He shrugged. "To be honest, that's why I went in today. To see if you'd be there."

"Oh. I'm sorry. I didn't remember."

"It's okay. Don't worry about it. But now that we've officially met, I thought I might—"

Trace stepped in right behind Skyler's shoulder and roughly tapped his arm. Skyler turned his head, face scrunched in confusion.

Oh, boy. I had no idea what was about to happen. But it was going to be something.

"You're standing in my space."

Skyler gaped at him. "I'm what?"

"You're standing where I'm supposed to be." Trace hadn't raised his voice, keeping it low and deep and smooth. His face was neutral. But an implied threat seemed to bleed out from his pores.

"*Excuse* me?"

My skin flushed. My pulse was racing out of control. "Trace, what're you doing?" I murmured. Other people on the dance floor were starting to stare. Yet Trace hadn't even looked at me, even though until this point his eyes had been glued to me all night.

What kind of stunt was this?

Skyler's grip tightened on my hips. "I'm dancing with Scarlett. You're just gonna have to wait."

"Afraid that's not possible."

"Man, are you serious right now?"

I stepped back from my dance partner, pushing on his hands so he'd let me go. "I'm sorry. I need to talk to Trace."

Skyler looked from Trace to me again, mouth open, eyes wide. I felt terrible. The poor guy was embarrassed. Heck, so was I, because Trace was being ridiculous. I *could not* figure him out.

But if Skyler had been about to ask me on a date, I would've disappointed him anyway.

I grabbed Trace's arm and led him off to the side, leaving Skyler behind us. "What's wrong with you? You need to apologize. You're going to be seeing him at the Last Refuge worksite."

"I didn't appreciate the way he was touching you."

I had to admit, Skyler's hand had been venturing further south than warranted. "Like that's any of your business."

"It is when you'd rather be dancing with me."

My jaw fell open, incredulous. "Do you think I'm playing games? I wasn't trying to make you jealous. I'm not that kind of girl. I was just enjoying my night."

"I don't play games either. Now's the time to tell me. If you'd rather dance with Mr. Peanut Butter Cup Fudge—"

"You know his name."

"Whatever. If you'd rather keep dancing with him, say so. Is that what you want? Or do you want to dance with *me*?"

Neon light reflected in his eyes. His jawline under his beard was sharp in the low light, his hair messy and flipped to one side. I'd been smelling cigarette smoke all night, but Trace smelled different. Fresh woodsmoke and pine, like the mountains at twilight. I shivered, though I didn't want to. I reacted so strongly to him. From the first moment I'd seen him, when it had just been animal attraction, I'd felt it. I wished I didn't. I wouldn't feel this confused.

"You said no when I asked you to dance before."

"Just answer the question."

"You," I bit out. "I'd rather dance with you."

"Then come here."

I didn't move. It took everything in me to stay still.

Then Trace took hold of my wrists. He pulled me, slowly but inevitably, until we were pressed together. I exhaled.

What was happening right now?

"Would you dance with me?" he whispered in my ear. "Please?"

Ugh, how could I possibly resist that? It wasn't fair. I was defenseless against this man.

A slow, sultry song started playing. He didn't bother leading me back to the dance floor. Trace put my hands on his chest, then held me at the waist. We swayed there in our dark corner. I felt his lean muscles. The strength in his embrace.

His nose brushed my temple like he was breathing me in, and he brought one hand up to bury his fingers in my hair. Trace moved our bodies together, somehow surrounding me and keeping me against him all at once. The way he danced was dirty and intimate at the same time.

He was absolutely *slaying* me.

I had to say something before he pulled me under completely. "You're a…decent dancer."

"Am I?"

His hips arched a bit closer. I held back a whimper. "Why wouldn't you dance with me before?"

"Because I don't feel in control of myself when I'm around you. I don't like feeling that way."

I appreciated the honesty. Yet that statement sobered me. Just what every girl wanted to hear. That I made him feel *bad*. "But you didn't like me dancing with anyone else, either."

"I want you to have a nice time. I just regretted that I couldn't give that to you."

"But you're trying now?"

He shrugged. "Seems I am."

I pulled back to look up at him. We both had lost the rhythm of the music. "I've been friendly since the moment you got to Hartley. And you've made it clear that you don't want anything from me. Yet the moment you think I'm upset or in danger, you swoop in. Forcing your way into my life. Making me think..." I shook my head. "What is with you, Trace Novo? Please give me a real answer and not some tortured hero nonsense." Maybe that was cruel of me to say, but he was jerking me around. I needed a straight answer. "If you've got issues, that's fine. I've got some too, even though I'm not comparing. But I don't know what you *want from me*."

His eyes flashed. With fury, longing, with frustration. With all the things he was holding in.

"Come with me." Trace turned, taking my arm and dragging me through the crowd.

"Where are we going?"

"Outside."

I had no idea what we were doing. But I couldn't help myself. Not when it came to him.

CHAPTER SEVEN

Trace

THE MOMENT we stepped outside the roadhouse, the noise fell away and the quiet of night descended. I pulled Scarlett around the side of the building, away from the main part of the parking lot. Then I advanced until she had the brick wall behind her.

Insects chirped in the trees. The music and voices were faint in the background. But the rush of blood in my ears was deafening.

"Why are we out here?" She was shivering. It was chilly tonight, common in the mountains even in summer. I shrugged off my canvas jacket and held it out to her without a word. She shrugged it on, pushing up the sleeves that had swallowed her hands.

"Too hard to talk in there," I said. "Too many people."

Her expression softened into concern. "I'm sorry. I didn't think about that. The noise was bothering you?"

"I didn't mean I was triggered." I was not okay with that look of pity on her face. I braced my arms to either side of her, staring down. "I'm not exactly the picture of stability at the moment. I know what everyone says, and I know what you think. But I'm *not weak*."

"I never said you—"

"Make no mistake. If someone touches you in a way that's not welcome, if someone hurts you, they'll answer to me, and do not *ever* doubt that I can back up those promises with action. Never doubt me." Those words had rushed out fast. I'd been holding them in for too long. I wasn't angry at her. I didn't blame her at all. But I couldn't take that kind of second-guessing from anyone except my own damn self. "So don't worry about what I want or what I need. Tell me what *you* need, so I can fucking go out there and get it, because I can't stop thinking about you, Scarlett. And I can't stay away from you. Even though I should."

Her eyes went round. She'd asked for a real answer. For honesty. There it was.

But she recovered quickly. Scarlett shifted her weight. Brushed her hair over her shoulder.

And I knew I was about to get an earful.

"Are you going to let me speak now?" she asked.

"It's why we're out here. To talk."

"Great. So let's talk. First of all? I would never say someone's weak just because they have trauma. Don't ever put those words in my mouth." She crossed her arms. My jacket dwarfed her. "Second. You asked what I want. I want to get to know you. I don't want to feel like you're avoiding me. I want to feel like I'm someone you respect and like having around you."

"It's not that simple. I've resisted because I'm not the kind of man you should want around. Not unless I'm protecting you."

"Why?"

"You'll have to take my word."

She straightened up, lifting her chin defiantly. "Then it's not fair for you to look at me the way you are now."

"What way?"

"Like you already know how good we'd be together."

I knew this was a mistake. But I couldn't hold this back. Not anymore.

"Scarlett. I have been trying for a long time not to kiss you. I'm about to lose that battle. If you don't want that, now's the time to stop me."

"I'm not stopping you," she whispered.

I hadn't even realized my hand was loosely gripping the side of her neck, thumb massaging the pulsing vein at her throat.

I dropped my head and kissed her.

My lips parted over hers. I tipped her head back and cradling it with my hands, and she opened up to me so beautifully. Like she was made to do it. My tongue slipped inside. Scarlett moaned. Her tongue stroked against mine, and that electric sensation sent a jolt of pure desire down my spine.

My cock bucked in my jeans, imagining sliding into another hot, wet part of her. Making her mine.

I'd had no clue how much I was aching for her until I gave in and felt it. I'd backed her up against the brick, and she grabbed onto my hips, pulling me to her as tight as we could get while still wearing clothes. It wasn't enough. I wanted the warmth of her body, the heat of us building as we moved together, sweat and arousal smoothing the friction. And she was right. We would be *so* good together.

God, how had I thought I could keep denying this? There was no possible way.

I was trying to figure out how fast I could get her into bed. Any bed. Hers, a hotel. Her taste and scent had me in a fog of lust. *Even if it's a bad idea,* my conscience whispered. *The worst.*

But suddenly, she was pushing me back and slipping out from between me and the wall. "I can't. We can't do this." Scarlett squeezed her eyes closed. "Tomorrow you'll go back to avoiding me, and it's giving me whiplash, Trace. Tell me I'm wrong."

Her eyes opened, and she waited.

I knew the words to say to convince her. She was right on the edge of indecision, and she just needed a little reassurance before she tumbled over and back into my arms. And then I'd have her. All night long. What I'd been aching for. What I couldn't deny.

But was she right? Was this my last chance to stop myself and do the upstanding thing?

Fuck me.

"I'll drive you home."

"No," she said sharply. Her hazel irises had gone glassy. She turned away from me. "I'll find my own way home. I'm going back inside."

She took off my jacket and shoved it at me. I let it fall into the dirt. Then she started marching back toward the roadhouse entrance.

"Are you going home alone tonight? Or are you hoping to find another man who'll make you forget how I just kissed you?"

She whirled around, hurt and indignation painted over her pretty face. "You have some nerve. For most of the last eight months you've been in Hartley, you didn't care what I did. Then suddenly, you've appointed yourself my protector and provider. Tonight you danced with me, *kissed* me, like I mean something to you. But you don't get to change those rules without *earning it*."

She disappeared around the corner of the building, and I heard the door slam as she went back inside.

CHAPTER EIGHT

Scarlett

I COULDN'T BELIEVE that man.

Of all the arrogant, alpha male bullcrap. Making demands like he owned me and nobody else could have me? *Really*?

"You all right, Scarlett? You're being unusually quiet. You seem preoccupied."

I looked up, my thoughts interrupted mid-rant. "What was that?"

Marco put his car into Park. He'd given me a ride home from the bar, and we'd just pulled up at my curb. "I think you may have proved my point. Want to talk about it?" His jaw worked around the gum he always seemed to be chewing.

Marco had been the bartender at the Hartley Saloon for years, and my friend since I'd arrived in Hartley. He'd sat next to me in social studies period. He still had the same ponytail and sharp features. Back then, Marco hadn't made fun of me for being the oldest kid in the eighth grade class. He'd always been adept at reading moods, an admirable quality in a bartender. But tonight, I didn't feel like sharing.

"Sorry. A lot on my mind."

"Does it have anything to do with Trace Novo's hang-dog look when we left the bar just now?"

"No comment," I grumbled, getting worked up again at the mention of Trace. *The nerve of that man.* "I'll see you around, Marco. Thanks for the ride."

I got out and stomped into my house, dumping my purse on the ground by the door. I marched into my kitchen, kicked off my shoes as I went, and started rinsing the dishes I'd left there from breakfast. Water flew as I stuffed them into the dishwasher. But I couldn't wash Trace from my thoughts. In fact, I was only getting angrier.

"And that kiss?" I said aloud. "Are you kidding me?" I looked over at my ficus plant, gesturing wildly with my arms for emphasis.

I had never been kissed like that before.

While we'd been dancing, I'd done everything in my power not to get pulled in. Yet he had cast some sort of spell over me. Those intense eyes, piercing me and putting me at his mercy. I'd fallen for it before, and I hadn't wanted to go through that again—thinking Trace wanted me only for him to pull away. But within a couple of songs, I'd been melting like the center of a lava cake in his hands.

And then he'd dragged me outside. Told me he couldn't stop thinking about me. Kissed me, wild and raw, like he was compelled by pure, untamed desire.

I had no idea where I'd summoned the strength to break that hypnotic kiss. Probably all those warnings he'd made that we *shouldn't*. It was a *bad idea*. He didn't really want to be kissing me. It was just a matter of time until he changed his mind again. And it *hurt*. I'd wanted Trace to be happy he was kissing me. I couldn't bear the thought that he'd regret me.

I didn't want a commitment or declarations of love from him. Trace was probably right that we were a bad idea, and that just made this worse. He was my best friend's brother. A fling between us might blow back on Jessi. And besides, I wasn't like her, waiting around to get swept up in a perfect love story. Marriage, kids, the full fairytale package—it wasn't for me. I'd always been able to keep sex and feelings separate.

Yet every time Trace and I were together, sparks flew. And I kept getting singed.

Finished with the dishes, I stomped into my living room and flopped onto my couch, being as dramatic as I could manage. But I already felt my frustration fading away.

I wasn't the only one hurting. I knew Trace's pain came from somewhere in his past. Somewhere deep. But unlike mine, his pain still seemed fresh, as if it had barely scabbed over. He had finally admitted tonight, in a roundabout way, that he was struggling. I didn't have some misguided belief that I could fix him. But if he would let me be his friend, I could at least support him. I wanted the best for Trace. Truly, I did.

Well, I could be supportive even if we weren't friends. Right? I'd give him a little space, and then check in with him soon. In a platonic, no-more-kissing way.

I heaved a sigh. *There*. That was settled. No more obsessing over him. I had other things to worry about, like that message from Virtue's brother at the compound.

I tugged my phone from my pocket to read it again. The words didn't reveal anything more than the first times I'd read them. My reply still sat there, no indication the kid had seen it. Trace had said his friend would try to pin down the sender's location, and I'd promised him I would wait to do anything else.

And then, as I was watching, the status of my reply switched over to *Seen*.

I sucked in a breath and sat up. Was Virtue's brother going to write something back? I stared so hard at the screen that my eyes watered.

Then I heard a creak that had sounded distinctly like the boards on my front porch.

My heart was already jumping to conclusions, imagining Trace had come to apologize. I could just picture him out there, struck by indecision over whether to ring my bell or not. Seemed like something he would do.

My socked feet took me to the door before I'd thought it through, and I opened it.

Nobody there.

"Trace? Are you out here?" I stepped out, and there was the same creak again as I put weight on the wooden boards of the porch.

He'd spied on me before when he was playing my protector. I didn't understand his need to hide. But I trusted his intentions. Trace was a good man underneath his bristly exterior.

As I stared into the dark, I smelled cigarette smoke.

Would Trace draw me outside like this in the middle of the night, then ghost me? Or would he tell me I was being stupid? I was acting like every girl in a horror movie who investigates a creepy noise.

Really, Scarlett? What the heck?

Right on cue, a rustling sound came from the grove of aspens to one side of my house.

I yelped and dashed back inside, locking my door quick. Heart going crazy, I ran into my bedroom closet and opened my safe. I took out my over-under shotgun. Checked that it was loaded and flipped the safety off. Then I rushed around the house to make sure every window was latched, the back door locked, and my curtains all closed.

Back in my living room, I sat on the floor and grabbed my phone. Even last winter, with all the madness that had gone on then, I hadn't been this freaked out. My rational brain still wasn't sure what to do, but my heart clearly did. Because my fingers were already thumbing to my contacts.

Trace picked up on the first ring. "Scarlett?"

I exhaled when I heard his voice, like some part of me was ready to collapse with relief.

"Is something wrong?" he asked.

"I think there's somebody outside my house. Can you —"

"Don't move. I'm on my way."

Five minutes later, there was a knock. "I'm at your place," Trace said into the phone. He'd stayed on the line with me, though it had barely taken any time for him to get here. He already must've been close by. Not on Refuge Mountain. "Let me in?"

"Coming."

I set down both my phone and the shotgun, got up, and went to unlock the front. And there he was, tall frame taking up my small wooden porch. His mouth was drawn with concern. He stepped in past me, closing the door and flipping the latch.

"You all right? Did you actually see someone?"

"I just heard a noise on my porch, and I thought…" I felt silly admitting that I'd thought it was Trace. "I thought someone was out there," I finished. "I went to check, but I realized how stupid that was. That's when I came inside and called you."

"I'm glad you did. And I'm glad I was just over on Main Street. You've locked everything up?"

"Yes."

"You mind if I double check?"

"Surprised you're asking permission."

The corner of his mouth quirked up. "Trying to be better about that."

I smiled sheepishly, remembering everything we'd said

outside the bar. But our argument seemed inconsequential right now. "Thank you for coming."

"You say that like there was any question. I'll always come if you need me."

I followed him as he made the rounds of my small house, confirming that every window and door was locked tight. I noticed a holster at his lower back, a Glock tucked into the leather. He definitely hadn't been wearing that before.

"Where'd the gun come from?" I asked.

"I keep it locked in my glove box. I was parked outside the diner when you called. I, um…" He glanced back at me. "I wasn't ready to go back to the mountain for the night. Wanted to make sure you got home safe."

I thought of the question he'd asked me outside the bar. *Are you going home alone tonight?* And my refusal to answer.

"You saw me catch a ride with Marco."

"Yeah. He didn't stay long."

"He's also not my type." I almost laughed, but Trace's frown only deepened. "Marco's a friend. I was never going to pick up some other guy."

"You were right. It wasn't my business." He shrugged. "But I'm glad you didn't."

I looked at the floor and chewed my lip. I was making a valiant effort not to think of that kiss, and it wasn't going well.

Focus, I told myself.

"Did you see anything on the camera that you've got near the diner? I assume you looked at the feed."

"I did. I confirmed you'd gone inside your house. Didn't see anything else suspicious. But how about you and I look at the footage together? See what we see?"

"That sounds good." I'd been mad about the camera before, but now I was happy to use it.

We went into the kitchen. Trace took a seat at my table

and pulled out his phone. I sat beside him, scooting the chair close enough for our knees to touch. I knew it was dumb, especially after the big fuss I'd made outside the bar. But I just…needed to feel him close.

While he pulled up the camera app, I fidgeted, too full of nerves to sit still. "Do you have to be in town to access this?" I asked. "Or do you have data coverage on Refuge Mountain?"

"I have a satellite connection."

"Oh. That's smart."

Trace was so full of contradictions. He liked living out in the wilderness, yet he was one of the more tech-savvy people I'd met. With his cameras and his contacts who could hack Instagram accounts. Aiden had hinted that Trace worked for the government before coming to Hartley. But it was this big mystery, and he hadn't been eager to enlighten me.

"Here we go." He tilted his phone screen so I could see it too. The camera had a wide view that included the mouth of my street. The front of my house was visible. The image was black and white, I guessed because it was nighttime.

As we watched, an SUV pulled onto the street, and I got out of it.

"There's Marco dropping you off," Trace said. "Once you'd gone in, I stopped watching."

"Because I was mad about the camera when you told me about it this morning?" One of the *many* times I had been annoyed at him today.

"You had a point. I should've told you about it before."

"Maybe. But I don't mind it now." I nudged him with my elbow. "Don't look so smug."

"Trying not to."

Having Trace here made me feel safe again. This was what Trace did. He lulled me with his warmth, until he got skittish and closed himself off. I was resigned to that fact. But he was here now, and I decided to focus on that.

I edged closer, leaning into his broad shoulder.

We watched the camera feed at double speed. Then Trace stopped it. Moved the time stamp back. The image was frozen on a dark figure walking toward my house, and I gasped, my hand going to Trace's forearm. "There really was somebody there. Oh my Lord."

He zoomed in on the figure, but the person had a hat pulled low and a dark coat. "Can't see his face. Do you recognize anything else about him? His frame or his gait?"

"No," I whispered, my throat tight. "It could be anyone. But I don't think it's a neighbor."

On the recording, the figure disappeared into the trees near my house. He stayed there for several minutes. Then reappeared beside my front porch, stepping onto it briefly before darting away. Probably because he'd heard me approaching the door.

Trace's big arm wrapped around me, drawing me against his side. I felt sick. My whole body was shaking. I didn't usually scare easily, but this was a lot. Seeing how close the guy had been to my home.

"You scared the guy away. You did well."

"But I opened the door. What if he'd tried to get inside instead of running?"

"Then you would've given him hell. I know how ornery you are. You might look like the unassuming owner of the local sweet shop, but you wouldn't hesitate to go for the jugular. Or better yet, the testicles. You keep that mean streak hidden. But I've seen you waving a can of bear mace."

That made me snicker, though I was still scared.

Trace was so serious all the time. Yet he could get me to laugh even at a moment like this.

His arm was a pleasant weight on my shoulders. I felt him

breathing against me. His heart beating. His scent filled my lungs. And before I knew it, I'd stopped shaking.

"You're good at this," I said.

"At what?"

"Making me feel better."

His arm stiffened. Trace drew away from me, and I wished I hadn't said anything. Why was it impossible for him to take the slightest compliment? To get close to me and stay there?

It made me wonder what would've happened if I'd let things play out earlier. Would he have taken me back here and slept with me, only to be gone by the morning?

Yeah. I knew the answer to that.

"I should walk a grid outside," he said. "See if the guy left any clues behind." He started to get up. "Lock up behind me."

"I'm going with you." I could tell he was about to say no. "You're not leaving me out. I want to help. And I'll feel safer if we stick together."

We both stood, facing one another. Trace looked down at me from his full height. But I wasn't going to cave.

"You didn't want me as your protector before," he said. "I remember several conversations today when you were pretty angry about me overstepping."

"I was right about a bunch of things, but not that specific issue. I can admit when I'm wrong." Maybe I'd walked away from him earlier, but I'd learned my lesson. I was safer when Trace was around. "I called you, didn't I? I do want your help. But I want to be involved."

"You're completely sure? You want me as your protector?"

"*Yes*, I'm sure." I barely held back an eye roll. Jessi had told me today about Aiden's idea for a team of "Protectors" for Last Refuge, and I knew Trace was supposed to be one of them. But he seemed to be emphasizing the point a little more than necessary.

"If we go out there, I'm in charge. I won't half-ass this. If I'm protecting you, I'm all in, and I won't hesitate to boss you around. I need to know you'll listen."

"Fine. If it's about my safety, I will defer to you."

He nodded once, his face solemn like he was taking some kind of vow. He headed for the door.

"Wait," I said. "I have conditions, too."

Trace slowly turned around, eyebrow cocked.

"You keep me informed."

"If it pertains to you and your protection, then yes, I'll keep you informed."

"No more spying on me without my permission. Or deleting things without telling me."

"I consider that part of keeping you informed. Can we go out there now?"

"One more thing."

"And that is?"

I lifted my chin. "I would like to hold your hand because it makes me feel better. *You* make me feel better. But it doesn't mean anything more than that, and I don't want you to be weird about it."

He laughed softly. "All right. Come on, then."

Trace held out his hand. I slid mine into it, and together, we went outside.

CHAPTER NINE

Trace

AN OWL HOOTED, and leaves rustled in a nighttime breeze. Otherwise, Scarlett's street was quiet. The moon was nearly the only light to see by, aside from the kitchen light shining through her window. There were no streetlights for another half block.

There were a lot of shadows. A lot of places to hide.

I squeezed her hand in mine as we walked around the outside of the house. I used the flashlight on my phone to scan the ground for footprints or anything unusual that the guy might've left.

The thought of some creep sneaking around Scarlett's home made fury boil in my veins. While I had been keeping a discreet eye on her for months, it was because I cared about her wellbeing. I'd never skulked around her house peering into her windows. And I had never disguised myself, either.

If I'd caught the guy in the act, he would have lost something vital. That was guaranteed.

I was kicking myself for not noticing the guy on the camera earlier, but I'd been trying to back off and give Scarlett space. Like she'd asked me to do. And that guy had gotten way too close to her without my having a clue. At least Scarlett had finally given me the go-ahead to protect her. I would've kept doing it anyway, to some extent. But having her permission would make the whole process easier. Sure as shit, this was difficult enough as it was.

I had to get hold of myself. Rein in my self control. Because I had a job to do.

But I found myself rubbing her hand with my thumb, trying to provide whatever additional comfort that I could.

This woman had gotten so far under my skin.

We reached a cluster of aspen trees. "On the video, it looked like he was hanging around over here for several minutes." I inhaled deeply. "You smell that?"

"Tobacco smoke. Same thing I smelled at the bar, and when I opened my front door earlier, too."

I studied the leaf-strewn ground until my light hit on a cigarette butt. "Bingo." I knelt to get a closer look. It was smoked halfway down to the filter, as if the person had abandoned it prematurely. Covering my hand with my jacket, I picked up the butt and lifted it to my nose. It was fresh. Likely the source of the lingering scent.

"Do you have experience as an investigator?" she asked. "In the work you did before?"

"No. But I'm trained in counter surveillance." I stood and showed the butt to Scarlett. "Could it have come from one of your neighbors?"

"I don't see why any of my neighbors would be smoking over here. And besides, they wouldn't just leave it here smoldering. It's a fire hazard."

With my sleeve covering my hand, I tucked the butt carefully into my pocket. "Seems likely it belongs to our suspect. It can't have been out here long, so maybe a lab can pull DNA from it. I'll see what I can arrange."

I found two more cigarette butts on the ground, not far

from the first. These were older. Smoked all the way down. Those times, the person hadn't been rushed.

Not at all what I wanted to see.

"He's been here before," she said. "Right?"

"That's what it looks like." I collected those as well, though finding DNA on them was less likely, and then I slid Scarlett's hand into mine again.

"It could be a coincidence," she said. "Maybe...maybe the person didn't mean anything by it."

"You believe that?"

She closed her eyes. "Probably not."

Either Scarlett had two creeps bothering her, or the online stalker wasn't keeping his activities to the internet. Even if we were wrong about that, and these cigarette butts meant nothing, we couldn't ignore the possibility. River had already confirmed the Instagram comments had been posted from Colorado.

As soon as we got back inside, I made sure once again that everything was locked up. "Got a plastic bag?" Scarlett fetched one from her pantry, and I stowed the cigarette butts inside it, placing the bag inside my jacket pocket.

"What should I do?" she asked.

I turned around and found her hugging her middle, eyes downcast. That wasn't the Scarlett I'd come to know since I'd gotten to Hartley. She was supposed to be smiling, her inner vibrancy shining outward. Not because she was obligated to be happy. I was the last guy to command a woman to smile. But for some piece of shit to take that smile away?

Not on my watch. That couldn't stand.

"We'll be cautious," I said, emphasizing the *we*. She wasn't alone in this. "You need devoted cameras. Can I order some for you?" I tamped down the urge to insist.

"I would appreciate that. Thank you."

Scarlett got her laptop, and we returned to her kitchen table. I pulled up a website I liked and ordered the equipment I would need to set up a camera system. "You need eyes on the front and back of the house, watching the entrances and exits. But I'd also like a camera aimed at that grove of aspens."

"Will I have access to the feeds?"

"You think I'd set it up any other way?"

She gave me a challenging look.

"You'll have primary access to everything," I assured her. "I can set up the app on your phone and computer. I'll need access as well, but you can decide how much. Do you want cameras inside the house?"

"You sure I have a choice?"

"You've always got a choice. But do you want my recommendation?"

She bit her lip. Returned my gaze.

I was testing her a little. Seeing how much she'd push back when it came to her safety. But I had to know if she was willing to follow my advice. If we couldn't agree now, when the stakes were relatively low, how would we work together in a dangerous moment?

I had no idea where this situation would take us. I intended to be ready, even for the worst.

"Set up whatever cameras you think are best," she said. "Just tell me how it will all work."

I nodded my approval. "I can do that."

"Look at us. Compromising and playing nice."

"I'm capable of listening. And so are you."

"So it seems."

I smirked.

The really crazy part was, my head felt clearer than it had in *months*. I had a real job to do, not just odd jobs at the diner or minding the Last Refuge site. I was using the skills I'd spent years honing. I was good at this. And I could admit that I needed it. Something to focus on.

Something worth defending.

After I finished placing the order, I closed Scarlett's laptop. "I put rush shipping on everything. It'll be a day or two." As I stood up, her expression returned to the anxiousness she'd been betraying all night.

"Will you stay here tonight? I'm scared he'll come back."

My chest expanded. I put my hand on her wrist, still unable to resist the slightest excuse to touch her. "Anything you need." That was what I had told her outside the bar tonight. Right before I'd kissed her senseless. That kiss had hardened my cock and set my blood on fire.

Not where my thoughts should be tracking after she'd just asked me to spend the night.

I cleared my throat, letting my hand drop. "Do you want me to take the guestroom? Or I could stay on the couch. That way, I'll have a view of the front and back door."

A mischievous glint appeared in her hazel eyes. "I have another idea." She vanished into her room, and I took the moment to scrub my thoughts of any dirty inclinations.

When Scarlett returned, she was holding a stack of blankets, a couple of sleeping bags, and pillows. "I thought we'd camp out on the living room floor."

"Works for me."

I helped her spread out the sleeping bags. Scarlett had changed into flannel pajamas in her room, but I decided to keep my street clothes on. I took my boots and coat off, leaving my jeans and T-shirt.

She crawled into her sleeping bag, settling in. The main lights in the house were off, and I was sure Scarlett was exhausted after the long day we'd had. But there was still more I needed to say before the night ended.

I sat on my sleeping bag beside her, resting my arms on my bent knees. "I wasn't happy with how we left things earlier at the bar."

"After you kissed me?"

"You kissed back. But yes."

She propped up on her elbow. "You weren't happy with which part?"

With you reacting like I'd hurt you. I never wanted to hurt her. But that was exactly what I'd done, regardless of my intentions.

"I started the kiss, so that's on me," I began. "We can't repeat it."

"I wasn't offering."

"Let me finish. You were right that I'd been avoiding you off and on since I moved to Hartley, and you deserve better than that. A lot better." *Just say it,* I told myself. "I would... like...us to be friends."

"Wow. You could barely get that out."

"I'm trying," I said, gritting my teeth. "But for this to work, I need you to trust me to handle myself. Sometimes, you might see me tense up more than usual. Just let me shake it off. Don't ask if I'm okay. I won't be coddled. If I need something, I'll let you know."

"Will you?"

I screwed up my lips. If I didn't think I was capable, I wouldn't have agreed to protect her. *Period.*

"Okay," she relented when I didn't answer. "I'll trust you. I would *never* think you're weak because you're struggling with something." Her voice lowered, and she looked at the ceiling. "I probably trust you more than anyone to help me. More than even Aiden or Owen. And I think it's because you've been through difficult things, too. Whatever they might be."

I was silent. And she was quiet too, like she was giving

me room to sit with what she'd just said. I hoped she understood that I wasn't holding back because of her.

She shifted around in her sleeping bag. "I'm glad we're friends now. Friends who hang out and share things about ourselves. My favorite color is red gingham, by the way."

"That's not a color."

"It's a color *and* a pattern. That's better."

I chuckled. This girl.

"Your turn," she said.

Did I have to? "Huh. Well. I guess my favorite color is blue. And my favorite book is *The Hobbit*. I've read it about fifteen times."

Her smile was soft. Sweet. A comfortable sensation warmed my center. "Tell me more about you," Scarlett said.

"Maybe later. Just don't ask to braid my hair."

She giggled. "Now I really want to do it."

"No," I grunted. I laid back, stuffing a pillow under my head. For a while, I listened to the wind outside and the sound of Scarlett's breathing. I knew she wasn't asleep.

Finally, she spoke again. "Trace?" she whispered.

"Yeah?"

"Please don't disappear again. Don't shut me out."

"I'll be right here. Whatever you need." As much as I was able.

"But..." she said, trailing off. Neither of us finished the sentence. But man, did that word echo.

But.

I would do anything in my power to give Scarlett what she needed. Except for one thing. And the bittersweet tinge to her smile in the dark told me that she knew it.

The only thing I wasn't capable of giving her was my whole self.

CHAPTER TEN

Scarlett

LAST REFUGE WAS OFFICIALLY under construction. And Trace and I were officially friends.

On Wednesday morning, I drove up to the base of Refuge Mountain and parked near the worksite. Trucks labeled with the Mayfield Construction logo were already here, and workers were dragging bricks and plaster out of the old ranch house to a dumpster. Piles of lumber and other materials waited nearby.

The foreman, Liam, tipped his hardhat when I walked past. "Morning," he said. "Are you looking for Skyler?"

"Oh, um," I stammered awkwardly. Had Skyler said something about me after our interrupted dance on Saturday night? I'd hoped he would drop by the sweet shop this week so I could smooth things over and ensure there were no hard feelings. But no such luck. I probably would've texted to apologize, but I didn't have his number. I had no interest in dating him, but I did hope to be friends.

It was entirely possible he wanted to put the whole thing behind him. If that was the case, so be it.

I had my own pressing issues to focus on.

"I actually came by to see Trace. Coffee delivery." I held

up the cardboard tray I'd brought with me, which held two house brews from the coffee shop on Main.

Since Trace had officially become my friend *and* my Protector with a capital P, we'd been spending more time together. More time in the last few days than in all the months that preceded. Trace had camped on my living room floor three nights in a row after the stalker incident, making sure I was safe. Then the new cameras had arrived, and he'd gotten them set up.

Today was the first time I'd turned the tables and visited his place, but I had a reason for that. News that I was anxious to share.

I said goodbye to Liam, then headed over to the row of cabins where Trace lived. I wasn't sure which one he occupied, but it didn't take long to figure out. There was a frilly curtain hanging in the window. I figured Jessi had added that. This place was her baby, so that didn't surprise me, aside from the fact that she'd want to make it nice for her brother.

The main building of the ranch would house the Last Refuge Tavern, and these cabins would become rustic guest cottages. The Inn would come later, built as an addition to the ranch. Last Refuge was a big project, so Jessi and Aiden were taking it in stages, rather than all at once.

But the space to shelter people in need was a high priority. It was possible we'd need it sooner than any of us had expected.

I rapped on the door. "Trace? Hope I'm not waking you, but—" The door flew open. Trace stood there, his hair messy and his feet bare. He wore a pair of gray sweatpants. And nothing else.

"Morning," he said, voice all gravelly. And wow, that made the whole effect of him even sexier.

"Hey."

"What are you doing up here? Everything okay?"

My eyes had glued themselves to the smooth, golden expanse of his torso. I'd seen him shirtless before, but in the morning mountain light? It was like a photo shoot. And how did the man smell this good without access to running water and plumbing? That wasn't normal.

Trace's hair fell across his cheek as his head tilted. "I thought we weren't supposed to look at each other that way."

So he was quoting me now? "What way is that?"

"Pretty sure you know."

"I have no clue what you're talking about." I forced my brain to get moving again and held out the coffees. "Brought caffeine for you."

"Thanks," he said, taking the coffee.

"I'm here because I got a new message on Instagram. It's from Virtue's brother at the compound. He finally wrote me back. He said his name is Toby."

"Did you read it?"

"Not yet. I saw the first line, then I came straight here. Thought we could read it together, and I didn't want to wait." Which seemed ridiculous now that I was standing here, and he was half-naked. But I hadn't wanted to read the message alone. It was still possible there was a connection to my stalker.

Or maybe you were looking for an excuse to come see him?

Okay, perhaps that was the case. But I'd been enjoying our newfound friendship. I'd been getting used to having him around. When he'd been staying over, I'd brought him candy from the sweet shop. And he'd ordered takeout from Jessi's Diner. We'd spent those evenings together, eating and relaxing.

After setting up the camera system at my place yesterday, he'd returned to his cabin for the night. And I'd *missed* him. His deadpan humor that appeared out of nowhere. The way he noticed how I was feeling, like he could read it in my body language. The little details about himself that he'd started dropping into conversation, like how his favorite holiday was Easter because he loved those cream-filled eggs. He was still quiet and brooding, but Lord knew I could carry on enough conversation for the both of us.

I liked being around him. He didn't just make me feel safe. I'd been having *fun*. And every new piece that Trace showed me of himself, I appreciated. Because I knew how difficult it was for him to open up at all.

He flipped his hair back out of his eyes. "Let me get dressed, and I'll be out in a sec. Unless you want to come in?"

"I might as well see what you've done with the place." I followed him inside. The noise and voices from the construction faded once he'd closed the door.

The interior of the cabin was small and quaint. Two tiny rooms with an open doorway between them. The front room had a low table with a computer and a solar-powered charger. A camping hot plate sat in the corner, plus some shelves that held dishes, utensils, and nonperishable food. Through the doorway, I spied a bedroll in the other room, as well as Trace's backpack.

No other electricity. No plumbing. He had a huge plastic tank of water that I assumed he had to fill in town or pump from a well. I loved camping way out in the wilderness, but for every day, this was another level of roughing it. I couldn't imagine how he stayed warm enough at night without a heater. There was an antique wood-burning stove, but I hadn't seen any firewood or pellets around, so I doubted he'd been using it.

And from his barely dressed state, I assumed he didn't bundle up in layers of PJs at night. Maybe he even slept naked.

Which was not something I should be imagining.

While Trace went to open up his backpack in the other room, I glanced over the paperbacks he'd stacked on his table. *The Hobbit* was among them. The creases in the spine showed it was well-loved.

"I'm changing my pants now," he announced. "Fair warning."

So of course, my eyeballs flew straight to his toned behind in boxer briefs just as he stepped out of his sweatpants.

Have. Mercy.

"It's good timing that you came by," Trace said as he changed. "I just got an update from River. He's my contact who's been helping me investigate your stalker."

"Yeah?" My voice cracked. I was facing away from him now, flipping through *The Hobbit* with my cheeks burning.

We were friends, and I was *not* being weird.

"River sent those cigarette butts we found to a lab. They're working on pulling DNA, but there's always a backlog, so it'll take a few days. He's still had no luck pinpointing the exact origin of the threatening comments. But as for *creekviewkid13*, River unmasked it easily. The IP address came from a cell phone outside Creekview, Colorado."

I gasped and turned around. Luckily, he had his jeans on and was just tugging down his long-sleeved Henley over his flat stomach. "The compound?" I asked. "Paradise Ranch?"

"That's what it looks like. An unregistered burner phone."

"Then Toby is telling the truth. He's Virtue's brother."

"Unless it's really the stalker, and he's trying to manipulate you."

"We have to read his new message." There was nowhere to sit, so I went into the other room and planted myself on top of Trace's blankets. This wasn't the time to get shy. Far more important matters demanded my attention.

Trace joined me on the blankets, watching as I pulled up

the latest message from *creekviewkid13*. My phone didn't have reception, but I'd taken a quick screenshot before I'd left home to make sure I'd have access to it.

Dear Miss Weston, My name is Tobias, but I go by Toby. I understand you want me to prove who I am. I would write a longer message cause there's a lot to say. But something happened yesterday and it's more important. Virtue is missing. Our sisters said she was gone from her bed, and nobody knows what happened to her. I think she ran off. I'm real scared about where she is and if she's okay. You escaped once, so maybe you can find her before anyone else does. Help her. Please. Just please believe me. I'm trusting you.

I covered my mouth with my hand, my stomach twisting up. "He sounds terrified."

"True. But he didn't give us anything specific to prove his claims."

I glared. "What do you expect? He's clearly using a phone without permission, so it can't be easy to send me anything at all. Everything about this message sounds authentic."

"I agree, and if this girl is really missing, that's concerning. But this could be a trick to lure you to the compound. It's an effective tactic. Use the name of a girl you once knew, give her a story that's similar to yours."

"Then why send me those creepy comments from the other anonymous account? Those only made me more suspicious. It's not the same person. I feel it."

"Your feeling isn't enough to keep you safe."

"You're right," I spit out. "I thought that was *your* job."

I stood up, pacing across the tiny square of space. Trace was being reasonable, and I shouldn't have been taking out my anger on him. But I couldn't stand the thought of Virtue being out in the woods, all alone, trying to make her way to freedom. If she was the same toddler I remembered, she would be fifteen. The same age I'd been when I'd escaped.

"I still don't know how I made it all the way to Hartley," I said. "It was like there was somebody watching over me, because so many things could've gone wrong. I could've been lost in the hills beyond the compound. Some sicko could've picked me up by the side of the road instead of that Good Samaritan. I was naive in a lot of ways back then, and I have no doubt Virtue is the same. There's no telling what could happen."

"Then what is it you want to do?" Trace asked softly.

"I have to go try to find her. Like Toby asked." I rubbed my hand over my mouth, ignoring the nausea that reared up in my throat. "I have to go to Paradise Ranch."

It terrified me to think of going back. It had been thirteen years, and I had never wanted to set foot in that place again. But if I turned my back on this girl and her brother, knowing what I did? How could I ever face myself in the mirror again?

Trace got up and stood in front of me, hands on my shoulders to stop my pacing. "I'll go there myself. I'll see what I can find out."

"It won't work without me. They'll never talk to you. Not in a million years. I know the people. I know the place."

"You sure they'll talk to you? Aren't you an apostate or something like that?"

"They won't be welcoming. But they're still my family. What else can I do but try?"

And my mother was there. I could see her again, something I'd never thought was possible.

Trace's expression hardened. "You're asking me to take you to the same people who would've forced you into a marriage. Who murdered your friend for helping you escape. You honestly think I'm going to put you in that kind of danger?"

"I am asking for your help. Not your permission."

There was a loud crash from outside, and I jumped. "Jeez, what was that?" I went over to the window and peeked out, but everything looked fine. It was just the demo. "They're really getting into it."

My brief flare of nerves faded. But when I turned around, Trace's eyes had gone distant, his body rigid. His tanned skin had gone pale.

Oh.

I almost asked if he was okay, but he'd asked me not to do that. So I just waited, and after a few more seconds, he dug his fingers into his hair. "There was someone I put at risk," he said hoarsely. "She had plenty of training. Our superiors decided she could manage it. So I let her go into a situation alone. And she didn't make it out." His Adam's apple bobbed as he swallowed. "I can't ever let something like that happen again."

I was shocked. This was more than Trace had ever mentioned about his former job. I could tell he was stuck in those memories, struggling to find his way out again.

A couple of feet separated us. I wanted to touch him, reach for his hand. I also knew Trace wouldn't want that comfort. So I walked toward him, not touching, but close enough I could feel his heat, and maybe he could feel mine.

He slowly breathed out. "I have no problem risking myself. But it's something completely different to risk you."

"I know this is a risk. And it does scare me. But if you're with me, I won't be going into it alone." *Please don't say no,* I thought.

Was I brave enough to go back to Paradise Ranch myself? Maybe. Probably. But I much preferred having Trace there beside me.

"I need to talk to Aiden. We'll need backup. We're not charging over to the compound without a plan."

"Does that mean you're saying yes, though? You'll go with me?"

"I'm certainly not letting you do it without me. I won't

abandon Virtue or Toby, either. If they're real, I'll do whatever I can to help them."

"Thank you." This time, I couldn't hold myself back. I hugged him, my cheek against his chest. Trace's spine stiffened, and I almost let go. But then he rested his hand on the small of my back.

"It'll be okay," he said.

We stood there a few minutes together as I soaked in the comfort. Though I wished he would've let me comfort him, too.

At the diner, I found Jessi in her tiny office, staring at a spreadsheet on her computer. "Hey, got a minute?" I asked.

She looked up and smiled. "For you, always." Then she noticed Trace behind me. "Big brother. Why does this visit feel a lot more serious all of a sudden?"

"I need to speak with Aiden."

"Is it urgent?" she asked.

I nodded, and at the same time Trace said, "Probably."

"He's upstairs." She pointed at the ceiling, where she and Aiden had their apartment. "What's going on?"

"Scarlett will tell you."

Trace left, headed for the stairwell, and I closed the door. Jessi came around to sit with me on the edge of the desk. "Scarlett, you look freaked out."

"I am, sugar. Things seem pretty bad at the moment."

"Tell me."

So I did. I told her everything.

I didn't want to burden Jessi with this. She was juggling a lot of plates already. Thankfully, she'd finally hired some employees for the diner. That was why she and Aiden weren't serving customers right now.

Aiden was always there for her, supporting her in every way. Yet I still wanted to protect my best friend. But that was just it. She was my best friend, and I knew she'd always have my back too.

I showed her the messages from *creekviewkid13*. Toby. "I remember his older sister from when I was still at the compound."

Jessi read Toby's messages with her brows drawn together.

"They want to force Virtue into a marriage with a man she didn't choose or want. That's also what happened to me. At least, they tried. When I was fifteen, my father was going to give me to another man to marry. That was bad enough, but this man Dawson Witkins, he was cruel too. I would've had no control over my body, my freedom. He would've owned me in every way. *That's* why I ran."

"Oh, sweetheart." Jessi hugged me. "I figured it was something like that. I'm so sorry, Scarlett. It's evil, stealing someone's freedom that way."

Jessi looked even more upset when I told her about my stalker—both the comments online and the person who had been outside my house.

But my friend was tough. And she had the biggest heart. Her next statement reminded me exactly why I loved her. "We're going to help Virtue," she said. "There's no question. That's what Last Refuge is all about. Helping people like her."

"That's how I feel too. This stalker thing is obnoxious, and I'm taking it seriously. But I won't let it stop me from doing what I can for Virtue."

"Agreed. So Aiden and Trace should go to Paradise Ranch. See if they can track down Virtue and bring her back here. The housing isn't ready at Last Refuge, but we'll find a place for her."

I smiled, squeezing my friend's hand. "We will. But I need to go to the compound myself. When you were in trouble, you always insisted on being right there in the middle of it. Facing down the people who wanted to hurt you. You didn't just sit back and let Aiden handle it without you."

"But you're my best friend," Jessi said. "Remember how you said you wanted to protect me then? Well, that's what I want now. It's more than just your physical safety. Are you sure it's healthy for you, mentally and emotionally, to go back there? After what you went through?"

"I have to. For Virtue. And...my mother is still there."

"Oh, Scarlett."

The truth was, those vicious comments online had taken their toll. The stalker's accusation that I didn't care about those I'd left behind. I *did* care. But I'd been living my life in Hartley as if the compound didn't exist anymore. "I'm the best hope that Virtue has. Toby hinted that Virtue is supposed to marry Dawson Witkins. I've been in her exact position. And the others at the compound, like her brother Toby, and anyone else who doesn't want that life..."

Would they want to leave? Would my mother want to leave if I asked her again, after over a decade had passed?

Jessi's gaze sharpened. "This is starting to sound like a much bigger mission than just getting Virtue to safety."

I shook my head. "I'm not trying to get ahead of myself. A lot of the people at the compound don't want to change, and they never will. But I can't keep hiding from my past. I'm going back there to face it. Even though I'm scared half to death. I'm especially afraid I'll bring the danger back to Hartley. To *you*."

"Don't worry about that. I've been known to kick some butt on occasion. And when that fails, I've got Aiden to protect me. And we've got Owen as well, should we decide to get law enforcement involved." She pulled me into a hug.

"Neither one of us is fearless all the time. That's why we lean on one another. We'll always be enough if we stick together." Jessi leaned back, smiling deviously. "And if we have our men with us."

My skin heated. "Trace isn't my man. We're friends, and it was hard enough to get him to agree to that."

"If you can get Trace out of his shell, I'm all for it. I trust him to watch out for you, but I trust you with him too. For what that's worth." Her eyes conveyed her meaning. Jessi was giving her blessing. I didn't need it because Trace and I weren't going there again. There would be no more sexy slow-dances or fiery kisses. But I appreciated it all the same.

"Thanks."

We both sat back, taking a breath after that intense moment. "We need to talk logistics," Jessi said. "But that's Aiden's purview. The Last Refuge Protectors are his idea, and he and Trace obviously have way more knowledge in that department than either of us. I have to defer to them. This could get dangerous, and I realize you're well aware of that. But listen to me, Scar. If something happens to you, I would *not* be okay. I can't lose you. So if you take some kind of impulsive, crazy risk, I'm not sure I could forgive you."

"Noted."

"Don't do anything I wouldn't do."

"Oh, I promise I'll be more careful than you would ever be."

We both laughed, and she pretended to punch my arm. "I'll hold you to that."

CHAPTER ELEVEN

Trace

I FOUND AIDEN UPSTAIRS, just as Jessi had said. Aiden was painting a newly constructed wall in a pale blue shade. This half of the apartment was covered in plastic, while they were living on the other side.

"A lot's different in here," I said.

Aiden glanced over. "Trying to wrap it up before Last Refuge is finished. But I've always liked to stay busy. More doing, less talking."

I grunted. "Fine by me."

"What's up? Unless you just came by to help me paint. That's a hint, by the way."

Smirking, I grabbed a roller and joined in, spreading blue over the wall. "The situation with Scarlett that we talked about? It's escalating." I'd already been texting with him over the last few days, sharing what he needed to know since this was a Protector assignment.

"What happened?" Aiden asked.

I updated him on Toby's message and Virtue going missing from Paradise Ranch. "Scarlett wants to help find this missing girl. But the timing is odd. Someone was harassing Scarlett online, watching her in real life, and then this *creekviewkid* account claims to desperately need her help. I don't like it."

"You think they're connected?"

"Can't discount the possibility. Of course, Scarlett doesn't care about the risk. She wants to go to Paradise Ranch to find Virtue. That's where Scarlett grew up, and she barely escaped the place the first time. I don't want her going back there, but she's pretty insistent."

"I've had those arguments with Jessi. I get it. So let's skip ahead, because we know Scarlett isn't going to back down."

"Agreed." I chuckled, thinking of how stubborn my sister and Scarlett could be, then returned to seriousness. "The people at this compound won't talk to an outsider. Scarlett has the best hope of getting someone there to open up. Of course, I'll be there with her. I may be able to find clues to the stalker. And if we can find Virtue, and the girl wants to come with us, we'll bring her back to Hartley. Help her start a new life."

"That's a lot for one mission. But it's all good by me. This is why we're starting the Protectors. To keep our loved ones safe, plus help innocent people. Our first official mission is here sooner than we might like, but we can do this. I just need you to tell me what you need from me."

"I thought you'd have stronger opinions about how this goes. The Protectors are your idea. Not mine. I'm not even sure I'll be staying in Hartley for the long term."

"What?" He frowned. "Please tell me there's a *but*. Because Jessi won't be happy to hear that."

"Just something I'm considering."

Aiden dumped his roller in the paint tray. "Look, I need you for this. If either of us should be in charge of the Protectors, it's you."

"How do you figure that?"

"I know there's a lot you can't tell me about your former

job. Or that you just *won't* tell me. I'll accept that. But you and I both know you're the one with the superior skills."

"You did fine when Jessi was in danger."

"I've been a civilian for seven years. I'm just a cook at this point. And a guy who'll do anything in the universe to make his woman happy. Jessi wants to make Last Refuge a reality, so I'm doing that. But I'm no leader."

I shifted my weight, glancing at the window. "You think I am?"

We had never spoken candidly about my issues. But Aiden had to be aware of it. He was neither stupid nor unobservant. I respected everything he had to offer. Both as my sister's life partner, and as a teammate. We'd worked well together in the past.

But if he thought I would be a good leader for the Protectors, he was a fool.

A leader should have a level head. A respect for hierarchy. Once upon a time, that had been me. But not any more.

Aiden needed to understand who he was dealing with.

"My last mission..." I tried to come up with the minimum I could tell him to get my point across. I'd already shared a bit with Scarlett today, and that wore on me. It was like pulling up stones from a vat of quicksand.

When Scarlett and I had been in my cabin, those memories had tried to drag me down into that suffocating darkness. I didn't want to go back there. But I had to get through it if Aiden and I were going to trust one another.

He cocked his head, waiting until I was ready to go on.

"In my former job, I wasn't out there serving justice on bad guys. Okay? I was gathering intelligence. I was part of a structure to feed a machine that ran on political capital. That machine didn't care about strict principles of right and wrong."

"You were CIA."

I didn't confirm. He didn't need me to. I was already violating all sorts of laws to tell him any of this. "I did my job, even if it was in shades of gray. But then I came across some intelligence that I couldn't ignore. A friend of mine was supposed to infiltrate a human trafficking ring. Not to stop it, but to exploit a foreign leader's connection to it. Blackmail, basically."

"Shit," he muttered.

"Yeah. My friend and I decided we were tired of gray. We defied orders and set our own mission parameters. Decided to do what was right."

We had intended to stop the trafficking ring. Free the victims. Even if our own government would burn us for it.

"You think I'd have a problem with that?" Aiden asked. "I don't give a fuck if you went against orders. I would've done the same in that circumstance."

"Just listen." I blinked away the shadows that feathered at the corners of my mind. "My friend was undercover. She..."

Blood on the walls. On my knees when I hit the floor.

Dammit, I felt like I was polluting this building by uttering these words here. Thinking these thoughts. But I kept going. "She was killed. Then I tracked down every last person involved in the trafficking ring. And I took care of them."

I had gone dark in more ways than one.

There was a long pause. I had closed my eyes, but I felt Aiden studying me.

"You did what you had to."

"Maybe. But if I'd done better, I might've saved innocent lives in the first place."

"Is that how you hurt your knee?"

I nodded. I'd limped away from that final mission having destroyed more than just my career. To the Agency, I was a dirty secret to be hushed up. And that meant I had to keep my superiors' secrets too.

It would've been easier for a lot of people if I had died while taking my revenge. But I hadn't. I was here. And somehow, I had people in my life who hadn't turned their backs on me. No matter how much of a pain in the ass I was.

"You're still dealing with all of it," Aiden said, more gently. "Can't blame you."

"My point is, with me involved, things could get messy." I didn't want that to happen, especially with Scarlett near. But if it *was* necessary? "If shit really hits the fan and we get caught, we'll all go down for it. So you deserve fair warning who you're partnering up with."

Then Aiden surprised me.

He laughed, long and hard. Something he didn't do often.

"I'm the last guy to have an issue with that. You know how I feel. If they're fighting dirty, we will too. If Jessi had given me the go-ahead, certain people would no longer be breathing. I would've had bodies to hide."

"And I would've been happy to help you dispose of them."

"Figured I could count on you." He grinned, then sobered. "But Trace, if you don't feel you're ready to be on the front lines, I can take this assignment. I'll go with Scarlett to Paradise Ranch. You can stay here with Jessi and provide backup and logistics support."

My body reacted viscerally. "If Scarlett's going with anyone, it's me. I don't trust anyone to protect her more than myself. No offense," I added.

He held up his hands. "All right, not a problem. It was just an offer."

"I can protect Scarlett. I won't let anything happen to her, and the same goes for Virtue if we can find her and get her out of there."

"Got it." Aiden nodded, accepting my assessment without

question. "I'm glad we're on the same page. No matter what, I've got your back. I know you've got mine. Whoever else we bring into the Protectors, we'll demand no less. But at some point, I'll need to know how committed you are. Whether or not you're staying or going."

A fair question.

In some ways, I had been living the past year as if I were a ghost. I'd felt untethered, restless, and I had to find my way forward.

Right now, every path I took seemed to lead to Scarlett. The woman I couldn't get out of my head. Who'd burrowed under my skin. The past few days of being her friend had been more vivid, more fulfilling, than anything I'd experienced in years, even before my career had blown up. She was filling in my faded outline with life and color. With reasons to actually wake up and look forward to my day.

I didn't deserve to be the man she came home to and welcomed into her bed. But whatever I *could* be for her, I would. For the time being.

That might not wash the blood from my hands, but it was something.

"I'm not sure where I'll end up. If it'll be Hartley or...elsewhere. Can I have a couple of months to decide?"

"Just keep me informed. And know that I'm here if you ever need me. Not just as Jessi's significant other." He grasped my hand in a warrior's grip, then pulled me into a hug. My second of the day. "Brothers?" he asked gruffly.

"Brothers."

It felt damn good to say that. And to mean it.

Aiden released me and stepped back. "So let's talk about what you'll need for this mission."

CHAPTER TWELVE

Trace

WE SET out the following morning in Scarlett's Jeep. I was driving, and I'd been a little surprised that she didn't put up a fight on that subject. But from the way she was staring out the window, lost in thought, I assumed she had other things on her mind.

The sky was overcast today, threatening rain. The road narrowed quickly as we approached the mountain pass, in some places not wide enough for two cars to pass side by side. But there wasn't a single other vehicle but ours—except for the one following us at a distance. Aiden's truck.

"I haven't been this way in a long time," she said with a shiver. "Never thought I would again."

"You don't have to do this. Say the word, and I'll take you back to Hartley. I can still visit the compound myself. Or take Aiden with me."

She shook her head. "I'm not having that conversation again. I'm *going*. I just don't know what kind of reception I'll get. If they'll turn me away at the door or spit on me or something."

I scowled. "If they do that, I'll see that they regret it."

"Easy, tiger." She smirked, and I was glad to see her anxiety tick down a few notches. "I'm a big girl. I don't care if they curse me. But I need to get inside and get info on Virtue."

We'd already planned our cover story. Scarlett would say she missed her mother and sisters and wanted to see them. I was posing as her adoptive brother. *If it was good enough for Jessi and Aiden, it's a good enough excuse for me,* Scarlett had remarked last night when we were planning. For reasons I still didn't quite get, Aiden had pretended to be me before I'd arrived in Hartley. Weird. But it had worked to confuse the bad guys who'd been after Jessi.

Today, Aiden would follow us and park off the road before we reached Creekview. He now had a satellite phone of his own, and I had mine, so we were prepared if I needed to call him for backup. But I also had a GPS tracker in Scarlett's Jeep, plus my personal weapon in the glove box and Scarlett's shotgun stowed beneath the seat.

We'd prepared for contingencies. But I hoped those plans would prove unnecessary.

"I keep wondering if we should've told Toby we were coming," Scarlett said.

We'd been over this. "It wouldn't be wise. If anyone knows we're coming, even him, it's more likely we'll meet resistance."

She bit her lip. "I can't even risk mentioning his name unless my mom and I are alone. If he's thirteen, he's old enough to live in the bachelor's house, so he's not allowed to speak to any unmarried women he's not related to."

"We'll be careful this visit," I said, repeating what I'd instructed last night and again this morning. "Get a feel for what's happening there. Assess the situation and recruit potential allies. We can go back later once we know more."

"But what if that's too late for Virtue?" She said this

quietly, facing the window again. I knew she didn't expect an answer. I didn't have one.

Her anxiety was back up to eleven.

"Hey." I held out my hand. "I'll be with you. We can do this."

She twined her fingers with mine. "Are you telling me to be more optimistic?"

"Exactly. You're a downer, Scarlett. Try being cheerful like me."

She snorted. "Distract me. *Please*. Tell me something new about you."

"I got bitten by a snake once in India. Thought I was going to die."

Her eyes bulged. "*What*? When were you in India? What kind of snake?"

"Can't tell you any of that. Classified."

"Your stories are the worst."

I felt the faint smile on my lips. Those muscles around my mouth had been getting more use lately.

We passed through the town of Creekview. It was even more of a blip than Hartley, with just a couple of run-down blocks on its main street. Hartley had livened up since I'd arrived in the winter. This place felt like a graveyard.

On we went, the road winding again. The landscape opened up in rolling hills, interspersed with grassy pastures. Aiden and I had studied the compound and its surroundings on Google Earth. It was a working cattle ranch spanning hundreds of acres.

"Beautiful," Scarlett breathed. Her hand was tight on mine. "It looks exactly the same."

"You're not the same, though."

"No. I'm not. And this time, you're with me. I know I said I'd do this even if I had to go alone. But I'm not sure that's true."

"You could've done it. But you don't have to."

The road cut through more hills, like we were threading through a maze. It was expansive and claustrophobic at the same time. The woods that covered those hills went on for miles. The kind of place a person could get lost in and never be found.

Was there a teenage girl hiding out here somewhere? And if so, how could we find her?

We passed through an open gate. A rusting metal sign proclaimed it Paradise Ranch. We drove on until a cluster of buildings appeared. Wisps of fog clung to the settlement, and rain dotted our windshield.

Scarlett sucked in a breath. "That's it. The compound."

People milled about, some turning to stare in our direction. The chapel was at the center of the settlement, with the other buildings arranged around it. Scarlett had told us that each family had its own large dwelling, and I saw the fences that separated them. In another area, Scarlett had pointed out a bunkhouse for the unmarried men over age thirteen. Plus the structures for the ranch operation.

Then a pickup roared onto the road, heading straight toward us. Several men sat packed inside, with more crowded into the bed. I tensed, wondering if they meant to stop us. But they didn't slow and went right past, faces glaring from the truck's windows. Dust puffed behind their tires. They were on their way somewhere in a hurry.

But despite their hostility, they hadn't looked all that surprised to see us.

"Where do you think they're headed?" I asked.

"No clue." She pointed to another building, this one a double-wide trailer. "That's the office." I pulled into a gravel lot, where several other vehicles were parked, and cut the engine.

Scarlett stared at her hands in her lap. "I remember

coming here with the Hartley sheriff when I was fifteen. When my own father called me a liar and impure."

"We can still turn around and leave, babe. This is your decision."

Her eyes widened, and I realized what I'd just called her. *Shit.*

"We're on a pet-name basis now?" she asked.

"Slipped out," I grunted. "Sorry."

"I didn't mind." Scarlett lifted her hand and smoothed it down my cheek. Her thumb moved over my whiskers, and a very inappropriate surge of arousal zapped down my spine.

Then her thumb pressed into my lower lip. That arousal went straight into my cock.

"Someone's probably watching us," I warned.

"I know. I have this strange urge to kiss you right now. Probably because I'm so *impure*."

"Scarlett." I was trying not to smile. Or pull her to me. "If you really want me to, I will kiss you. But our brother-sister cover story won't go over as well."

"Exactly the issue that Jessi and Aiden ran into." She patted my cheek instead, eyes bright with mischief. "I'm ready," she said. "Let's go."

When we stepped out of the Jeep, there was already a man in his thirties striding out of the office to meet us. His expression was cautious and diplomatic. The guy assigned to speak to outsiders, I figured. He didn't introduce himself, and though he glanced over us both, I didn't get the sense that he recognized Scarlett.

"Can I help you folks?" There was a defensiveness to his tone. I spotted curtains moving in the office, plus more eyes watching from nearby buildings. They were nervous about something. But was that general standoffishness, or something more specific?

I thought of that truck speeding down the road past us.

The guy was looking to me for an answer, probably because I was male. So I nodded for Scarlett to speak.

"My name is Scar—Um, Serenity. I used to live here. I'd like to see my mother Felicity and my sisters. Elder Tyler is my father."

He reared back slightly in shock. He knew the names, but not specifically that we'd been coming. Which was good.

"And you?" he asked me.

"I'm Trace, her big brother. Adoptive, obviously. Just here to look out for her." I tried to convey harmlessness through my stance and my tone. Bullshit, all of it. Because I meant a world of harm to anyone who had hurt Scarlett. Whether they'd find that out depended on what they did next.

"Do you have a name?" I asked.

He didn't respond to that. "Come inside."

He spun on his heel and headed back into the office. I lifted my eyebrows at Scarlett, placing my hand on her lower back as we followed. "Mr. Friendly, isn't he?" I commented.

"No surprise there."

The office was sparse and functional. A desk with a computer. A couple of stiff-backed chairs against one wall, lined up in a sort of waiting area. I imagined this was all of the compound that most outsiders got to see. They probably handled deliveries and other business here.

Mr. Friendly rounded the desk and picked up a landline phone. He spoke quietly into it. We stood, waiting for his decision on what to do with us.

"You good?" I whispered to Scarlett. She was trembling slightly.

"Fine."

Mr. Friendly lowered the phone. "Serenity, I'll take you to speak to your mother. She's waiting at Elder Tyler's house."

Her reaction was almost invisible, but I still caught it. *Her father's house*. "Can't her mother come here?" I asked.

"That's impossible," Mr Friendly said.

"Then I'm going with her."

"That's impossible, too. You'll have to wait here. If she wants to see her family, this is the only way. It's up to you."

I could understand why the elders had chosen Mr. Friendly for this job. He had a backbone, I gave him that. Actually, I was surprised he had agreed to Scarlett's request so easily. I'd been expecting more follow-up questions.

My eyes drilled into him hard. Was this a trap? Should I grab Scarlett and get her the hell out of here?

But then she wouldn't learn anything about Virtue or Toby. She wouldn't see her mother.

"I'll go." Scarlett cast a glance at me that said, *I'll be fine*. Mr. Friendly escorted Scarlett through another door, and she was out of my sight.

I breathed out slowly, trying to ignore the opposition that reared up in my gut. I had known this mission could get dicey. So many unknowns. I didn't like it. Not at all. But Scarlett had been right about one thing. We had no other way to get the info we needed. It was a calculated risk. One I had agreed to.

But did this guy really think I was going to sit here and wait patiently?

Hell. No.

Another man stepped into the office. This one bigger and burlier. He crossed his arms over his chest and stood by the wall without a word, glaring at me. Then the front door to the office opened again, and two more big guys walked in.

Now this could be a problem.

For them, anyway.

Out of caution, I'd left my weapons in the Jeep. I didn't like going into this unarmed. But I had other methods at my disposal. All my training and instincts were firing for the first time in two years. And despite the danger, it felt *good*. Like stretching out after being trapped in one confined space for too long.

I sat quietly for a while, twiddling my thumbs. The other guys shuffled their feet.

"I saw a truck full of people moving pretty fast out of here this morning," I said conversationally. "What was that about?"

No response.

"And the guy who met us outside the office when we first pulled up. The friendly one. He seemed to be expecting visitors, but not us. Have you been expecting anyone?"

No answer.

Then I stood abruptly. All three of my babysitters snapped to attention. "I need to use the bathroom," I said.

They glanced at each other. "You have to stay here," one said.

"I get that, but this is an emergency. I really need to take a piss."

They stared.

"There must be a bathroom in this office, right?" I asked.

"That's not for you."

"But you don't want me to do it right here, do you?" I gestured at the office with its cheap carpeting. "I'm telling you. Emergency."

"Too bad."

"I drank a lot of coffee, and it was a long drive. What part don't you understand?"

"The answer is *no*."

I reached for my zipper.

That did the trick. The guy who'd spoken jerked forward, cursing under his breath. "Okay, *stop*." He had a look of pure disgust on his face. "I'll take you. Just wait a dang minute."

There. Was that so hard?

We went outside. Two of the babysitters came along,

while the other stayed behind in the office. We walked across the gravel toward a sprawling barn. One of the men pushed me toward a wooden side building. "The can is in there. Just hurry it up."

"You don't want to come in with me?"

There was that revulsion again, which helped ensure they stayed out here rather than keeping an eye on me.

"Suit yourself," I muttered. I opened the door and went in. There was a toilet and a rickety old sink. Neither had been cleaned in a while. But there was also a window, and that was all I cared about. The view showed the back of another building with a small yard between. No other sign of life.

I turned on the faucet, water splashing into the metal basin. The window frame squeaked as I opened it. Nobody came to investigate. I pushed it the rest of the way, stepped onto the toilet, and slipped silently through the opening. My shoes whispered against the dirt as I landed outside.

Now, I had to find Elder Tyler's house.

"Psst. *Hey*."

I turned sharply. There was a scrawny teenager pressed up against a wall, hidden by shadows. The kid had big eyes, which kept darting around. His sleeves were too long, and he'd rolled them up a few times.

"You came here with Scarlett?" he whispered.

"Are you Toby?"

He put a finger to his mouth to shush me. "This way. Hurry." Toby stuck his head around a corner, then darted out, waving for me to follow. He led me around the next building to another door, which opened into some kind of storage room full of miscellaneous tools and equipment. It smelled like metal. Toby didn't turn on a light, and sunlight painted stripes across one interior wall.

"We don't have long," I said. "Any moment they'll realize I left the bathroom."

Toby whirled around. His fists were clenched, and a scowl darkened his childlike face. "What's your name?" he demanded. The poor kid looked like he hadn't slept in a while. He was scrappy and courageous, but he was also overwhelmed.

"I'm Trace. A friend of Scarlett's. You told Scarlett your sister is missing, right?" He hesitated, so I added, "Scarlett and I are a package deal. If you trust her, you trust me. You'll have to decide quick. Because I'm guessing if you get caught with me, you'll be in trouble."

His lip trembled. "They've been out searching for Virtue. If they get to her, they'll hurt her. That's all I care about. Just making sure she's safe."

So that explained the flurry of activity. Search parties were out, and Virtue had been missing for at least a couple of days at this point. The elders probably feared Virtue would make contact with outsiders, like Scarlett had thirteen years ago.

"Where could she have gone?" I asked.

"The woods. She was mad at me." He wiped his eyes. "I knew Virtue was planning to run away before her marriage to Elder Dawson. I just didn't know when. I told her I'd contacted Scarlett Weston for help, and Virtue was furious with me." His voice broke. "She was gone the next morning."

"And you're sure she ran? She wasn't taken?"

"Why else would they be searching so hard?" He dropped his voice low, and I had to lean in. "Elder Dawson has been raging. He and the others have been questioning everyone."

"Including you?"

The scowl returned. "I won't tell a soul what I know. I wouldn't give up my sister. Ever."

"You haven't told anyone else that you contacted Scarlett?"

"*No*, I swear I haven't. The only reason I knew her name was I heard Elder Dawson talking about her."

Voices shouted somewhere nearby. I wondered if that was about me. Surely they'd noticed I had disappeared. Toby heard them too. He sent a panicked glance at the door, and I rested a hand on his shoulder. "Hold on, you heard Dawson mention *Scarlett's* name?" I repeated. "When?"

He blinked. "It was about a month ago. He was on his cell phone in his personal study, and I was making a supply delivery to his house. He didn't know I was there. I was in the hall and heard Dawson mention Serenity. He said that her new name was Scarlett Weston. That she was living in Hartley." Toby licked his lips, clearly trying to keep his scattered thoughts together. "I have a pay-as-you-go phone I bought in Creekside. That's how I get online. When I got back to my bunk, I looked up Scarlett Weston, and that's when I found her Instagram account. Everyone here knows about Serenity. We're not supposed to talk about her except as a bad example, but we do. I thought Scarlett could help us. Help my sister. I didn't know another soul who could." His eyes lifted like he was searching for reassurance.

"You were right to ask for help."

"I was scared I did the wrong thing. Virtue was so mad."

"No, kid. You're doing great. And you're not alone, okay? We are going to sort this out. Now listen. Do you have any idea who Dawson was talking to on the phone about Scarlett?"

He shook his head. "But I think it was an outsider. From the way they were talking. That's how it sounded."

"Okay." I wanted to ask more, but we didn't have time. "What about you? Do you want to leave the compound? Yes or no. I can help you escape, but only if you're sure."

He hesitated. "Maybe. I...don't know. We have to find Virtue first. Please."

"I'm going to try. I want you to contact me directly if you

get more info, or if anything else happens. Do you have somewhere to write down my number?"

"I'll remember," he said eagerly. "I'm good with numbers. I keep my phone hidden, but I'll put down your contact tonight."

I recited my satellite phone number, and Toby repeated it a few times, committing the digits to his mind. "Begin your message with the word *Freebird*. That way, I'll know it's from you." I patted his shoulder again. "Virtue needs you to stay strong. You've been doing great so far. Just keep going a while longer."

"'Kay. I'll do my best. Um, thank you. You don't know how much this means."

"I do know," I assured him. "I need to go now. When we get outside, can you point me to where Elder Tyler lives?"

"You can't go there. They won't let you in."

I'll go wherever I want to, kid, I thought. I had plenty of experience moving unseen. "Just point me to where it is. After that, keep your head down and don't tell anyone about talking to me."

His scrappy attitude made a resurgence. "Do you think I'm crazy?"

"Only in a good way." There was nothing wrong with being a little crazy if that was what it took to do something brave.

We carefully stole outside after making sure the coast was clear. Toby directed me toward Elder Tyler's property, then scampered off. The rainy, foggy mist was heavier, coating everything in dampness. The sky had turned an ominous dark gray.

I really hoped I'd run into Dawson. I was just dying to meet the SOB who had tried to make Scarlett's life hell.

It was about time that I returned that favor.

CHAPTER THIRTEEN

Scarlett

FOR THE FIRST time in thirteen years, I stepped over the threshold of my father's house. But my father wasn't waiting in the living room for me. And neither was my mother.

Mercy, my father's first wife, stood there with her hands clasped in front of her plain blue dress. "Hello, Serenity." She looked older, but she wore the same style of dress I remembered. And the same pinched expression on her face.

The man who'd escorted me was already gone, and the door to the house shut behind me. Instead of answering her, I glanced around the room. This place looked smaller than I remembered.

No, that wasn't it. I was bigger. So much bigger than this place.

I held my head high. "I came here to speak to my mom. Where's Felicity?"

Her eyes moved over me with distaste, taking in my jeans and plaid shirt. "I never expected to see you again."

That wasn't an answer to my question, but I played along. "I didn't expect to come back. Yet here I am."

"And why is that? I'm sure you must have some reason.

Not just that you wanted to see your family, because you scrubbed your hands of us long ago."

I struggled to keep my anger down. Years ago, Mercy had told me I should be honored that Dawson had chosen me. That I should be honored to serve him. I tasted bile as I looked at her, remembering her callous treatment of me and my mom.

Yet not everything about this place had been bad. I'd played with my younger sisters and brothers right over there behind the sofa. Jacks and hide and seek. Part of me did miss them. If I'd believed I could save them, I would've returned earlier, like I had tried to do when I'd brought the sheriff here.

But I did feel guilty for leaving them, even now. And I hated that Mercy was playing upon that.

"I did care. I do. But I couldn't be true to myself and stay here. Don't forget that you all turned your backs on me."

"Because you were a sinner and a disgrace. You think I would allow you to see your sisters or anyone else who could be corrupted? You can't just turn up here and expect to be welcomed."

"Fine," I snapped. "At least let me see my mom. You must have a heart in there somewhere, Mercy. Let Felicity see her only child."

"Felicity is dead."

I gasped.

"She died five years ago. You really shouldn't have come."

I wanted to cry and scream and demand to know everything that had happened. My mother hadn't wanted to leave the compound, and I thought I had accepted it. But *dead*? That word crowded out everything else in my mind.

It couldn't be true. *Please, don't let it be true.*

"How?" I choked out.

"A fever took her. Your father called a doctor out, but it

was no use." Mercy went over to pick up a small cardboard box. "These are Felicity's things. When I heard you'd shown up a few minutes ago, I had them fetched from the cellar. Probably should've gotten rid of them a while ago." She thrust the box at me.

With trembling hands, I accepted it. A folded quilt was on top, thinned with age. My mother had made it with scraps of fabric from every color of the rainbow. Hearts interspersed between diamonds and squares. The sight of that quilt filled me with aching memories. My mom holding me at night. Tucking me in to bed. Singing "You Are My Sunshine." I'd had my half-siblings, but my mom and I had shared a special bond. And I'd left her alone.

I couldn't let myself cry. Not here, not now.

I wished Trace were here with me.

"I know you think I was too hard on you," Mercy said. "But you girls have to be strong. That's our lot in life. Our burden to bear."

I didn't want to hear a sermon from her. Yet she had a point. I had been tough enough when I left this place to survive on my own. I had been lucky enough to find good people to take me in. But if I had been weaker, I never would've made it that far.

Be strong, I told myself. I had escaped, and I was grown now. Virtue was still out there somewhere in need of a rescue. But Mercy wasn't going to tell me anything useful about Virtue's whereabouts. I already knew that. So I'd find another way. There was nothing else for me here.

"Thank you for giving me this," I said. "You didn't have to do that."

She shrugged like she didn't care and didn't want my thanks. "You should go now. Don't come back."

"Trust me, I won't. I can see myself out." I turned to leave.

But Mercy and I were no longer alone in the room.

Dawson Witkins stood blocking the door, leering at me.

Every drop of blood in my body turned to ice. "What's he doing in here?" No man except my father was allowed in this house. It was absolutely forbidden, unless a whole lot more had changed since I'd left than I'd realized.

Dawson didn't answer me. Neither did Mercy. She hadn't said a *thing*. Hadn't even betrayed it in her eyes. He must've already been in the kitchen when I'd come inside, because I hadn't heard the door open.

"It's been a long time," he said.

Objectively speaking, Dawson was a handsome man. Thick dark hair, a square jaw. But his heart and soul were ugly.

"You're allowing this, Mercy?" When I glanced behind me, I caught the swish of Mercy's skirt as she left the room. Leaving me alone with him.

A trap. This had been a trap, just like Trace had warned me it could be.

Now I needed Trace's help. I had no way to let him know.

Dawson walked toward me. I backed up against the sofa, the box of my mother's things in front of me. "Don't you dare touch me."

"I have every right to touch you. You belong to me. You have all this time, even if you ran away. You were prettier back then, though. That's a shame." He crowded me against the back of the couch, forcing the box out of my hands. It thudded onto the floor. He grasped a lock of my hair and spun it around his finger. "How many men have you let defile you, *Scarlett?*"

I slapped his hand away. "Stop."

He knows my name, I realized with a shiver of revulsion and fear.

"Are you here because of Virtue?" he asked. "Did you

have something to do with that girl running off? I swear if you did, I'm going to find out."

"I don't know what you're talking about. I only came to see my mother."

"Didn't know she was dead, huh?" He held my chin to make me look at him. "Felicity was weak. Not so defiant as you. But at least she knew how to accept her fate."

"You'd better let me go. I'm warning you."

Dawson pressed up against me. "Because you brought that big guy to protect you? Where is he now? You're alone plenty, Scarlett. In that little yellow house of yours in Hartley. Or the candy shop." He brought his lips to my ear. "You think I don't know how to find you? Did you think you wouldn't be punished for the promises you broke?"

No. No, no. "You left those comments. You were watching me? That was *you?*"

"I'm your rightful husband. You're mine to do with what I please. You've got punishment coming to you for every betrayal, every lie."

"Don't!" I pushed him away, but Dawson grabbed my shoulder and shoved me up against the nearby wall, face first. He held my hands behind me.

"And when I decide, I'm going to take you back. And there's nothing you'll be able to do about—"

His words dissolved into thick, desperate choking sounds. *What the heck was going on?*

Dawson wrenched away from me, and I turned.

Trace had his arms draped almost casually around Dawson's neck. Dawson's eyes bulged. He clawed at the grip squeezing the breath out of him. And Trace didn't say a single thing. His expression was completely blank. He just kept his grip clamped on Dawson's throat until the other man's eyes rolled back and he passed out.

It had taken a matter of seconds.

Distantly, I was aware of Trace dropping Dawson onto the ground behind a couch. Then he came over to me, his hands gently touching either side of my face. I was shivering all over.

"Hey. Look at me, babe. I've got you now. You hear me?"

"Y-yes. How did you get here? You were in the office."

"I'll always come to find you."

I wanted to collapse against him. But his calm, steady tone sank into me. His words. *I'll always come to find you.*

He smoothed the hair from my forehead. "We need to go now. People are looking for me, and I assume they'll wonder what happened to Dawson soon. I didn't see anyone on my way in here, but there could be people upstairs."

My brain was sluggish, still trying to sort through all that had just happened. "It was a trap. Letting me in to speak to Mercy. My mother..." I shook my head. I had to focus. "I didn't find out anything about where Virtue could be."

"That's okay. I found Toby, but we gotta move. I'll explain later. After we're out of here." He grabbed my hand and tugged me toward the window. Trace checked the view through the glass, then opened it and helped me climb out. There was no one in the yard. As if they'd all vanished, and with horror, I understood why.

Mercy had sent everyone away because Dawson was here. Here for *me*.

I didn't want to think about what might've happened if Trace hadn't appeared.

Rain pattered on our heads. Thunder rumbled as we climbed my father's fence, then made our way from one building to another, using them for cover. I heard voices yelling, feet running, but they were still distant. Briefly, my brain tried to think about my mom, but nope. I couldn't handle that right now. I was barely keeping hold of the quilt, which I'd grabbed before we left. I'd had to leave the rest of the box behind.

Trace moved like a silent predator. Like he had a sixth sense, hiding us in shadows and around corners when anyone approached. Graceful, but pretty damn intimidating too.

How much did I even know about him? About the kind of training and experience that would allow him to move that way? Or choke out Dawson without breaking a sweat?

What else had Trace done in his past?

Whatever it was, I was grateful. I had never seen anyone so fierce. So beautiful in his dedication. And he was here protecting *me*. I'd never felt more lucky.

I held on tight to his hand, and there wasn't another person in the world who I wanted more by my side.

Trace had stopped, and he was doing something with his phone. "Are you calling Aiden?" I asked.

"Sending an SOS. He'll be on his way. But we need to get to your Jeep and get out of here. Even with Aiden, we'll be outnumbered."

We were about to run again, but Trace suddenly pushed me against a wall, his large body blanketing mine. A pickup roared past.

"It's clear," Trace said.

The rain had picked up, wind lashing at my face. Wetting my hair and clothes. The voices got louder as we neared the office building, where my Jeep was parked.

We had to stop again. Trace seemed to be looking for an opening.

I rubbed the moisture from my eyes. "We can cut through the woods," I said, "and go around. It'll get us closer to the Jeep without going past the office. But we'll have to cut through that pasture." I pointed.

His gaze was dark. Intense. "All right. When I give you

the signal, run. Don't slow down and don't look back. Got it?"

"Yes."

He took the quilt from my hands. "Go."

I almost tried to take the quilt back, but I had the feeling this was one of those moments not to question his orders.

I dashed toward the slatted fence. Climbed over it and ran across the grassy pasture. *Come on, Scarlett. Move those legs, sugar.* I hadn't spent all those hours trail running for nothing. I focused on the woods ahead of me. When I reached the next fence, I leaped over and didn't slow down until I'd reached the cover of the trees.

I turned around, and Trace was right behind me. He held my mom's quilt like a football tucked under his arm. "Keep moving." His hand was heavy on my shoulder, guiding me gently but firmly along.

We ran through the woods, far enough in the trees that we wouldn't be seen easily from the compound. But I knew where I was going. I knew these woods. It was like muscle memory. Those nights I'd sneaked out to visit with Kenny. Stealing small doses of freedom.

There were more shouts, even more frantic than before, and I wondered if they'd found Dawson.

We approached the edge of the trees. "There," I said. My Jeep sat parked in front of the office. There was a man guarding my vehicle with a rifle in his hands. But the road was clear if we could just get past him and get going.

"How do we get to the Jeep?" I whispered. "We're unarmed."

"I'll handle it." Trace dug my keys from his pocket and passed them over. "Head for the driver's side. Get the Jeep started. The moment I'm inside, drive."

I nodded, breathing hard. Adrenaline coursed through me, and cold raindrops slid down my back. "Got it."

And in that moment, Trace actually smiled.

"You take the quilt this time. I'm assuming it's important to you." He put it in my hands, and before I could answer, he was moving toward the guy with the rifle, who'd just glanced in the other direction. My heart leaped into my throat.

Driver's side. Get the engine started. Go.

I ran again. Didn't pause until I'd yanked the Jeep open and climbed inside. I had the soft top down already. My mother's quilt landed somewhere in the backseat.

Seatbelt, I thought.

Rain pattered on the soft top. I heard a shout and a loud smack behind me. The engine roared to life. And suddenly, Trace was jumping into the passenger seat, and I had the car in gear.

Everything was happening so fast.

"*Go,*" Trace commanded, reaching under the seat. His hand came up with my shotgun.

"Seatbelt," I reminded him.

"Yeah, I got it, babe. Just go!"

I reversed into a turn, then steered the Jeep away from the compound. Rain poured and splashed on the road. Thank goodness for four-wheel drive.

But then Trace cursed. And I saw it.

The metal gate that had been open earlier? It was now closed.

"What do we do?"

"Don't slow down. Hit the gas."

"Oh, heck." My eyes went to the rearview mirror. A truck was on the road behind us. I hit the accelerator.

"Steer left."

"Left?" I said. "There's a *fence there.*"

"It's wood, and it's old. We'll be fine."

We sped down the unpaved road, bouncing in our seats.

That closed metal gate was coming up way too fast. I got ready to steer left.

"Oh gosh. Oh jeez."

"How is it that you curse *less* when we're running for our lives?" Trace reached for the steering wheel and gripped it, helping me keep it steady. At the last moment, we aimed for the wooden fence to the left of the gate.

There was a huge crash as we slammed into it, the old wood giving way. And then we were through, bumping on the wet grass of a pasture. My poor Jeep.

I went through a puddle, sending up a huge spray of water. The Jeep bucked, throwing us around. Trace's hand stayed on the wheel with mine.

We were driving parallel to the road now. A quick glance showed the pickup had tried to follow, but it was much slower. Then it stopped altogether, its tires trapped in the muck. Maybe it had a 4x4, but my Jeep could off-road like a champ even in these conditions.

But to get back to Hartley, we needed to be *on* the road to get through the mountain pass. Not stuck in a pasture that belonged to the compound. "What now?"

"Aim for that section of fence," Trace ordered, pointing. I could barely see it for the downpour. My wipers whipped back and forth across the glass.

"Which one?"

"*That* one."

Oh, heck. I gunned the accelerator again. The Jeep roared up the slight embankment, plowing through the wooden slats and jostling us when we landed, steering to straighten up.

Holy crap, that had been close.

We sped down the road. "I can't see if anyone's following us," I said. "Storm's too bad."

"If they are, they had to stop to open the gate. We've got a head start."

The road climbed again as we entered the hills, twisting and turning. I had to slow down around the curves. Trace had his satellite phone out. "Aiden got our message. He's—"

A loud snap and a *ping* against metal interrupted him.

I checked the rearview. Another pickup was just visible in the rain. This one clearly had a bigger engine than my Jeep, because it was gaining ground fast.

"They're shooting at us!" I cried.

"I noticed."

"You're the guy with all the jokes now, huh?"

The gunman in the pickup shot at us again. It missed. Trace looked back, the shotgun in his hands. The pickup was closing in. Trace leaned out the passenger window. Fired. Cracks appeared in the pickup's windshield, and it dropped back.

I was coming to another curve in the road, and I was going way too fast. We had to slow down.

But before I could do anything, I heard another shot, and the steering wheel jerked. The Jeep swerved. We'd just lost a tire. I screamed. Trace grabbed for the wheel, trying to help me steady it as I braked, but it was too late.

The Jeep careened off the road.

And a steep drop-off was barreling toward us.

I managed to skid us to a stop. The pickup roared past us on the road before the driver braked. But I had no doubt they were coming back. My poor, poor Jeep. She didn't deserve this treatment.

"Out of the car," Trace said.

I threw open the door. We both jumped out through the driver's side. Rain cascaded over my head and arms, pouring down my face. We were inches from that slope.

Trace grabbed hold of my arm and pulled me along. I

scrambled, shoes sliding on the wet ground as I tried to keep up. He was taking us toward the woods. At the same time, he pointed his handgun behind him and fired. I had no idea where the shotgun had gone. I could barely process everything that was happening at this point.

And of course, the jerks had to keep shooting at us.

"Get to the trees." Trace shoved me to the side as he twisted his upper body, returning fire.

And suddenly, I lost my footing. My foot hit a slick, muddy patch and kept on going. The ground seemed to vanish.

"Trace!" I screamed. But he was gone from my view in an instant.

I was careening down a muddy hillside, with no way to stop my fall.

CHAPTER FOURTEEN

Trace

ONE MOMENT, I'd had my hand on Scarlett. And the next, she was just *gone*.

I'd been laying down cover for us to get to the woods. My aim was less than perfect with the deluge pouring on us and screwing up my visibility. But that had meant the other guy was having trouble too. Except for that shot to our tire. *Luck*.

I'd looked away from her for a split second, but that was all it took. She slipped and slid right off that drop-off.

I fired twice more, keeping our pursuers back.

And then, I jumped.

I slid down the slope after Scarlett. It was mostly loose dirt turned to mud, with rainwater sluicing down in thick streams. I saw her trying to grab onto stray plants, and finally, she got hold of a scrubby bush. My boot heels dug into the muck, slowing my fall, and I managed to work my way toward her.

When I reached her, Scarlett's eyes were wider than I'd ever seen. "I thought I was going to break my neck."

Then don't look behind you, I thought. Because if she'd gone much farther, she would've fallen down a sheer cliff about forty feet to the rocky ground below.

"We need to go toward the trees," I said. "It's more level there."

Another gunshot sounded high above us, though we were too far away unless the guy had a sniper rifle. But still, it got us both moving.

Once we reached the trees, Scarlett rested against a trunk to catch her breath. "You in one piece?" I asked.

"Yeah, I'm okay." Scarlett's hair was plastered to her forehead and cheeks, and her clothes were so wet with mud they clung to every curve of her body. I was in no better shape.

"Let's put some more distance between us and the shooter."

We kept going through the woods. Finally I said, "We've lost them by now," wiping my face as rain continued to pour. "At least the storm is washing away our tracks."

"See? I totally meant to fall down that hillside. One of my spy tactics."

"It was unpredictable."

"At least I have that going for me."

I still had my handgun. It was wet like everything else, but it was a Glock, so it wouldn't jam. I hoped my phone was that reliant.

But as I searched my pockets, I couldn't find the sat phone. A complication I really did not need. "Dammit."

Scarlett looked up. "What is it?"

"The satellite phone. I must've dropped it."

"I've got my phone," she said, taking it out. "It's supposed to be waterproof. But no signal. Of-freaking-course."

"Okay. This isn't ideal. It'll be harder to find Aiden. He'll go to our last GPS coordinates. But we'll sort it out." Aiden would have called Owen by now—the mission had gone off the rails enough for that—and the sheriff would have his deputies combing the hills for us soon. But with this much ground to cover? There was a reason the searchers from the compound hadn't found Virtue yet, assuming she was out here.

"Are *you* okay?" Scarlett asked. "You seem like it. But I wasn't sure if those gunshots...if the noise..."

"All good," I said tightly.

"Don't be mad. I know I'm not supposed to ask how you are, but after a gun battle and a car chase, that must entitle me to a freebie. Anybody would be affected by all that. I certainly am."

"I'm not *anybody*."

She sighed. "I don't know the right things to say."

"It's fine, Scarlett." I'd almost called her *babe* again. I needed to stop that. "Let's keep moving."

She frowned at me, but she didn't argue. "When I thought about how that visit to the compound could go, I never would've expected I'd end up here. Out in these woods again."

"You made it out once. And you're not alone this time," I added, echoing what she'd said on the drive here.

"At the moment, I would settle for getting this mud off of me. I feel disgusting."

She didn't look that bad, but I understood what she meant. "I'll see what I can do."

We walked for a while, picking our way through the woods. My knee ached, especially with the dampness. But I'd dealt with worse. It wasn't safe yet to head back to the road, so I aimed us in the direction of Hartley based on the position of the sun, which had peeked out from behind the clouds.

Scarlett wiped her face, smearing the mud. "You said you found Toby."

"I did, yes." I recounted what he'd told me about Virtue.

"He's a brave kid, just like his older sister. He thought Virtue was upset that he'd contacted you."

"How did he find out I was in Hartley?"

This was going to disturb her, but I didn't feel right keeping it back. "He overheard Dawson talking about you on the phone."

"*What?*"

"From the sounds of it, Dawson has someone watching you in Hartley. He knew you'd changed your name. That could explain your stalker."

She looked ill, but not that surprised. "Dawson said he knew about my life in Hartley and could take me back whenever he wanted. He said things that sounded like the Instagram comments. He said…" She cleared her throat. "He said he'll make sure I'm punished."

I reached over, letting my hand rest briefly on her back. "Sorry it took me a while to get there. I had to talk to Toby first. He told me how to reach your father's house."

"You were there when I needed you, and that's what matters. Thank you again for finding me. You seem to have a knack for that."

But I still thought I should've been there sooner. "I'm not going to let Dawson get near you in Hartley."

"I trust you. But what about everyone else at the compound who are still at the mercy of Dawson and the other elders? I've been living my life as if I didn't care about them. Like I'd forgotten them." Streaks appeared in the dirt on her face. "My mother died. Five years ago."

"Shit, I'm sorry."

"I didn't even know. I should've tried again to go back for her. *Something*."

"She made her choices, though."

"She *had* no choices," Scarlett said harshly, wiping at her cheeks. "I just can't forget about them again. Kids like Toby. There must be something more I can do."

"They might not want to leave. I asked Toby point-blank if he wanted my help to escape, and he wasn't sure." I'd given him my number to contact me. I'd have to replace the phone as soon as I returned to Hartley. Hopefully I wouldn't miss a message from the kid.

"I don't know what to do!" Scarlett said. "But it's not right that people like Virtue and Toby and my mom just keep hurting and nobody does anything about it."

I couldn't say anything to that because words wouldn't be enough. I agreed with her. And I was damned impressed at her strength. After all she'd been through today, Scarlett was thinking more about the others left at the compound than about herself.

When I'd found Dawson with his hands on her, I had wanted to choke the life out of him so that he never entertained another sick thought. Never cursed this county with his foul breath. No doubt he had a vicious headache and a bruised larynx. But he deserved true justice.

Maybe I'd still get the chance to deliver it.

But right now, it was my job to take care of Scarlett. She wasn't focused on her own safety, but that was my top priority. Once we were back in Hartley, safe and sound, we'd decide what to do next about Dawson and the compound.

Because this wasn't over. Not by a long shot.

After about an hour of walking, the rain let up, replaced by sun. The mud had started drying to our skin. And it itched like hell. Yet the birds were chirping, and raindrops glittered on the leaves of the trees. Beauty was all around us. Peacefulness.

My protective instincts were like a shield around us, telling me that we were safe here. There wasn't another human for miles.

I knew Scarlett must be hungry and thirsty, but she didn't complain. I'd already checked on her phone, hoping to pick up a signal, but there hadn't been one yet. Then finally, after several more miles, I stopped.

"Hear that?" I asked.

She cocked her head, listening. "Oh, thank God."

We followed the sound of rushing water to a creek. It wasn't a good idea to drink the water without any way to purify it. Not unless we really got desperate. But at least we could clean up.

We found a side pocket where the creek wasn't moving too fast, near an abandoned beaver dam. Scarlett toed off her shoes and socks, set her phone on a rock, and waded right in. The water was knee deep. "*Gah,* that's cold." I chuckled as she danced around. "Aren't you getting in?"

I got rid of my boots and the items in my pockets and waded in after her. Yeah, that was chilly.

She scrubbed her face, hair, and exposed skin. Then she stripped off her mud-drenched shirt to clean it in the water. Scarlett stood in profile, her white cotton bra wet and translucent.

Damn.

I realized I was just standing there, staring. And a certain part of me was waking up in response to the view. She started to turn toward me, so I knelt in the frigid creek, cringing as my erection deflated. Yet my cock tried to rally when my eyes landed on her breasts again. Her hard nipples strained the wet fabric.

Bet those would fit perfectly in my mouth, that taut flesh hardening even more when I sucked...

I stuck my head under the water.

When I came up for a breath, I rubbed the mud from my clothes, avoiding my needy cock. I'd worn technical fabrics, which washed clean fairly easily and would dry fast. My face and hair were next. I paid extra attention to the mud stuck in my beard, even though I wouldn't have cared if I were alone.

Then I went ahead and shrugged out of my soaked shirt. After scrubbing the biggest patches of dirt from it, I returned to the bank, squeezing the water from my hair. I wrung out my shirt and draped it over a tree branch. I thought about doing the same with my pants. But I kept them on to cover my scars, even if the wet fabric against my skin wouldn't do me any favors.

When I turned, Scarlett had her pants off and was hanging her clothes on another tree.

She might as well have been naked for all those undergarments did to cover her.

"Fuck," I muttered.

She looked over. "Problem?" Her damp hair was slicked back, and the cold water had left her cheeks and lips bright pink. Her intelligent eyes and the twist to her mouth told me she knew exactly what my issue was.

"I'm really trying to be on my best behavior here."

If I had been in this same situation with any other beautiful woman, I would've kept my control. I wasn't an animal. But Scarlett was one of the most resilient women I'd ever met, and I'd served with some incredible badasses who happened to be female.

Everything about her drew me in. Made me want to bask in her sunshine. Make her smile when she was troubled.

Make her moan with all the pleasure she deserved.

I bit down on my tongue, but a frustrated moan still snuck out of me. "How about you stay over there, and I stay over here. And when we've dried off and I'm...calm, we'll keep moving. We need to get back to the road so we can find Aiden and return to civilization before nightfall."

"Or…"

"Or what?"

Scarlett walked toward me, giving me a full-on view, and my cock filled to aching hardness in half a second. It had to be obvious, given the way my pants were plastered to my crotch.

She stopped inches away from me. Her finger trailed over my cockhead through the fabric of my pants. I growled, grabbing her wrist to stop her hand. "Scarlett, I'm serious. This is not the time for games."

"It's not a game. It's something we both need."

"What do we need?" My voice was hoarse. My control was nearly shot.

"A release."

My cock jerked. I closed my mouth on a groan. "A release? You want me to give that to you?"

Shouldn't have asked that, I told myself. *You should stop this. Walk away. Don't you dare claim this woman because she can never be yours.*

"Yes," she said simply.

I knew my own strength. And I wasn't strong enough in this moment to make the honorable choice.

I pulled her to me, hands moving over her bare skin. "Oh Trace, warm me up," she murmured, just before I slanted my mouth down on hers.

My tongue pushed past her lips. The taste I'd been craving since the last time. I groaned, and my need only increased. My cock was painfully hard.

I'd been trying not to want this with her, but I did. Every fucking minute, I wanted Scarlett.

I was going to take what I wanted.

I went to my knees, and I brought her down with me.

Probably being rougher than I should. Scarlett sprawled on her back in the short, damp grass. Her eyes were wide with surprise, but her gaze roved over my chest and my tented pants with open lust. I crawled over her. Hooked her bra straps and tugged the undergarment to her stomach to reveal her gorgeous curves. I licked my lips, mouth filling with saliva at the sight of her.

I bent down. My tongue swirled around one nipple before sucking it hard into my mouth.

"*Yes.*" Scarlett's hands reached to thread into my hair, trying to keep me in place, but we were doing this my way. I took her hands and pressed them into the ground above her head.

Then I went back to kissing and sucking on her tits while she made needy sounds.

This was going to be quick and dirty because I didn't have the self control available to draw this out. We didn't have the time. And besides, if I stopped to think too much about this, I wouldn't be able to go through with it. I'd have to face how wrong it was.

I'd saved her earlier at the compound, and she was probably feeling vulnerable. She had an instinctual, deep-seated fear that I'd abandon her and she'd be alone again—like she had been the first time she ran from the compound—and I was a bastard to take advantage of that. She was hopped up on adrenaline and fear, and that was a cocktail that translated far too easily into sex. No wonder she craved a release. And needed *me* to provide it.

But if she'd been in her right mind, she would've known better. When I'd kissed her outside the bar, she'd been the one to stop it. She knew that sex with me wouldn't lead us anywhere good.

So nope, I wasn't thinking about any of that.

The *yes* from her lips had opened the floodgates. Unless she changed her mind, nothing was stopping me.

I shifted to hold both her wrists to the ground, while my other hand moved down her body to her panties. The fabric was thin, soaked from rain and creek water, so it was nothing to tear it and shove the remnants to the side. My fingers met the slickness at her core.

Scarlett's spine arched. She cried out. "God, Trace, *yes*."

"Shhh," I urged. I was confident nobody was around, we were safe, but no need to tempt fate.

My fingers worked fast. Testing first to discover what made her eyes roll back, then slid in and out of her, over and around her clit. She couldn't stay quiet, so I bent down to feed my tongue into her mouth.

She sucked it as she moaned and shook and came apart.

Then I straightened up, still kneeling to either side of her. I pushed my wet pants and briefs down enough to free my erection. It popped out, angry and aching. My fist shuttled up and down over my length in a blur. On the fourth stroke, my release painted her stomach.

For a too-brief moment, I was flying on that high. I dropped forward to kiss Scarlett. Feasted on her lips. She was perfect. So soft and delicate beneath me, hands resting on my thighs. My sweet, beautiful, wicked Scarlett.

A pause. We both breathed, and the creek babbled peacefully.

Within seconds, reality and regret came crashing in.

"Scarlett. I..."

Her lips pursed, her blissful expression erased in an instant. "Don't say it. Don't say we shouldn't have done that. I've heard enough today about all my many inadequacies and mistakes."

Damn it, I didn't want her thinking that. Even if I

shouldn't have lost control just now, I could never allow her to feel guilty or used over it. The fault was mine. Not hers.

"I'll clean you up." I used my hands to wipe her stomach as best I could, then went to the creek to rinse off. When I turned back to her, she had her bra back in place and was walking to the tree that held her clothes. Her panties were in tatters.

I tucked myself away and zipped my pants, walking over to her. She was struggling with the damp fabric of her shirt. "Let me." I carefully helped her get her arms into the sleeves and tugged the rest down her torso, smoothing it into place. "I was too rough with you."

"I enjoyed every second of it," she said defiantly. "It's my body, and I can give it to whoever I choose." Her voice wavered, and I realized she was speaking to more than just me.

"Yes. You can."

"So don't tell me I did something wrong. We both wanted it. Neither of us has anything to feel guilty about, and I *refuse* to let you suggest otherwise."

"Then I won't. C'mere." I drew her into my arms and kissed her head. "You're one of the sexiest women I've ever met. I'm a lucky guy that you chose to share that with me."

Scarlett relaxed against me, letting me hold her. Her cheek was mashed against my chest. I hadn't put my shirt back on. I hoped my skin was warm and dry, even if I couldn't say much for the rest of me.

"Thank you," she said.

"You don't need to thank me."

"Why not? You've been taking care of me. Driving me a little nuts too, but at every moment that counts, you're there for me. Even when it's difficult for you."

"Don't make me sound selfless."

"I think in a lot of ways, you are."

I exhaled through my nose.

"You don't believe me, do you? Think of the ways you've helped Jessi. Helped me. You're a Protector, and that comes naturally to you. Even when you try to hide from it." Scarlett lifted her head to look up at me. Her palm rested on my pectoral, as if she was seeking out my heartbeat. "Why can't you see how good a man you are?"

I didn't want to argue with Scarlett, especially right now.

"Aiden and Owen will be out looking for us," I said. "We need to get reception on your phone and tell them where we are. I don't want to be stuck in the woods overnight with no shelter and no supplies."

I gently removed her hand from my chest. Started to back away. But she didn't let me. Her arms circled my waist, and she rubbed small circles into my back.

She laid her cheek on my chest again and nuzzled into me.

I closed my eyes as tingles spread across my skin, starting at her fingertips on my back and then moving outward. It was pleasant. Gentle and comforting in a way I didn't usually want. And that gentle sensation was enough to send cracks through the barriers I kept around me.

That terrified me. But strangely, a part of me longed for it, too. The same part that wished I could be the man Scarlett thought I was.

Maybe, if she believed it that much…I could. If I could figure out how.

CHAPTER FIFTEEN
Scarlett

IT WAS late afternoon when we found the cabin.

We were miles away from the compound by now. Trace had brought us closer to the road so we would stay close to where Aiden might find us. But we didn't risk staying *too* close to it either. The men from the compound could easily be patrolling for us.

When I had escaped at fifteen years old, I'd had supplies and a compass with me that I'd stolen from my father's study. Trace and I had nothing but my phone. My device had a compass built in, but we hardly needed it. Trace seemed to have a compass in his head.

Every few minutes, he would check for cell reception. No luck yet. But we were climbing higher as the elevation rose. If we could get to a good open space that was high enough, we'd probably be able to hit a cell tower.

We stopped at another creek for sips of water because I was dying of thirst, and Trace made us move on quickly. As we made our way, we were both silent. But my mind was working in overtime.

I couldn't stop myself from picturing Trace above me, nearly naked and stroking himself. Or looming over me as he held my arms down and pleasured me. A shiver of desire made my limbs quake with an aftershock.

That had been the hottest encounter of my life. Who knew that danger could be such an aphrodisiac?

Trace glanced over at me. "Doing all right? Are you cold?"

He must've noticed the way I'd been shivering. "I'm okay. My clothes are almost dry. My panties are bunched up all weird though."

He made a choked sound and looked away, checking the phone for a signal again instead. I tried not to laugh. It was that or get angry at him, and I was so tired of it.

It was true about my undies. They belonged in a trashcan after Trace had destroyed them. Which I'd been into, by the way. But I wasn't about to start littering in a pristine forest.

I just didn't get why he had to be so awkward about it. Yes, we'd broken our friends-only rule. But we'd both wanted it. Why did it have to be such a big deal? Why did he have to act like I was some fragile, innocent flower and he had sullied me? It was nonsense.

If Trace wanted to keep his inner struggle to himself, fine. But the regret I'd seen in his face after his orgasm faded? I hadn't deserved that.

Of course, then he had soothed the sting by being kind and chivalrous and sincere, in that sexy, infuriating way he had about him. Ugh, I didn't know what to do with him. Everything in me wanted to stay close, and not just because he was protecting me. It was because he cared about people like Virtue and Toby. He cared about what was right. Trace had been through enough in his life to harden him, and he was hurting underneath. But he still managed to comfort me. Make me laugh.

I just wanted to do the same for him. I wanted him to see the truth. That he was wonderful, and that anybody was lucky to have him around. Even if he could be infuriating.

Suddenly, Trace barred his arm in front of me.

"What is it?" I whispered.

He held a finger to his lips, then pointed. I could just make out the edge of a rustic wooden structure. Ruins of old mining cabins were common in the mountains. But from here, I couldn't tell if it was some abandoned home from a hundred years ago or a more modern shelter. Or if it was occupied.

We carefully moved closer. The space around the cabin had been cleared of debris, and there were distinct footsteps leading in and out of the entrance. Some looked recent, imprinted into the still-damp dirt.

"Do you know this place?" Trace whispered in my ear. "Does it belong to the compound?"

"Not that I know of. I had no idea this was here." I hadn't come across it during my trek through these woods thirteen years ago. Not that it was so surprising, because you'd have to be pretty close to spot it. It had been out here long enough for the forest to grow in around it. The roof was made of corrugated metal that had rusted through in places, and somebody had been patching it up with plastic and duct tape.

A blanket hung in the window, and something about that blanket set off an ache in my heart. It was a quilt. It reminded me of the one my mother had made.

I grabbed Trace's shirt. "What if it's her? Virtue?"

"I'll check it out."

"Don't scare her."

He frowned. "I have no intention to. But we don't know that it's her. It could be anyone." He drew his gun and handed it to me. "Stay here."

"Seriously? Trace—"

He was already dashing across the small clearing. He pressed himself against the wall of the cabin, then went still. Listening. I was distracted a moment, just watching him. I'd never seen a man run so gracefully one moment and keep himself so motionless the next. Like he demanded complete control of his body and senses. No wonder it wasn't easy for him to surrender that control, even for a moment.

But what was I doing just standing here?

Did he really think I'd let him leave me behind? After all we'd been through?

Trace turned to peer at the window. Then he approached the door. Opened the latch and stepped inside.

I crossed the clearing and went in right behind him, latching the door closed behind us.

"I told you to stay there." He hadn't turned around. He was bent over a small nest of blankets on the floor.

I stuck his handgun into the back of my waistband. "I thought that was just a suggestion."

He gave me a sardonic look over his shoulder.

The cabin was tiny, just one room, and barely that. One of the walls was sagging precariously. Whoever was staying here had stacked up some supplies near the bed. There were a few dishes, a first aid kit, and a change of clothes neatly folded.

And as I stepped closer, I saw Trace pick up a rag doll from the nest of blankets. My heart nearly broke open.

There was a girl living here, judging by the fabric of her spare clothes. Just a kid.

But where was she? What if the people from the compound had gotten to her?

A rustling sound came from outside. In a blink, Trace was up and pressing me to one side of the door. His hand went to the small of my back, reaching for the gun, though he didn't draw it. Whoever was outside was moving slowly, and paused right outside the door.

The latch shifted. The door cracked open.

A teenage girl stepped inside, wearing a backpack. She'd combed her hair back and fastened it into a tangled ponytail.

Her face was drawn with exhaustion. She kept her eyes down, using a stripped branch as a walking stick. Her right foot was injured. She could barely put her weight on it.

Trace and I weren't breathing. He had kept his body positioned over mine. But I didn't need protecting. That poor girl did. I couldn't believe we'd found her.

This had to be Virtue.

I was about to say something, hoping to make her aware of us without terrifying her. But then her head snapped up, and her eyes fixed on us. She cried out, trying to lunge for the door.

"Virtue, wait. I'm Scarlett Weston. You're safe. We're not going to hurt you."

"Like I haven't heard that before." She stopped in the doorway, teeth clenched in pain and terror as she looked back at me.

"I've been where you are now," I said. "My name used to be Serenity. I grew up at the compound."

Her eyes flashed as Trace moved, but he had shifted backward, putting himself behind me. "We spoke to your brother today," Trace said. "Toby's been worried about you. He asked Scarlett to help find you."

"Did you lead them here to take me back? I'd sooner die."

"And I'd sooner die than let them do that to you," I replied. "I know what your freedom must mean to you. And I know what you're going through. Please, let us help."

Then all the fight seemed to leave her, and she slumped against the doorframe. "I can't believe my little brother, sending out messages like that. I told him it was stupid. I didn't think you'd actually…come."

"Just wish I'd gotten here sooner." I held out my hand. "Would you sit down? That looks painful."

She eyed me suspiciously, gaze flitting to Trace behind me.

"Trace?" I said. "Maybe you could check the signal on my phone again."

He nodded, understanding what I was really asking. To be alone so that Virtue and I could talk. She wasn't going to let her guard down around him.

But then she spoke up. "I've got a bag with some food outside. I strung it up in a tree to keep bears away from the cabin."

"I'll find it." He gave Virtue a soft smile. She shuffled out of the way so he could leave, and I shut the door.

The poor girl was putting on a brave front, but she was shaking. Her eyes were red. Filling rapidly with tears. I felt her distress all the way to my bones because I had been in her place. I knew how this felt. To have come so far and still fear that you weren't strong enough to carry through.

Because it was all *too much*.

"Come on. Let's sit." I helped her over to her blankets. Virtue lowered herself down and snatched up the rag doll like she didn't want me to see it. My heart tugged again.

"Can I sit with you?" I asked. When she nodded, I joined her, leaning my back against the wall. "Your mom is Patience, right?"

"Yes. How'd you know?"

"I remember you from before I left. The mothers used to group all the little ones together, rotating which family cared for them during the day while the other girls and moms did chores."

"We still do it that way."

I wasn't surprised. The place had seemed unchanged. "It was usually my job to watch the littles. You were two, last I remember."

She wasn't looking at me, but I could tell she was listening.

"You were rambunctious. You'd run around exploring

everything, and when you got tired out, you insisted on being held. Had a pair of lungs on you, that's for sure. You weren't afraid of anything except being by yourself."

She looked down at the doll in her lap. "You were my age when you left. Fifteen."

"Yep. I was supposed to marry Dawson Witkins, and I decided to run instead." I didn't mention Kenny getting caught because that part of the story was too awful. "I was alone until some good people from Hartley stepped up. They helped me. I've lived there ever since."

"And now you want to help me?"

"I do."

Her lips drew up skeptically. "What about that man? Who is he?"

"That's Trace. I trust him completely. He's a good friend of mine, and I brought him here to protect us. He went with me to Paradise Ranch today looking for you."

Her nose wrinkled. "You really went back there after getting away? That's dumb."

I shrugged, holding back my smile. "Probably. I did it anyway."

"Guess I'm dumb too. Toby didn't want me to run away by myself, but yeah. I did anyway. I wanted him to stay out of it because I was scared he'd get into trouble."

"Did you know this cabin was here?"

"I used to sneak out at night to explore. I'd go further and further in the woods, imagining I could keep going forever and never go back. I'd seen my older sisters getting married off, and I didn't want that. I found this place one of those nights. I started storing supplies here a little at a time. Whatever I could sneak without anyone noticing it was gone."

"It must've taken you all night to get out here and then back. Especially without them realizing it. You're amazing."

Her cheeks pinked. "Toby caught me coming back one

night, and I didn't want to tell him what I was up to. I didn't want to put him in any danger. But he kind of guessed. My little brother knows me better than anyone. So I told him what I was planning. Then he moved into the bachelor house, and must've decided he was a grown-up man whose job it was to save me. That's why Toby contacted you. We'd heard about Serenity. There were sermons about you."

I barked a laugh at that. "Really? I'm honored."

Virtue snickered, and that small grin warmed my insides far more than my own laughter. "It had the opposite effect of what they hoped. The elders meant you to be a cautionary tale, but it made me believe I could do it. Sometimes they said you died in the woods. But other times, people talked about how you'd betrayed your family by bringing outsiders. Police who wanted to tear us apart and destroy our way of life. So obviously you'd made it, right? If you'd brought the sheriff?"

I nodded. "Sure did."

"Then Toby figured out your new name was Scarlett Weston. He thought you might be able to help us."

"But you weren't in favor of contacting me?"

"I was afraid of anyone knowing." Her chin wobbled. "I thought I could do it on my own. Get to Hartley, like you did. Then I twisted my ankle. I never would've stayed here this long otherwise. For the past couple days, I thought any moment they'd find me. Or I'd starve here."

"Good thing we found you first."

Suddenly, Virtue burst into tears. She covered her eyes, hiccuping. "Sorry."

"Hey, there's no reason to be sorry." I opened my arms, and she fell into me, hiding her face against my shoulder as she cried. Her whole body shook. "You are so brave. So strong. But nobody can be strong all the time. Trace and I are going to look after you. You're not alone anymore."

Slowly, the worst sobs subsided. But hot tears kept rolling down her cheeks.

"When you were little, you used to like when I sang to you," I said.

Every Friday, my sisters and I would have to sing to our father after dinner. I'd usually had the solos, and I'd hated it. But I'd found joy singing to the littles like Virtue when I cared for them. It had been a gift I was giving, not something being forced or judged.

"I think I remember that," she whispered, voice blurry. "Would you? Sing to me?"

I closed my eyes and hummed the first melody that appeared in my mind. "Bridge Over Troubled Water." I opened my mouth and let the words flow out of me.

And soon, Virtue started singing too.

Her voice trembled at first, but slowly got stronger and clearer. We were both keeping our volume down because of the danger of the sound carrying. But we needed this. The words and the melody uplifted our hearts. Took us far away from this cabin. To somewhere we'd always be safe.

CHAPTER SIXTEEN

Scarlett

VIRTUE'S BREATHING had evened out, and I thought maybe she was asleep. But then we heard a sound at the front door of the cabin, the latch opening. Virtue sat up, stiff and straight.

Trace's tall silhouette appeared, outlined against the dying daylight. "Just me," he said.

"Did you get reception?" I asked.

He shook his head. "Not yet. No signal. Found the food, though." He lifted a cloth bag. "Nice work tying it up, Virtue. Smart."

She glanced away, chewing on her lower lip.

"Are you hungry?" I asked. Then my stomach betrayed me by growling.

Virtue gave me a knowing look. "You clearly are. I've got granola, crackers, beef jerky. Apples too."

"Water purifying tablets?" Trace asked.

She rolled her eyes like the teenager she was. "Of course. Those took forever to stock up."

Virtue shared her water and food with us. I tried not to take much, but even a few mouthfuls perked me up. Trace ate and drank even more sparingly than me, which was ridiculous considering he was twice my size. The guy was a camel.

As we ate, Virtue watched Trace from the corner of her vision. He'd taken up a spot on the opposite side of the cabin from us, seated against the wall on the ground. He was probably the first adult male she'd seen who wasn't from the compound. There was discomfort there, but curiosity too. And after a while, her courage took over.

"Um, Mr. Trace?" she began. I noticed that she'd tucked her doll under the top blanket.

"Trace is fine."

"You really talked to my brother? How is he?"

Trace recounted the conversation he'd had with Toby at the compound. How the boy's biggest concern was Virtue's safety, and how Toby regretted that they'd argued.

"Did anyone see you with him?"

"No, I was careful."

She took a shaky breath. "I miss him. The last time we spoke, I said things that weren't nice, telling him he was too much of a kid to help me. I should've believed in him. I should've taken him with me."

I put my hand over hers. "You did the right thing. It's much easier for one person to slip away unnoticed." I knew that all too well. "If we can get him out of there, we will. And anyone else who wants to leave, too."

"But how?"

"Toby has my number," Trace said. "I need to get a new phone set up, but I'll do that as soon as we're back in Hartley."

"When are we leaving? What's going to happen when we get there? Where will I stay?"

Now that she'd gotten going, Virtue couldn't stop asking questions. And of course, I didn't blame her. I remembered how uncertain I had felt at this stage. She was starting all over again.

This was exactly why Jessi had wanted to build Last Refuge. People like Virtue. I was once again beyond grateful for my best friend's incredible heart. And her business sense, too, because starting a place like Last Refuge meant nothing without money behind it. That was just reality.

"Let's take your questions one at a time," I said. I nodded at Trace. "What do you think? When should we leave here?"

He was sitting with his legs bent, and he clasped his hands between his knees. "The sun's going down, so we'll have to stay tonight. It's not safe hiking in the dark. We'll move at first light."

"But my ankle," Virtue reminded him. "I can barely walk."

Trace and I exchanged a silent look.

"I'll carry you," I said.

Her eyes cut to me. "Wait, *you*? Are you sure?"

"Yep. I'm strong. Check out these guns." I flexed a bicep. Both Virtue and Trace were covering their laughter. "Hey!" I protested.

Virtue flung her hand in Trace's direction. "Just make him carry me. We'll move faster that way."

I heaved an extra-deep sigh. "Fine, I guess." Reverse psychology, for the win. Now she wouldn't be nervous about Trace carrying her. "Trace, are you sure you can handle that?"

He shrugged. "I've got it. No problem."

Virtue flopped back against her blankets. "I'm so ready to get out of this dingy little cabin. I want a bath. And a big, fat hamburger."

With the ice broken, Virtue seemed to relax around Trace for the rest of the evening. She even let him check her ankle. She didn't take her eyes off him as his long fingers gently inspected and he asked about her pain. I couldn't stop staring at the man, either. The way he was so careful with her. His voice had dropped to a low, smooth register. He declared the ankle sprained, but most likely not broken. We would need to get her an x-ray, not to mention a full hospital exam.

Trace refilled her water bottle, and we ate some more crackers as we settled in. Virtue had a solar-powered lantern, which lit the cabin with a soft glow. I told her about each business on Hartley's Main Street. About Aiden's delicious cooking at the diner, Jessi's desserts. Virtue was especially interested in my sweet shop. I promised to take her to pick out whatever she wanted. She listened with wide eyes, looking far younger than fifteen.

She was almost grown, yet still a kid, and I wanted nothing more than to give her back the childhood that had been stolen from her.

"You can stay at my house for the time being," I said. "I have a guestroom."

"Really?"

The temperature had dropped past chilly. We were curled up together under the blankets, though Virtue had passed one over for Trace where he sat across from us. His handgun rested on the dirt beside him.

"Sure. But Jessi and Aiden are building a place called Last Refuge. It's not finished yet, but they'll have housing for people who need help. Jobs and training, things like that." My brows drew together. "Of course, you'll need to go to school."

Reality was coming at me in a rush. Virtue was a minor, and her parents were back at the compound. Could she somehow be emancipated? I'd have to talk to a lawyer about that. Finding her had been such a daunting task that I hadn't figured out the rest. When I'd left the compound at her age, my saviors had done everything unofficially.

The legalities didn't matter to me. I'd do whatever I could to make sure Virtue could start her new life.

Virtue perked up. "High school? I've seen so many TikToks about what it's like."

"*TikTok*? How are you on there?" I asked.

"I have my ways."

"Keep going like you are, and you'll be the mayor of Hartley in a few years, Virtue," Trace said. "I have no doubt you're clever enough for that."

She blushed, and her eyelashes fluttered. "Except I won't be called Virtue. You changed your name, Scarlett. I thought maybe I could do that too."

"You absolutely can. Have you picked one? You don't have to tell us if you're not ready."

"I'm still thinking about it."

"Take your time. It's an important choice."

She bit her lip. "I'll decide after we get to Hartley."

"That'll be tomorrow." At least, I really hoped so. "Better get some rest. It could be another long day."

"Will you sing to me again?"

My eyes found Trace in the dim light. His dark irises were watching me. I was self-conscious about singing in front of him. But I said, "Of course."

I sang quietly as she drifted to sleep. One heartfelt song to the next. When her breathing was slow and regular, I finally looked over at Trace again. I had felt his gaze on me unwaveringly the whole time as I sang. He was still sitting up.

"You need rest too," I said.

"I'll rest when we're back in Hartley."

I wiggled, trying not to jostle Virtue. "Well, there's no way I'll be able to sleep with you staring at me."

"I can't help myself. You're too beautiful."

The breath left my chest in a whoosh. And inexplicably, anger burned in its place. "Don't say that to me."

He flinched almost imperceptibly.

Trace had been wonderful to Virtue. He'd saved me today. He'd been a hero to both of us. But when I had strayed too close to intimacy with him by the creek, Trace had pushed me away once again.

And now, to my absolute mortification, hot tears started rolling down my cheeks.

Trace cursed. He stood up and walked over to me, kneeling in the dirt beside the makeshift bed. His thumb brushed over my cheek, but more tears kept coming. "Babe. Please don't cry."

Ugh, he was killing me. "I'm just feeling a lot," I said. "It was a rough day, and I need to let it out. You can ignore me."

I was crying for the childhood Virtue should've had. That *I* should've had. For Toby being left behind at the compound. For my sisters and nieces. For the other innocent kids who hadn't known any other life.

And I was crying for the astonishing man in front of me who had no idea how incredible he was. I wished I could take all of that pain away and banish it from the earth.

"I'm an asshole in plenty of ways. But I could never ignore you." Trace bent at the waist, sitting closer so he could put his arm around me. It was a little awkward with me lying down. But instantly, I was warmer. Downright toasty.

It was torture.

I wasn't in love with the man. That wasn't part of my makeup, and I was glad for it. If those pieces of my heart hadn't been warped years ago, I would've been in so much trouble with him. But I still had feelings, and Trace Novo had a way of playing on every one.

He was close enough that I felt his exhales on my cheek. "Tell me what you need. What can I do?"

"I need things that are impossible," I murmured.

"*Scarlett*." That was all he said. Just my name. But that

single word had never held so much meaning inside it. Longing and confusion and frustration.

Neither one of us knew how to fix everything that was broken.

His lips brushed the corner of my eye. My cheekbone. I reached up to thread my fingers through his hair, my palm grazing his beard along the way. It felt so nice. So right. Didn't he feel it? Would he change his mind in five minutes, telling me we shouldn't touch like this?

Why did I keep coming back?

This man was my weakness.

I turned my head. His lips found mine. We pressed our mouths together with soft and gentle kisses. It was chaste. Far more relaxing than provocative. Neither one of us would allow more with Virtue asleep here with us.

But how could anything that felt so purely good be wrong?

I broke the kiss. My fingers slid up and down his neck, caressing the skin there before sliding up into his hair again. It had always felt nice when my mother did this. Simple affection.

Predictably, he tensed.

"Please," I said. "Let me. This is what I need." I needed him to let me in, just this tiny bit. Not to fix him or change him. Just because he mattered to me.

I needed him to accept what I offered instead of turning away.

For a solid minute, he didn't move. As if he was right on the border and couldn't decide which way to go. But finally, he turned into my touch, the puff of his exhale shifting the hairs at my forehead.

He let me caress him. Comfort him. The way he'd so often comforted me.

Virtue slept to my left, and Trace was sitting to my right.

Eventually, I fell asleep. Soothed by the knowledge that Trace was there. Our guardian angel with bent wings, sheltering us. But I hoped I'd given a little of that goodness back to him.

CHAPTER SEVENTEEN

Trace

AFTER SCARLETT WAS ASLEEP, I got up silently and went outside. The clearing was dark. Quiet, except for the humming of insects. The air was frigid compared to the cocoon of the cabin, especially when I'd been right next to Scarlett and Virtue. Keeping them warm and sharing their warmth in turn.

But the cold didn't bother me. I'd been hoping the fresh air would shock some clarity into my mind. It wasn't giving me the answers I'd wanted.

I was so fucked.

I'd been sitting for hours, so I stretched my back, looking up at the sky. The stars were a thick blanket overhead. Glimmers of light in a vast, unknown ocean. Stunningly beautiful. But nowhere near as beautiful as the woman I'd left inside that cabin.

Scarlett blew me away, time and again. Her courage and tenacity. Her sheer goodness. The electric quality of her touch.

Even earlier today, I had been fighting it.

But when I'd finally relaxed into that kind, generous

contact, the sweetness that she gave so easily, I'd already been lost. There was no coming back from that.

"I tried," I said to the night sky. "I really tried."

Eight months ago, I'd limped into Hartley, scarred and defeated. I'd meant to pay penance for what I'd done. The blood on my hands. The blackened, damaged parts of my soul. I'd thought I could do that by devoting myself to my sister. Then I'd tried to be selfless as I watched over Scarlett. I was just supposed to protect her.

It had been easier to maintain some kind of distance between us when I'd pretended it was a passing attraction I felt for her. Yet I kept on slipping, like that night outside the bar after we danced. And what happened today by the creek.

We'd become friends because it had been impossible to deny her. And I'd told myself, *That's it. You can't have more*. But the closer I'd gotten to her, the more I'd given in to this soul-deep yearning. And the more selfish I had become.

I wanted to hold her so tightly we'd never be apart. And I also wanted to run as fast and as far as possible, because she deserved much better than me.

But it was clear which of those options I would choose. Over and over again. This was a test I would always fail. What I felt for Scarlett wasn't just a physical craving. It was so much worse.

When I'd been sitting in the cabin, listening to her sing Virtue to sleep, something had broken open inside of me. Something I had tried to keep locked away. But those barriers around my heart had rusted through like the roof over the cabin behind me.

I could see where this was going. I was on my way to falling for her. Right off the edge of that cliff.

I went back inside, taking up a post near the door, my gun within reach. Sleep wasn't an option for me with things as they were. So instead, I would sit up all night to make sure

Scarlett and Virtue stayed secure and safe. Maybe I'd failed to keep my heart distant, but I would never let them come to harm.

It was a long night. Just me and my spiraling thoughts.

As dawn came, I slipped outside again to replenish our water bottle in a nearby creek, adding a purification tablet. I splashed icy water on my face. I would get Scarlett and Virtue back to Hartley today if it was the last thing I did.

Rustling in the nearby brush made me whirl around.

A family of deer stood in the clearing. A buck, a doe, and a fawn. They froze, just like I was. We stared at one another. I didn't move. Didn't breathe. Slowly, they approached the creek and drank. As if I wasn't even there. A serene feeling washed over me. The dawn light, the babbling of the creek, the animals. This was why I loved being out in the wilderness, away from humanity's ills and the reminders of my past. Here, nothing mattered except the present moment.

I wished Scarlett were here next to me, so she could see it.

Dammit. I really had it bad.

When I returned to the cabin, Scarlett was sitting up and rubbing her eyes. Virtue was still asleep. "Is it time to go?" Scarlett asked.

I handed her the water bottle. She sipped at it, probably intending to save most of it for Virtue. "Yes," I said. "But we can let Virtue sleep five more minutes." This was probably the best night's sleep she had managed since running away.

"Good. She needs it." Scarlett got up and walked over to me. She held out the water bottle. I capped it without drinking and set it aside. My hand reached out for hers. I brought it to my lips to kiss it. She watched me curiously, but didn't say anything. She pulled her hand from my grasp and slowly threaded her fingers into my hair instead.

I didn't flinch. Didn't try to pull away.

This touch wasn't sexual. And it wasn't pitying, either,

which I never could've tolerated. Scarlett's touch was caring. Affectionate, like she'd been last night. I wasn't good at this kind of thing, despite what Scarlett seemed to think, and I couldn't say I deserved to be on the receiving end of it. But I kept on gravitating toward her. Unable to resist.

I'd been able to reach out platonically in certain situations, of course, like trying my best to comfort Jessi. Or reassuring Toby yesterday. Even a hug with friends like Aiden or River. But those had been little more than gestures. For most of my adult life, the only thing close to mutual intimacy I'd experienced was during sex. It was possible there was something messed up about that. I'd never stopped to think about it before.

All I knew was that I was quickly becoming addicted to Scarlett's touch. Even if she would've been better off giving it to someone else.

Or maybe not. The thought of her touching some other man this way made my jaw clench.

"You want me to stop," she said. "Don't you." She sighed with disappointment and dropped her hand. I gripped the back of her neck so she wouldn't leave.

"No. Touch me all you want. However you want."

"Really? You didn't like it before. Last night you were just doing me a favor."

"I want everything you give me." *Whether or not I should,* I added silently. Her eyes drifted to my mouth. I leaned toward her, my breath ragged in my chest.

I'd vowed to protect her. But I didn't know how to save her from *me*.

"It's morning already?" came a bleary voice from behind us.

Scarlett turned around as I stepped back to a more appropriate distance.

Virtue got up and had some water and granola. She and

Scarlett went outside to use the restroom. Meanwhile, I packed up Virtue's things in the cabin. Soon we were on our way, with Scarlett carrying the pack. Virtue rode piggyback, arms slung over my shoulders. She had Scarlett's cell phone and was checking it every few minutes for reception. We had to conserve the battery, which was getting low, yet another concern adding to my long list of them.

"Do you have hard candy at your sweet shop?" Virtue asked.

Scarlett smiled. "Yep. The old-fashioned kinds. Caramels too. But my favorites are the filled chocolates. I hand-paint them."

"Wow." Virtue swung her legs. "Trace, what kind of candy is your favorite?" She was far more comfortable with me than she'd been yesterday. That had to be a kid thing. Adapting so fast.

"I like the milk chocolate-covered marshmallows Scarlett makes," I said.

The woman beside me laughed. "You really do have a sweet tooth."

"Why is that funny?"

"Because you seem like someone who'd like dark chocolate," Virtue supplied. "The kind that's supposed to be for baking because it has no sugar."

That was probably fair.

Scarlett cackled. "Don't worry, Trace. I'll make some extra chocolate-covered marshmallows just for you." Her eyes lingered on me, and anticipation swirled in my stomach.

After we were safely in Hartley and Virtue was secure, how soon could Scarlett and I be alone? I probably needed food and rest. But I needed her more, and I could finally admit it. At least to myself.

When we reached a high ridge, Virtue shouted, "We've got bars!" Her uninjured leg kicked and caught me in the side. Ouch. The girl had some strength. I set her down, and she waved the phone in front of my face. "Look!"

I took the phone. Text and voicemail notifications started rolling in. I thumbed to Scarlett's contacts and found Aiden's number. He answered before the first ring had finished.

"Scarlett? Trace?"

"It's us," I said. I had him on speaker. "We're safe."

Jessi piped in next. She and Aiden were talking over each other. But once she'd confirmed that Scarlett and I were both okay—hadn't I just said that?—she let Aiden take over. "Where are you?" he asked. "We've been looking for you since yesterday. Where's your sat phone?"

"Lost it. We had a small detour, but we're on our way again. Scarlett and I aren't alone. We have a friend with us." I didn't feel comfortable saying more than that over the phone. But I was sure Aiden could connect the dots.

He paused, then said, "Copy that. I'll let Owen know."

I pulled up our GPS coordinates on Scarlett's phone. Data was slow, but it finally cooperated. Aiden and I sorted out a meeting place, and I headed back toward the road. I left Scarlett and Virtue hidden among the trees as I scoped things out. No sign of anyone from the compound.

And then an SUV marked Hartley Sheriff's Department pulled up. Sheriff Owen Douglas was driving, cowboy hat and all. I stepped out of the woods and waved him down. A second SUV was following, driven by Deputy Marsh, a young female officer. Aiden sat next to her.

A thousand pounds of weight left my shoulders.

Still, I didn't fully relax even as Owen and Aiden both got out and strode over to me. I called out to Scarlett and Virtue, who emerged from the trees. I went to carry Virtue to the road, where I set her on her feet.

Aiden hugged Scarlett first, then turned to me. "Never been so glad to see *you*," he said, slapping me on the back.

"Same."

"Took you long enough. Do you have any idea how worried Jessi has been? She's been nearly out of her mind."

Scarlett shared a look with me. Aiden was predictable. His number one priority was always Jessi. But I was starting to understand where he was coming from.

Virtue stood behind me, hovering in my shadow.

"Everyone, this is Virtue," I said. "That's Aiden. Deputy Marsh. Sheriff Douglas. All friends of mine and Scarlett's. You can trust them."

She was nervous, but she shook each of their hands. "You're taking me back to Hartley?"

Owen touched the brim of his hat. "That's right, miss. We're here to help you."

Scarlett steered Virtue toward the sheriff's SUV. "I'll get her settled."

"We have a shit ton to debrief about," Owen muttered to me. "We found the Jeep. Towed it."

"Good." I waited until Scarlett and Virtue were inside the vehicle. Then I turned to the sheriff. "We do need to talk about everything, but not in front of the girl. Let's get the women to the hospital first. Virtue needs to get checked out and treated. Plus Scarlett needs water and food."

"That's what I was planning on." Owen nodded at his deputy. "Marsh, can you call ahead? Let County General know we're coming?"

"Yes, Sheriff." Deputy Marsh got back in her SUV to use her phone.

Owen readjusted his hat, lowering his voice. "Trace, what kind of injuries does the girl have? How bad are we talking here? I've held back from arresting everybody at that Paradise Ranch because I was biding my time until we found you, but I'll send every deputy and the regional SWAT to clear that place out if I have to."

Aiden scowled as he waited for my response.

"I don't think she was attacked. Not like that. She ran before they could marry her off. Sprained her ankle, and she could be suffering from exposure and shock. But I think that's it."

Owen gave me a single nod. He and Aiden had relaxed slightly. "I'll arrange for a forensic investigator to question her, if it seems warranted."

"Let's go," Aiden said. "I'll tell Jessi to meet us at the hospital. If we don't get there soon with you and Scarlett safe and sound, I'm never going to hear the end of it."

"*Finally.*" Jessi ran toward us. "I'm so glad to see you two safe." She hugged me, the embrace brief but fierce, and then turned to Scarlett. "What do you need? I've got drinks and sandwiches from the diner. And changes of clothes."

"I knew you were my best friend for a reason," Scarlett said.

While Jessi tugged Scarlett over to the waiting room seats, I stepped over to a quiet corner with Aiden and Owen. Virtue was already in a hospital room being examined. Deputy Marsh had gone with her. But the nurses had shooed Scarlett away for the time being so they could treat Virtue in private. They'd promised to call Scarlett back in a little while.

"You sure you want to do this now?" Aiden asked me. "No offense, but you look like week-old shit. And you smell worse."

"Harsh," Owen muttered. "But true."

"Apologies to your delicate noses. But I'd rather talk."

I'd downed a water bottle on the drive here, and I was used to functioning on no sleep. After the rain, mud, and sweat, I wasn't pleasant to be around if you had a working olfactory sense.

There was also my knee. It hurt like hell, and I needed to ice it. But I was far more concerned with the danger still facing Virtue and Scarlett.

My eyes roved across the waiting room to linger on her. Unlike me, Scarlett's beauty hadn't been dimmed by the ordeal of the last day. I wanted to check on her. Touch her.

I was hopeless.

"I found Virtue's younger brother, Toby. Or I should say he found me. I'll need a new sat phone with my old number, by the way. In case Toby tries to contact me."

I quickly recounted where Scarlett and I had been for the last day. Aiden had told Owen some of it, but obviously neither of them knew the exact details of how our visit to the compound had gone sideways. "After I left Toby, I went to find Scarlett. An elder named Dawson Witkins was trying to intimidate her. I dealt with him."

Owen folded his arms. "*Dealt* with him?"

"He's breathing." For now. "But his other friends at the compound weren't happy."

"Sounds like you kicked the hornet's nest," Aiden said.

"Pretty much. They chased after us, shot out the Jeep's tire. Road was already slick from the storm. We had to abandon the Jeep and slid down a muddy slope. A few hours after that, we chanced upon the cabin where Virtue was staying. It was lucky, really. We never would've found her otherwise."

Aiden explained what had happened after he'd followed my GPS signal to Scarlett's Jeep. He'd found it by the side of the road, pocked with gunshots, tire blown. And rain-smeared footprints in the mud had led to a steep slope. "Whoever attacked you had already left the scene. I called

Owen and told him what was up. We arranged to have the Jeep towed to a repair shop, but couldn't pick up your trail."

"There was a quilt in the back of the Jeep," I interrupted. "It's important to Scarlett." That much had been obvious, though she hadn't explained why.

Owen nodded. "I'll make a note to one of my deputies. See that she receives it."

"We've been looking for you ever since," Aiden said, resuming his story. "I was sure you'd gotten Scarlett somewhere safe, and I had no doubt we'd hear from you at some point."

"But you could've let me know what you were doing beforehand," Owen added. "Might have saved some time."

"Really, Sheriff?" I asked. "You sure about that?"

Owen didn't know about the Last Refuge Protectors. Aiden and I knew the score, and I was beyond cynical about the drawbacks of government involvement. I'd seen what happened when the "good" guys abandoned right and wrong and lines got blurred. Owen wasn't like that. But he was an idealist. He didn't wear a white cowboy hat for nothing.

When dealing with men like Dawson Witkins, men who would twist every advantage and technicality to prey upon the innocent, there was no room for idealism. Besides, a guy wearing a sheriff's badge tended to think he should be in charge.

"I'm not thrilled that you went to Paradise Ranch to help this girl without a word to me," Owen said. "I guessed you and Scarlett were up to something. I got that vibe the night we spoke at the bar. I just didn't know it would get this messy. But I'm a hell of a lot less happy about men in my county forcing underage girls into marriages or trying to gun down my citizens. I'm not a fan of *that* at all. What they did was brazen, and I don't intend to let it go. In case there's any doubt."

Aiden looked at me, like he was saying, *This is your show, man.*

"I don't intend to let it go either," I said. "But they've been forcing girls into marriage a lot longer than this. Your predecessor is the one who helped Scarlett after she escaped over a decade ago. You must have heard about that. *Sheriff.*"

"I've heard rumors. I didn't know exactly what had happened to Scarlett until now, but word travels. Some people have claimed that teenage girls leave Paradise Ranch, and new ones arrive. There have been whispers about it being a polygamist cult. I've sent deputies there to check it out. But that place is closed off. Insular. They keep to themselves, and they don't talk. Without more to go on, some specific evidence of wrongdoing and witnesses to back it up, there was nothing I could do. But that's exactly my point. We have the possibility of testimony from multiple witnesses this time. Starting with this kid Toby. You could've come to me."

I remained skeptical, but I moved on. "Dawson Witkins is up to more than you know. This all started with that stalker harassing Scarlett online and potentially following her in town. We now think Witkins hired the guy. He'd found out about Scarlett's new identity. How, I don't know. Witkins threatened her yesterday and made it clear he doesn't intend to leave her alone. If I hadn't shown up when I did, he would've made good on those threats." I lifted my hand when Owen opened his mouth. I wasn't done yet. "But we *can't* make a move on them yet. We're not ready. If we go after Witkins and his co-conspirators now, they'll close ranks like they have before. And they might use the legal process against us to force Virtue back to Paradise Ranch. She's a minor. Her parents still have rights, whether or not they deserve them."

"I'll get Child Protective Services involved. I won't let that happen."

"Bullshit."

Owen stepped into my space, fists clenched. "Excuse me?"

We were toe-to-toe. I had an inch on him, and I knew how to use my presence to get my way. But Sheriff Douglas was no slouch, either.

"You can't guarantee what'll happen in a courtroom, Sheriff. I don't trust that bureaucracy. I'm going to keep Virtue safe on my own terms. Aiden and I will gather the intel we need, and we're going to do this our way."

Aiden was nodding along, but Owen just bristled further. "You're not the law of this county, Novo. You're not anything but a private citizen. *None* of these decisions are up to you."

I noticed Scarlett and Jessi watching from across the waiting room. They couldn't hear what we'd been saying, but the tension between us was clear. If we weren't careful, more people around here would pick up on it. As it was, gossip would be flying around Hartley about our confrontation at the hospital and the injured girl we'd brought in today.

How long until Dawson Witkins heard? Or until his spy reported back to him?

"Then I'm asking you as a friend," I said quietly. "You're someone who cares about what happens to women like Scarlett and Virtue and the kids back at that compound. Give Aiden and me a chance to prepare and plan this out. So that when we go in, we take them down *for good*."

Owen looked between me and Aiden. "You have anything to add, Shelborne?"

Aiden shrugged and shook his head. "I'm just the chef."

Owen snorted, and just like that, the tension broke.

"All right," Owen said. "I will trust you with this. We'll sit on the evidence we have so far and wait. Will Virtue be staying with Scarlett?"

"For the time being, yes."

"Then I'll increase my deputies' patrols in the streets nearby. I can't spare anybody given how stretched we are already, but I'll make it work. But what about this stalker situation? That's even more pressing with Virtue staying at Scarlett's."

"I'm working on it." I didn't feel like explaining my investigation with River or the new camera setup at Scarlett's place. I didn't work for Owen. I wasn't his deputy.

"You'll make sure Scarlett and Virtue are both protected?" he asked.

"To my last breath." That was the one thing in this world I was sure of. "That's all you need to know."

Aiden touched my shoulder. "And I've got Trace's back, for what that's worth."

Owen gave us each an unamused look. "I certainly hope that next time, you'll bring me in before it comes to that. I'll be in touch."

Aiden stood beside me as we watched him storm out of the waiting room.

"Let me know what you need from me, boss," Aiden murmured. "I knew you were the man to lead the Protectors. Thanks for proving me right."

"Lord knows you enjoy being right."

He clapped me on the back and smirked. "You'd think I would be used to it by now."

"But I haven't agreed to anything. I still haven't decided whether I'm staying in Hartley long term or not." I had reasons to stay, and I could now admit to myself that Scarlett was first among them. But that didn't mean I should.

"We'll see."

I was done talking about it. I looked for a bathroom to clean myself up a little.

CHAPTER EIGHTEEN

Scarlett

"DID you know they have Netflix in here?" Virtue asked, brandishing a TV remote. "I watched a whole movie about penguins."

I sat on the edge of her bed. "Sounds fun."

The nurses had finally let me into Virtue's hospital room. She was upbeat and comfortable, with an IV giving her fluids and her cheeks flushed from being washed. Her injured ankle was elevated. The x-ray had shown no broken bones, thank goodness. Aside from dehydration, scrapes, and a severe sprain, she was physically healthy.

The doctor still wanted her to stay overnight for observation. But contrary to what I'd expected, Virtue didn't seem upset in the least.

"Do you think they'll let me watch as long as I want? Or do they have a lights-out time?"

"I bet you could talk those nurses into anything." They'd been doting on her.

Virtue frowned at the remote. "Toby should get to see this, too. He'd love watching all these shows."

"I sent him a message from my Instagram, letting him know you're safe. I'm sure he'll get in touch when he can."

Jessi and I had been camped out in the waiting room all afternoon, while Trace and Aiden had been running errands. The men had picked up a regular phone from the gas station for Trace. But he had to special order a new satellite phone. In the meantime, Toby could still reach us through my Instagram account, and I'd written him to share my cell number.

"I hope he's all right," Virtue said.

"We have no reason to think he isn't. He's smart and resourceful. I'm sure he's being careful."

She nodded, but looked unconvinced.

I fluffed up her pillows. "I like Netflix too. Are you sure you don't want me to stay the night with you? It's no trouble at all."

"No way. You need to sleep, Scarlett. In a real bed." Her brows drew down, and I could just imagine her lecturing her younger siblings. She reminded me of myself at fifteen. "I'll see you when you're back tomorrow. Besides, Keira said she'd stick around. So I won't be alone. She's really nice."

"Keira? Oh, Deputy Marsh."

"Yeah. She went to get us some food for dinner. Mac and cheese. It's my favorite."

"I'll have to remember that for when I bring you back to my place." I gave her a hug. "Until tomorrow."

"Bring candy from your shop?"

"You got it."

She was already pushing the buttons on the remote and scrolling through Netflix's offerings. "See you later. Oh, and say hi to Trace for me." She paused and looked up. "I'll see him tomorrow too, right?"

"I'll make sure you do."

I left Virtue's room, saying hello to Deputy Marsh in the hallway, who'd just arrived with a container of home-cooked food. "Thanks for staying with her," I said.

Keira smiled. "No trouble at all. Virtue's a sweetheart. My

little sister is the same age. Sheriff Douglas will be back later as well. We'll take good care of her."

"That's a relief." It was still hard to leave Virtue here, but she was right. I needed rest. I couldn't care for her if I didn't care for myself.

Jessi was out in the waiting room, along with Aiden and Trace. "Will you come to the diner for a while?" she asked me. "You didn't even eat the sandwiches I brought."

"You can stop fussing. I'm okay, I promise. I just want to go home and sleep. I'm beat."

"At least take these with you." Jessi held out the food she'd brought. Then she glanced at her brother. "Should I drop you both off?"

Trace nodded, eyes locked on me. "I left my car at Scarlett's yesterday. You can take us to her place. We'll figure it out from there."

My place. But was that really just to get his car? Or was he going to stay?

Things between me and Trace had changed radically in the last twenty-four hours. We had shared a *lot*. Kisses and truths and that sexy interlude by a creek that I wouldn't soon forget. But I still didn't know where we stood. In front of his sister was not the right time for that conversation.

But if the choice was between Trace going to Refuge Mountain or staying with me, I knew which I preferred.

About half an hour later, Jessi had dropped us off. Trace walked me to my front porch. It was early evening now, the sun sinking.

It felt like a million years had passed since we'd set out for the compound yesterday morning.

"Do you want to come in?" I asked.

I'd asked that same question the last time we stood here. That had been weeks ago. Before anything had happened between us. Yet the chemistry I'd felt that day had only increased.

I knew the taste of his kiss. The bliss that overtook his face when he let go of that compulsive need for control. But which Trace was standing here with me? The kind, generous man who seemed to need me as much as I needed him? Or the stoic warrior who closed himself off to all comfort and feeling?

"I'll come in. I should check around your house for anything suspicious."

I sighed. "Is that the only reason?"

He didn't respond as I unlocked the door. I'd lost my keys, but Jessi had thoughtfully turned over my spare set at the hospital. Trace looked dour and pensive as we walked inside. I stopped in the kitchen, while Trace walked through the house to check for bad guys. I appreciated it, and he was being smart. But I didn't want to think about danger and stalkers right now.

Me? My needs were pretty simple at the moment. Virtue was safe at the hospital now, and I was so thankful for that. But I needed Trace beside me. I needed to capture a little of the peace I'd felt with him last night in that isolated cabin, when everything had been wrong and yet the two of us had felt *right*.

I removed our sandwiches from the paper Jessi had wrapped them in and set them on plates. I added some cut fruit from my fridge, because I was craving anything fresh. All I'd eaten at the hospital was a bag of chips.

A few minutes later, Trace walked into the kitchen. I had my back to him, but I heard his footsteps.

"Everything looks secure." His tone was gruff.

"Good to hear," I said tightly.

There was a pause. I felt him behind me.

Then I inhaled in surprise as he wrapped his arms around my waist and pulled me against him, my back to his chest. I immediately relaxed into him. Trace dropped a soft kiss to my neck.

"But that wasn't the only reason I came inside," he whispered.

My eyes sank closed. When I brought my hand up to stroke his cheek, he made a rumbly sound. Almost a purr. This unreservedly affectionate side to Trace was new. But I wanted it desperately.

He turned me around in his arms so I faced him. Trace was many things, but descriptors like *hesitant* rarely described him. At least, that wasn't the outward persona he showed the world.

Yet that was the look on his face now. Racked with uncertainty.

Then he kissed my mouth, slow but thorough, his tongue tracing my lower lip before he pulled back. "I don't know what to do about you," he said.

"Why does it have to be complicated? Spend the night with me. Sex is optional, but I'm down." I was too worn out to be anything less than candid. "Tomorrow, we'll go together to see Virtue at the hospital."

"Scarlett..." He had that tone in his voice that usually preceded words like *should* and *bad idea*.

"Don't overthink it. Do you *want* to stay?"

He kissed the top of my head and put his cheek against mine. "Yeah. Of course I do."

"Then why does anything else matter?"

Don't go, I thought. *Not when we both need each other this much.*

"I want you, Scarlett. I want you so much it's killing me,

and I'm tired of fighting it. This is one area that I'm not as strong as I should be, and I'm not proud of that fact."

"You wish you didn't want me?"

"I wish I wasn't capable of hurting you. I don't want that for you. So I'm putting this in your hands, babe. You make the choice."

I already had.

I didn't understand why he was so convinced he'd hurt me. That he was *bad* for me. Did he worry I'd fall in love with him, and he couldn't return those feelings?

I fit myself into his embrace, and he automatically tightened his arms around me. "Trace, I need you to know something about me. I'm not..." I cleared my throat. "I'm not like Jessi."

"In what way?"

I wasn't sure how to explain this.

I'd always been fascinated by the idea of romance. I listened to sappy love songs and read romance novels. I liked to see those happy, healthy relationships built on trust instead of subjugation. But I hadn't even been sure those *existed* in real life until Jessi and Aiden. My adoptive parents had been wonderful, but they'd acted more like good friends to each other than lovers.

"The connection that Jessi talks about having with Aiden," I said. "Being so in love that you can't function without that other person. Wanting *forever*. I don't know what it would feel like." My voice faltered because I had never confessed this to anyone. If I'd told Jessi, she would've said I just hadn't met the right person yet. That I shouldn't give up on a happily ever after. The marriage, the kids, the Labrador mix. But I had never needed those things. I didn't need anyone else to complete me.

Trace was just listening, rubbing small circles into my

back. So I went on. "Sexual desire has never been a problem. I've had *plenty* of sex, and I've thoroughly enjoyed it. "

He made a growly sound, hands gripping me possessively. "I don't need details."

I snickered. "Wasn't going to give them. I'm just saying, I haven't been a cloistered nun. I've dated. I like touch and being close to someone. And I do have love in my life, but it's with family and friends."

"Nothing wrong with that," he said softly.

"I agree. Who knows. Maybe I would've turned out this way even if my past had been different. Maybe this is just how I'm made." I lifted my head to look at him. "Just know, I don't expect anything *more* from you. Call it friends with benefits. Or don't call it anything at all. We don't have to worry about what this is or what it means, or even if it's a bad idea. We can give this to each other." I touched his cheek, fingertips smoothing along his beard and over his lips. I felt so warm, so steady with his arms around me. "Let's just *be*."

He kissed my fingers as they brushed over his lips. "You're very convincing."

"I like getting my way."

"So do I."

With a swift movement, Trace dropped his hands to my hips and lifted me, setting me on the counter beside our plates. He gripped the back of my neck and tugged me toward him. His kiss was claiming and gentle at the same time. Lips and tongue saying more than his words had. This wasn't a frantic moment like outside the bar or by the creek. We weren't rushing past any doubts. I wasn't asking for forever, and he knew that now. Maybe this time, he was really *in this* with me. Even if it was just for one night.

But I still had to make sure.

I drew back, our noses brushing. "Is that a yes?" I asked. "You're staying with me tonight? No regrets?"

He licked his lips like he was chasing the taste of me. "I'll stay. I'm with you. There is nowhere else in this world I'd rather be."

Exactly what I'd wanted to hear.

Trace leaned in again. My legs wrapped around his waist, my hands in his hair. I got lost in his kisses. Some shallow and soft, others so intense my toes curled. He did things with his tongue that hypnotized me. His long fingers cradled the back of my head, his other hand massaging my hip and thigh. His skin was slightly salty. Trace's scent was more pronounced than usual. But it wasn't unpleasant. The opposite, actually.

He smelled like sex. The more I inhaled him, the more arousal coiled low in my belly.

Me, though? I was a bit ripe for my tastes. And various parts of me could benefit from a razor. At least Jessi had brought us travel toothbrush kits at the hospital. I owed that woman.

When we stopped to catch our breaths, I said, "I could use a shower."

He hummed. "Same here. But you need to eat first. I'm neglecting you."

"I don't feel neglected." Desire had turned me languid, relaxed, even as I felt the need for relief. I knew Trace would give that to me.

He grabbed a plate and scooted it across the counter to me. Picked up a sandwich and held it out. I took a bite. Then Trace took one. We polished off that sandwich, and did the same with the second, Trace alternating between feeding me and himself. Nobody had ever fed me before. I would've been annoyed if another man had tried it. But from Trace, it felt natural. I liked when he took care of me. I was a sucker for it.

The fruit was next, followed by glasses of water. "Shower?" I asked.

"Yes. But separate. That'll be faster. I want to get you laid out on your bed as soon as possible."

"Oh really. What'll you do to me?"

He dropped a kiss to my jaw. "Explore you with my hands. My mouth. I've been waiting a long time for the privilege of knowing every inch of you."

A shiver of anticipation wound through me. "A long time, huh?"

"Since the moment I saw you."

I sat back. "Is that so?"

He held my chin with his fingers. "I tried to stay away because I knew what would happen if I let myself get too close." Trace brought his lips to my ear. His beard tickled the sensitive skin there. "I'd have to have you."

I stroked my hands up and down his chest over his shirt. There was a familiar subtext beneath what he'd said. His fear that he was "bad" for me. But he wasn't letting his fears stand as a barrier between us anymore. As far as I knew, he hadn't dealt with those issues.

Was *I* doing the right thing? Was I pushing him for an intimacy he wasn't actually ready for?

Don't overthink it, I reminded myself. Exactly what I'd told him.

Our mouths met again, drawn together by an irresistible force. Minutes passed before I'd even realized it. Trace was the one to pull away with a frustrated groan. "Okay, showers now. I'll use the guest bath. Then I'm taking you to your bed."

"Copy that."

He smiled at me fondly, and my heart thumped in my chest. *Wow*. I didn't think I'd ever seen him smile like that. Like it came from inside him. Like he meant it.

Trace headed for the guest bath, while I jumped into mine. I tried to be quick, but a girl had certain expectations for herself. When he got to exploring in a few minutes, I wanted to be smooth and well prepared.

Then I combed through the tangles that had built up in the woods, brushed my teeth again. Dabbed perfume on my pulse points. Tugged on a fresh T-shirt that I'd brought into the bathroom with me, leaving nothing on underneath.

Finally, I went into my bedroom. The lights were out. Trace was sprawled on top of my covers, hair damp, wearing the change of clothes Jessi had brought for him.

He was sound asleep.

Smiling, I crawled onto the mattress beside him. I smoothed a few strands of hair from his face. He would no doubt protest if I said this aloud, but he was beautiful. All masculine lines and intensity, even in sleep, but still beautiful. I kissed his forehead and then snuggled in beside him.

Trace made a groany, growly sound, his arm lifting and snaking around me. He didn't wake up. I felt warm. Secure.

I followed him into sleep.

I woke up in the dark. But I felt Trace next to me. His body, his breath. The steadiness of his presence.

A nightlight from my bathroom gave the space a faint glow. I shifted my head to look at Trace. He was blinking his eyes. He drew an inhale, rubbing his face with the hand that wasn't wrapped around me. "Damn. I fell asleep."

I laughed. "We were both exhausted."

"What time is it?"

I glanced at my alarm clock. "Three. You want to go back to sleep?"

"Nope." Trace rolled us both, so I was on my back. He

hovered on his elbows above me. His head dropped to kiss the skin above my T-shirt collar. His whiskers created pleasant friction on my neck. "How about you?"

"Mmmm. Not tired at all."

His thigh nudged between my legs. Trace had sweats on, but I felt his erection against my hip. His hand moved down to the bare skin of my thigh and stroked upward. Along my hip. My stomach. His fingers were calloused and rough as they pushed my shirt up.

"Already naked under here," he commented. "I like it."

"You know me. So impure. I'm a bad influence."

He chuckled, and I was glad he got my dark humor. "That might be. But I still need to know that you're ready for me."

"I've been ready for you since the first time we kissed."

"I seem to remember you stopping things that night. Not me."

"We had a few more things to work out. I'm glad I waited."

"Me too. But you need to know what you're getting into. When I take you this first time, I'm not gonna be gentle." His fingers tugged my nipple hard to emphasize his point.

A shiver of desire throbbed in my clit. I brought my hand to the bulge at his crotch and squeezed. "Baby, I don't want you to be."

He groaned, hips moving to press his still-covered erection against my palm.

Trace worked my T-shirt over my head and tossed it to the floor. His shirt followed. His skin and muscles were hot beneath my hands. His scent was fresh from his shower, but still *him* underneath. That earthy smokiness.

I pushed his sweats down over his hips. I wanted to see him better, see all of him for the first time. But I didn't want to break the spell between us by turning on any more lights. I just wanted to enjoy this moment with Trace and banish the rest of the world for a while. I truly had meant what I'd said earlier. Nothing else had to matter but the two of us, right here and now.

He stopped me from taking his sweats all the way off. But when he pressed his body to mine, it still felt divine. His mixture of hard and soft. The brush of his hair on my cheek combined with the scratch of his whiskers as we kissed. Languidly, Trace's tongue explored my mouth in slow but fierce kisses.

My hands slid into his hair and massaged his scalp. I liked the way his longer strands felt slipping between my fingers. He seemed to enjoy it, too, making those purring noises again as we kissed. I was already addicted to the sound. I loved making him feel good. It felt like something he was giving *me*.

I bent my knees to wrap my legs around him, drawing him closer.

But Trace had other ideas. He slid downward, moving his kisses to my breasts. He sucked my nipples until I was panting, and then his lips trailed down my stomach. All the way until he pressed his face into the cleft between my legs.

"*Oh*," I moaned.

"The smell of you. It makes me wild."

With a sudden, almost violent movement, he flipped me onto my stomach. I gasped, bouncing against the mattress. I felt him shifting as he shoved his sweats off.

And then he blanketed me with his naked body, his hard cock rutting against my lower back. The move was so raw. Possessing.

"*Trace*." My voice was hoarse with lust.

"This all right?" He kissed the back of my neck.

"It's perfect. Don't stop."

Trace's hands held me in place, while his erection slid against my skin. As if he couldn't wait to rub me with his scent. His gruff moans were *everything*. I felt claimed, even though he wasn't inside me yet. *Owned*. And I loved it. Because this was my choice. I had as much control in this moment as Trace did.

After several heady moments, he lifted off of me and flipped me onto my back again. "I had every intention of making this last, but I don't think I can. I need to get inside you. If that's what you want too."

I was so turned on, it was difficult to get my brain to string together the words. "Yes. Inside me. Please."

He bent my legs and widened them. His erection rocked against me again, but now *right* where I wanted it. "You're nice and wet," he breathed. "You do want it, don't you? Want my cock?"

"Trace. *Please*." I grabbed for his biceps.

"You want me to use a condom? I'm fine either way."

"No, I'm good. I trust you."

On a single thrust, he pushed himself all the way in.

I gasped. Cried out. It had been a while for me, and he was big. Trace paused, kissing along my forehead. "You okay, babe?"

"You don't like me asking you that question. In the bedroom, that goes both ways." I closed my eyes, trying to concentrate, even though the pleasure centers of my brain were shooting off like fireworks. He felt incredible inside me. But I had to say this. "I will tell you if I don't like something. Barring that, I want everything you've got. Don't you dare hold anything back."

He lowered his upper body and whispered, "Roger that."

Then he pulled his hips back and thrust them forward again. All I could do was hold on.

He was rough, like he'd said he would be. Yet Trace's eyes didn't leave mine, shining in the low light. He was entirely focused on me. Like he was tracking every sound that I made, every reaction. But not because he was worried about me or doubted I wanted this.

Every time I moaned, a wicked fire lit up his gaze.

Without warning, he pulled out. Rolled me over once again. But before I could protest, his cock pushed back inside my pussy, picking up that same intense rhythm. I had never felt so primal. Uninhibited.

I glanced over my shoulder and saw Trace with his head thrown back. Nothing but pleasure on his face.

This was what I loved most about sex. The freedom to simply feel. But it was *more* with Trace. Moment by moment, he was letting go of his tightly wound need for control, and it was an incredible thing to experience for me, too. Knowing I was giving that to him.

"Trace. I'm close."

He tugged my hips up so he could reach beneath me. His fingers slid between my legs to just above where we were joined, and he massaged my most sensitive spot.

I shattered. A wave of euphoria crested and broke.

Trace let out a hoarse cry, bending over so his chest was to my back while his hips continued to move. He kissed my temple, and his hair slipped over my cheek as his cock pulsed inside me.

"*Scarlett.*"

On his lips, my name sounded like a prayer.

CHAPTER NINETEEN

Trace

I LOWERED myself to the mattress beside Scarlett. She shifted so she lay on her side, facing me. She was panting. Her auburn hair spilled everywhere, on the pillow and over her shoulders. I wound a lock around my fingers. Her hair had always looked soft, but the strands had a substance to them, too. Like thick strands of silk.

She was the sexiest thing I'd ever seen. I put my arms around her, tugging her until her body was fitting against mine.

"You're not even winded," she said. "Aren't you worn out?"

"It's called stamina."

Her lips formed an O, and she smacked my abs.

"Ouch. Hey."

"I'm going to test that claim, stud. I'll be the judge of how much stamina you have."

"Looking forward to it. Hope you can handle me." I tried to kiss her, but she wiggled away.

"I'll show you how I handle you." Scarlett swung her leg over my waist, pushing down my shoulders to climb on top of me. And then the woman started tickling my ribs.

So of course, I had to knock her over and get in some naked tickling of my own.

Soon we were both laughing. Which turned into more kissing. I couldn't stop touching her. I was thirty-two, not twenty-two, so my cock hadn't rallied yet. But he was definitely getting ideas.

Her fingertips brushed the corner of my mouth. "I like to see that," she said.

"See what?"

"You smiling."

It felt good. Enjoying Scarlett this way. Just existing in the present moment with her, my soul unburdened for the first time in a while. But as soon as I noticed it, the feeling fled.

Scarlett's own smile faltered. So I kissed her again. I wanted that moment back. Even if it was fleeting.

We can give this to each other.

Earlier, I had almost turned her down when she'd asked me to stay the night. I wanted her like crazy. That was beyond obvious to us both. But I'd still been holding onto my resistance, what little there was left.

Then she'd told me she wasn't looking for love or forever. It had bothered me to hear it, only because she deserved someone who'd care for her like that. But I also knew that I couldn't possibly give that to her. So her confession had absolved me of those last threads of guilt.

She didn't want anything more from me than pleasure. A few benefits thrown into our friendship. That much, I could handle.

My secret—one among many—was that I *did* have feelings for her. But whenever I eventually had to walk away, Scarlett wouldn't get hurt, and that was all that mattered to me.

Our kisses were slow and comfortable, not leading to more just yet. Finally I lay back, covering us both with the sheets, and Scarlett put her head on my chest. "I need to ask you something," I said.

"You can ask me anything."

"It's a request. If I'm ever asleep next to you again, and I seem like I'm having a nightmare, I need you not to touch me. Don't try to wake me. Just leave me be."

"Nightmares?" Scarlett tried to sit up, her hair slipping over her shoulder. I eased her back down.

"Hopefully it won't be an issue. I just didn't want to catch you unaware." I was annoyed at myself for falling asleep here at all. I'd been under deep, no dreams. But still, I hated to think I could've scared her. For that very reason, I'd avoided sleeping in her house before. Even when I'd stayed here all night in her living room.

When I woke from a nightmare, I didn't always know what was happening right away. What if I struck out? Hurt her?

A mass of something dark and bitter gathered in my chest.

"Do you have nightmares a lot?" she asked.

"They come and go. And before you say it, no, I don't wanna talk about it. But that's nothing about you. It's just me."

Right after everything had blown up, and I'd been in the hospital with my knee getting pieced back together, the nightmares had been nonstop. Nearly unbearable. That was when I'd tried therapy, and it hadn't done a thing. But was that because of the particular therapist? Or because of my own despondency? I didn't know. I'd refused drugs and further counseling. Closed myself off from my friends.

I'd felt myself fading. And I hadn't cared.

Since moving to Hartley, things had been easier. Probably because I'd spent so much of the last eight months away from other people. I could go for weeks at a time without any nightmares cropping up, even though my sleep habits were still a disaster.

Could I actually sleep in a bed with Scarlett on purpose? I didn't know.

But I was surprised to find that I wanted it. While this thing between us lasted, I wanted anything with this woman that I could have. So long as her heart wasn't at risk.

It took a moment, but finally she nodded. "If that's what you need, then I'll do what you asked." She still had concern in her voice, but I was relieved that she didn't push the subject.

Scarlett sat up again, and this time I let her. "I'm starving," she said. "I'm pretty sure I have some cake in the freezer. Or better yet, hot chocolate with marshmallows. Oh! Hot chocolate with marshmallows *and* whipped cream."

"Hot chocolate sounds great." I sat up beside her and kissed her shoulder. "If we're getting up, I wanted to check the footage on your cameras. Haven't had a chance yet."

"Okay. Just let me shower, and I'll be right there," she said, sauntering naked into her bathroom. "Unless you want to come with?"

Nnngh. A very tempting offer.

"I'm fine. I'll clean up on my own." I admired her backside, my cock half-hard again. But I'd just told her about the nightmare thing, and I didn't want to broach the subject of my scars too. If she saw me naked under bright lights, that was going to come up.

Just...not yet.

Once she was in the bathroom, I grabbed my sweats from the floor.

I opened Scarlett's laptop on her kitchen table. When I'd set up the cameras before, I'd installed an app on her computer to monitor them. And she'd given me her password, a sign of trust that might not have been warranted.

Just one of the many ways she'd given me her trust. I wanted to live up to that.

While I waited for her laptop to boot up, I checked my email. There was a message from River, bugging me to call. It had come in half an hour ago. I wrote back, giving him my temporary phone number and explaining my sat phone was lost.

Next I logged onto Scarlett's Instagram, but saw no messages from Toby.

By the time Scarlett brought over two mugs of hot chocolate, piled high with tiny marshmallows and whipped cream, I'd finished my review of the camera footage from the last day.

"Anything?" Scarlett asked. She'd put her T-shirt back on, her legs once again bare.

"Nothing concerning. No sign that your cigarette-smoking stalker has been around." That was good news, but it had only been a week since he'd last been here. It was possible he'd gotten scared off by the presence of the cameras. But stalkers were motivated by obsession. Obsessive behavior didn't stop cold turkey.

The alternative was that Dawson Witkins had hired the guy to watch Scarlett. And if that were true, I couldn't imagine the guy would give up easily in that case either. Not if he was getting paid.

We would just have to wait until I picked up his trail again.

"A package got delivered to your porch, though," I said. The doorbell camera had shown a sheriff's deputy dropping it off, and I was pretty sure I knew what it was.

"Really?" Scarlett went to the door, opening it when I nodded for her to go ahead. There was a small cardboard box outside, the flaps folded closed. She came back in, and I locked the door behind her.

"Oh my gosh. I was worried about whether I'd get this back." She left the box by the door, pulling out the colorful quilt that was tucked inside. It was dirty and a little torn on one edge. But otherwise intact.

Scarlett took the quilt into the living room and sat on her couch. I brought our hot chocolates over to the coffee table. She was staring at the blanket in her lap with a mixture of emotions on her face.

"My mom made this. My stepmother gave it to me yesterday. Well, I don't know what to call Mercy now. Not that it matters." Her hands trembled, and I placed my own over her wrist.

"I'm sorry about your mother. What happened to her?"

"A fever, I guess? That's what Mercy said."

"We haven't talked much about what happened at your father's house." With fleeing the compound and then finding Virtue, we'd been preoccupied. But I should've said something before now. She'd just found out about her mother's death.

"Don't really want to talk about it," she said.

Now *that* sounded familiar.

I put my arm around her shoulders. "I lost my mom as well. It's one of the worst things for anyone."

"How old were you?"

"Six."

Her eyes darted to mine. "Trace. I'm sorry."

"My dad was a good provider, but not affectionate. Maybe that's why I'm not so touchy-feely. With anyone but you." Jessi was my half-sister, and we'd spent most of our childhoods apart.

"But you like affection?"

I brushed my nose against her hair. "Yeah, babe. With you, I do."

We kissed. She tasted like chocolate and cream.

"I've been trying not to think about my mom," Scarlett said. "I need to focus on Virtue."

"How long are you planning for her to stay here?"

"As long as she needs. But I'll have to figure out something more permanent. She's still a kid, and she needs a parent. I wouldn't be any good at that. When I left the compound, I was lucky enough to find people to take me in. Treat me like their daughter. I want the same for Virtue."

"You did pretty well with her at the cabin."

"So did you."

Scarlett's fingers grazed over my face. We kissed again, but this time, the moment grew heated. Our tongues met. Danced. Our hands wandered. I pulled her into my lap, gently moving the quilt to one side of the couch. Scarlett rocked herself against my erection. And I was very pleased to find she was still naked under that shirt.

She smelled great from her shower, but I wanted my scent on her again. I was raring to go for round two.

Then my phone made an annoying buzzing noise on the kitchen table.

"Is that important?" she asked.

"No. I know who's writing me at this hour. I'll deal with him in a little while."

But Scarlett was already off my lap and grabbing my phone. She held it up. "It's River. He says, *Are you alive? I doubt you're asleep. I need proof of life or I might decide to fly out to Hartley tomorrow. You still owe me that trip, by the way.*"

Grumbling, I held out my hand for the phone. "I must've missed some texts from him yesterday. He's dramatic."

"He's helping investigate the stalker, right?" She plopped onto the couch. "I want to meet him."

"Are you sure about that? He can be a pain in the ass."

"I have a hunch he'll say the same thing about you." She

shrugged. "Unless you don't want me to meet him. If he's *super top-secret*." Scarlett sipped her hot chocolate.

"Fine. I'll call him." I held up my phone and started a video call using a heavily encrypted app.

She set her cocoa mug on the table. "Wait, are you calling him *now*? I'm not even dressed."

"Neither am I." I pulled her closer, lifting her so she was sitting on my thigh, both of us facing my phone screen.

"*Trace—*"

River's face appeared. His chin was dark with stubble, and his hair had that crazy look it got when he'd been awake for a few days. "Novo, why is it so hard for you to respond to a simple—Oh. Well, hello." River pushed his glasses up his nose, grinning. "Who do we have here?"

I rolled my eyes. "Riv, this is Scarlett Weston. Scarlett, meet River Kwon. Sorry I missed your messages. A lot's been going on."

"Never mind. I get it now. You were otherwise engaged." He rested his chin in his hand. "So, Scarlett. What's your story?"

She giggled. "Trace didn't tell me you were so handsome. When exactly are you planning to visit?"

"Hey," I complained. "I'm right here." Suddenly I didn't find Scarlett's T-shirt ensemble and sex-mussed hair so amusing.

She put her arm around my neck and kissed my cheek. "Just getting you back for putting me on camera."

"I like her," River said. "Okay, enough fun. I have updates on your stalker, Scarlett. The lab finished with those cigarette butts Trace sent."

"Did they pull the DNA?"

"From one of the samples, yeah. The other two had been outdoors for too long. DNA degrades quickly when exposed to the elements."

Scarlett leaned toward the camera. "What about fingerprints?"

River shook his head. "Very hard to get from paper, and impossible when it's been outdoors like that."

"How soon can you check the DNA sample against CODIS?" I asked. CODIS was the national DNA database maintained by the FBI.

"That's going to be more complicated."

"But the database is connected to the internet, right? That's your thing. Do your magic." I waved my fingers like I was typing on a keyboard. I was fairly adept when it came to technology, but nothing like River. What he could do with a computer seemed like witchcraft to me.

River glanced at Scarlett, and I knew what he was thinking. Could we trust her to keep this quiet? Paranoia was a necessary side effect of the career River and I had chosen. The methods he'd already used to help the stalker investigation weren't entirely...legal.

But Scarlett wasn't just anyone.

"She's good," I said. "You can speak freely."

"All right." *I'm trusting you on this,* his eyes said. "You wanted me to keep this unofficial and off the books. But my tech can't just upload a sample to CODIS without an active law enforcement case. I can't hack the FBI's database, either. That's out of the question. I don't want black armored vehicles to show up at my door and disappear me."

Scarlett made a funny sound in her throat. Like she couldn't tell if River was joking. "Can't Owen start a case for us?" she asked. "He's the sheriff of Hartley."

I squeezed her hip. "Then we'll have even more complications to deal with."

"I'll keep working on it," River said. "It'll happen. It's just going to take some time, that's all."

I nodded. "Thanks, man. I have another favor to ask. This one might be easier."

River grabbed an energy drink and took a gulp. "Lay it on me."

"There's a guy named Dawson Witkins. Lives here in Hartley County. I want to know everything about him."

"He's the man I would've been forced to marry thirteen years ago," Scarlett explained. "I grew up in a cult, and he's now one of the elders. We just saved an underage girl who would've been his latest wife."

I stroked my fingers over her knee below the view of the camera. She reached for my hand and held it.

River's brows shot up, but otherwise he took this news in stride. "Got it. He's a sick asshole. What else do I need to know about him?"

"Somehow Dawson figured out my new identity. We think he hired the guy who's been stalking me. I can tell you more about it if you need the details. Or Trace can. He knows pretty much everything."

"Get me as many personal details on Witkins as you can. And then I'll work my magic. Like Trace said." River waved his fingers.

"Thank you. Your help means the world to me."

"Anything for a friend of Trace's."

"When you make it to Hartley, I'll show my gratitude with something sweet." She winked.

"Wow. I like the sound of that."

"That's enough," I grumbled. "Hanging up now." My thumb punched the end button.

Scarlett was laughing. "You're so easy to rile."

I tossed my phone behind the couch and grabbed her by the hips, pulling her more fully onto my lap. Her round ass was against my crotch, her back to my chest. My fingertips went for her ribs in the ticklish spots I'd found earlier, and she howled. She kicked and tried to squirm away. Well, she wasn't trying all that hard.

She stopped fighting altogether when her butt nudged against something that *was* hard. My cock pressed between her cheeks through my sweatpants.

Scarlett turned her head to the side, arm lifting so she could palm the back of my neck. I kissed her as my hands slid beneath her shirt. Palming her breasts. Flicking her nipples with my thumbs. She moaned on my tongue.

Then I moved my hand down to her soft wetness. She arched her back. "Yes. Right there."

"Want me to make you feel good?" My tongue dragged along her lower lip as my fingers worked.

"Wait. No."

Immediately, I lifted my hands. Was something wrong? But when she stood up and faced me, she was smiling. Scarlett fingered the hem of her T-shirt. Her eyes glided over my bare chest. The tent in my sweatpants. "I wanted to see you," she said. "You're gorgeous."

A brief flash of self-consciousness coursed through my insides. "Not like you."

She pulled her tee up and off. It landed on the rug at her feet. She stood between my spread knees and let me look my fill. Scarlett was soft and supple and perfect. Another bolt of lust made my cock jump.

I pulled down my sweats just enough to expose my erection, giving it a quick stroke. "You want this?"

She nodded.

"Climb on."

Scarlett crawled onto my lap, kneeling to either side of my hips. I notched myself at her entrance. Our eyes locked, and that contact didn't break as she sat, my shaft pushing inside her tightness. Her hands went to my face, mine to her back.

At first, we didn't move. Just enjoyed being as close as we could get.

"So good," she whispered. "Better than anyone else I've had."

"Same here." Even if I'd tried—and I wasn't—I couldn't have conjured another woman's face. Scarlett was all I could see.

And while I never enjoyed thinking of her with another man, I appreciated that Scarlett's sexuality was important to her. She owned that part of herself. I was a very, very lucky guy. I'd said it before, but damn, I really felt it.

I felt a lot more things with her than I was used to.

She rocked against me, and I took over. Setting a rhythm. Spreading kisses over her collarbone and the tops of her breasts as they swayed. Bending to tongue her sensitive nipples until she whimpered. She couldn't have been any more beautiful.

I wasn't rough this time. We were in no hurry. I tried to show her everything with my body that I couldn't say to her in words.

That I wanted this to last. That I wished I could give her everything in the world that she needed.

She whispered my name against my ear, voice drenched in pleasure. And for a split second, I almost believed that I could be the right man for her. That I could always, always stay, and that she could want me to.

CHAPTER TWENTY

Scarlett

WHEN WE WALKED into Virtue's hospital room the next morning, she was sitting on her bed, dressed in jeans and a sweatshirt. An orthopedic boot encased her foot to keep her injured ankle steady.

"Hi," Virtue said excitedly. "We're playing hearts. Sheriff Douglas taught me."

Owen sat in the guest chair. He looked up from laying down a card on a tray between them. "She's already beating the stuffing out of me."

"And it's not even Thanksgiving yet," Virtue quipped.

Owen cackled. "Better watch out for this one."

I walked over to the bed and gave Virtue a hug. "Sorry to interrupt the game. I brought you something." She took hold of the gift bag I held out.

"*Scarlett's Sweet Shop*? You brought candy?"

"Of course I did."

"She was going to forget," Trace said, "but I reminded her."

What a kiss-up. I shook my head. "Don't believe a word of it."

Trace stood at the foot of the hospital bed, smiling at me. In fact, he'd been smiling all morning.

After staying up for most of the night, getting tangled up in each other, we'd slept in. And of course, the man was far too tempting for me to resist. Especially when we were already in my bed, mostly naked. A couple more orgasms woke me right up. Stamina indeed.

But by then, we'd been running late. I had once again asked Trace to shower with me, but he'd insisted on showering alone in the guest bath. I didn't know what his deal was with sharing a shower. Didn't he like to conserve water? He was probably right though. We would've been even later getting here.

Virtue dug right into the candy bag. I'd brought a little of everything. Fancy filled chocolates, sea-salt caramels, packets of fudge. "Look at all this stuff," she said. "I knew I liked you, Scarlett, but now you're officially my favorite person. Will you adopt me? Please?" My whole body went still with shock. But Virtue went on like she had no clue about the effect her words had on me. "Ooo, chocolate-covered marshmallows? I know who'll want these." She held them out to Trace.

"Thanks." He took the cellophane bag. Owen looked on with a curious light in his eye, dare I say envious, until Trace opened the baggie and held it out.

Meanwhile, I forced myself to move on from Virtue's slip about adopting her.

The two men each bit into a chocolate-covered marshmallow, making identical little grunts of satisfaction. I knew Trace had a sweet tooth, but I hadn't realized the same was true of the Hartley sheriff. I'd rarely seen Owen in my shop. But it seemed like a lot of the men in Hartley had a secret sugar craving and needed someone else to treat them.

Interesting.

Virtue seemed to think so too, because she was snickering.

"We didn't just bring candy," Trace said, tucking the rest of his marshmallows away. "We have news. Toby wrote us."

"Is he okay?" Virtue asked, mouth full of double-chocolate fudge.

The message from Toby had come into Scarlett's Instagram just before we'd left for the hospital. He'd said he was safe, but that Paradise Ranch had been on lockdown since Trace and I had fled during the storm. "Toby doesn't think anyone suspects him," Trace said. "He said he's being careful. But he wants to stay there so he can report on what Dawson Witkins and the elders do next."

Virtue pushed the rest of the candy aside. "I don't want my brother trying to protect me. He's thirteen. He shouldn't be playing secret agent."

Trace sat on the end of the bed. "But we can't force him to leave if he doesn't want to. In fact, having eyes on the compound would be an asset. If he wants to help us, I think you should let him."

Virtue scowled at Trace like he'd betrayed her.

Very deliberately, she turned to Owen. "Sheriff Douglas, can't you go get my brother? Our parents don't care about Toby or any of us. They've got him working as a ranch hand. Isn't that…child labor or something?"

"Well, there's a process," Owen said carefully. "Child labor is complicated when you're talking about a family business. I worked on my grandpa's ranch when I was Toby's age."

So the cowboy hat wasn't just a fashion statement. Yet another detail I hadn't known about Owen. I assumed he was referring to his dad's side of the family. His mother's family had ruled Hartley until recently, and they were bad news.

Virtue's face scrunched up. "Fine, whatever. Maybe it's not child labor. But there must be *some* way. Please."

Trace stood and crossed his arms, shifting from foot to foot.

"If we suspect Toby is being neglected or abused," Owen said, "I would call Child Protective Services to investigate. I'd drive out to Paradise Ranch myself if you tell me Toby is in danger. Has that happened? Do you think Toby's being abused?"

Tears had filled the girl's eyes. I rushed to her side, reaching for her hand.

"No," she finally said. "They never starved us or laid hands on us."

But physical abuse wasn't the only way to snuff out the light in someone's heart. Virtue knew that, and so did I.

"When it's time," I said, "and the minute Toby says yes, we will get him. Okay?"

She nodded, eyes on her lap. "Do I leave the hospital today?"

"Yep. You're coming back to my house, if that still sounds all right."

"Yeah." She lifted her gaze to Trace. "Are you coming too?" Her tone was brittle, and I couldn't tell if she was still mad at him or not.

"Sure. I'll be there. Unless you say otherwise."

Virtue huffed and fell dramatically against her pillows. "If anyone *should* be protecting us, it's the old guy who's bigger than me and Scarlett put together."

Trace put his hands on his hips. "Did you say *old*?"

Owen and I were both trying not to laugh. Then Virtue started giggling, and the rest of us lost it.

Half an hour later, Virtue had shared her candy and said goodbyes to several nurses, orderlies, and doctors. But my brain had returned to the words she'd dropped so casually into our conversation. Virtue had been kidding. Right? It had been a throwaway comment. Every kid wanted to live at a candy shop.

As we piled into Trace's car and headed to my house, my mind continued to spin those two words around and around.

Adopt me.

Virtue crutched up my front steps. I unlocked the door, and Trace followed us both inside, carrying her backpack.

"I really get my own room?" she asked.

"You do. Want to go there first?"

"Definitely."

We left Trace in the living room. I led her down the hall to the guestroom. Virtue was slower with her crutches, but then she stopped in the doorway and stared.

"What do you think?" I asked. "Seem okay?"

I'd set up the bed with brightly colored linens. The walls already had framed prints of Colorado landscapes. The room tended to get hot in the afternoon from the angle of the sun, but with the temperatures cooling off, that wouldn't be a problem for long. Plus, the sunlight made it cozy. At least I thought so.

"I love it," she whispered. She went further into the room. There was a duffel sitting on the bed. "Is that for me?"

"Yep. Jessi dropped it off. Just some things you might need, but of course we can get more. Let me know."

Virtue sat down, pulled the duffel closer, and opened it. Jessi had packed clothes inside, the sizes based on my best guesstimate of Virtue's measurements. I'd added some hand-me-downs of my own. There was a notebook and a set of colored pens. An assortment of shampoo, soap, deodorant, and tampons.

"This is amazing. Thank you."

I leaned against the doorframe. "Jessi and Aiden were going to bring some lunch by the house. If you're hungry."

"Can I just hang out in my room for a while?"

"Of course, sugar." I wanted to cross the room and give her a hug. But would that be too much? She probably wanted to be alone. I remembered those first few days after I escaped. I'd had so many emotions to process. "Let me know if you need anything. I'll be in the kitchen."

Virtue opened her notebook, selecting a colored pen from the pack. "'Kay."

"Door open or closed?"

"Closed."

Crap, I thought. *Why did I ask that?* Would she be okay with the door closed? What if something happened? I glanced at the window, knowing that I'd locked it.

And now I was just standing here, and that was weird. Virtue looked up, and I gave her an awkward smile, backing out of the room.

After I closed the door, I leaned my forehead against it. Rescuing Virtue had seemed like the biggest obstacle in my way. But wow, that was nothing to taking care of her. Providing for the health, safety, and happiness of this girl.

I had no idea what the heck I was doing. And I had been a teenage girl. I *knew* it was only getting harder from here.

In the kitchen, Jessi was unpacking glass containers from a bag. "We're having lasagna and garlic bread. I opted for comfort food."

"Sounds perfect." I heard Trace and Aiden talking in the living room. "Jessi, do you think, um, we could talk for a sec?"

A crease appeared on her forehead. "Sure. What's wrong?"

My vision was feathering, and my insides were twisting into a configuration that couldn't possibly be healthy.

I dropped my voice to a murmur. "I am *freaking out*."

She grabbed my wrist. "Okay, come with me." She took me into the mudroom-slash-laundry room by the back door. "What's the matter?"

I opened my mouth, and everything poured out. "Does Virtue need a phone? Is it safe for her to be on social media? What about vegetables? I gotta say, I'm not that great about fiber content in my diet, but now I'm potentially affecting the digestive system of a growing person. Am I supposed to talk to her about dating? Or heaven help me, *sex*?" I was nearly hyperventilating. "I didn't think this through. I thought I'd give her a place to stay for a few weeks and support her until we found something more permanent. But what if I screw up? I am not the right person to be taking care of a child. Do you know how much candy I eat?"

Jessi's eyes were wide. She didn't move. I was worried I'd broken her. But after a moment, she came unstuck and put her hands on my shoulders. "Let's start by just breathing. We can't tackle the rest of your list if you've passed out. Here. Lean against the washing machine."

She rubbed circles into my back while I calmed down, bit by bit. Enough that I could breathe, anyway.

"Let's start with vegetables, because that's easiest. Virtue is old enough to pick foods herself, and if you make healthy choices available and set a good example, you'll be fine. Candy and dessert make life better, so no worries there as long as you've got balance. The social media and sex stuff is tougher. Oof, really tough. But you can handle things as they come up. Just talk to her and be honest and caring. Exactly who you are all the time, Scarlett. You'll figure it out. And you don't have to do it by yourself. You've got me and Aiden and Trace. And so many other people here in Hartley, too."

I glanced at the doorway, making sure nobody else was listening. "What if someone from Paradise Ranch tries to take her away? What if they hurt her?" That was my deepest fear of all. That I wouldn't be able to protect her.

"You know that Aiden and Trace wouldn't let that happen. Neither would Owen. But even if all of them were gone, you and I would put up a hell of a fight on our own. We might not have the title of Protectors, but that doesn't mean we won't defend our own. Virtue is one of us now. Anybody tries to touch her, they'll answer to us. Same thing if that stalker of yours comes back. We'll shut him down." Jessi smoothed my hair from my face. "But you see? The fact you're worrying shows that you *are* the right person for this. You'll do anything for that girl. You *are* enough."

"Maybe."

"I'm certain." She laughed. "You know, I've been planning to ask if you'd take over running the diner once Last Refuge opens. As a co-owner, of course. I could see you with a little business empire on Main Street. But I guess this isn't the best time?"

"You want me to be as overworked as you are? I don't have an Aiden to help me manage it all." Trace and I had a good thing going at the moment, but that was different.

"It's just an idea. We can revisit that later on once you're more settled. Or not. Just know I'm here. Always. That's what best friends are for."

"I thought it was to talk me down off a ledge when I'm panicking."

"That too. You've done the same for me. And I'm sure you will again."

I sighed. "No problem. Just let me know ahead of time, and I'll pencil you in."

Her smile beamed.

That night, I left Virtue's room, gently closing the door. Trace was at the kitchen counter, studying the various camera feeds on my computer. As he'd been doing off and on all day. He looked up as I came in.

"Aiden and Jessi went home?" I asked.

"Yep. Virtue's asleep?"

"Finally. It wasn't easy for her to relax." I'd sat with her until she'd drifted off. She'd been restless and scared, though she hadn't wanted to admit it. Instead, she'd asked a million questions about Hartley and high school and what was going to happen next. I had done my best to answer, even though I felt almost as uncertain.

Was this how parents felt? Trying to convince their kids they were in control of everything, while inside being terrified at how little control they really had?

"Your turn to relax." Trace opened his arms, and I walked right in. He ran his hands down my back and kissed my forehead.

"That feels good," I said.

"It's been hours since I touched you. Missed it."

"Me too."

"Wasn't sure if I should in front of Jessi."

I closed my eyes, nestling into his chest. "I haven't told her about...what we're doing. It doesn't need to be a secret, necessarily. I just don't want to give Jessi the wrong idea. And there's Virtue to think of as well. But if you'd rather tell them—"

"You're thinking a lot about everybody but yourself." His finger hooked my chin, tilting my head. "How are you doing?"

I was exhausted, through and through. But I didn't want sleep. "Kiss me?"

Trace turned us both so I was backed against the counter. His kisses were soft, yet still intense. I loved how he could surround me with his warmth, his scent, his strength. It wasn't just his size or the way he touched me. It was this aura around him. The confidence that he'd do anything to protect me. Protect *us*, because he wasn't just *my* Protector anymore.

I wanted to take him to my bed and enjoy that comfort all night. Let him massage every knot of tension from my body. If I'd asked, he would've gladly agreed.

But we weren't alone in this house. This was Virtue's first night here, and she could wake up needing something.

I put my hand on his chest, separating us by an inch before things got too heated. "I wish we could."

He dropped his forehead to mine. "Me too. Now's not the time. But I'll need to get you alone again soon, because I haven't had close to enough of you."

We kissed a while longer, as long as we dared. Which was a terrible idea because it was even more difficult to pull away. Why did the man have to be so irresistible? With those big hands wandering over my curves like he was mapping out what he wanted to do with them…

Finally, Trace put his hands on my shoulders and backed up until I was at arm's length. "No more of that. I should probably sleep in the living room."

"Agreed." Aside from the obvious temptation, I didn't want Virtue to know he'd slept in my bed. She'd make certain assumptions about our relationship being a permanent thing. A sex talk with her might be unavoidable, but I didn't want the context to be *my* sex life.

But I was glad he was sleeping here. I didn't want him to go back to his cabin on Refuge Mountain yet.

Trace had pajamas here from the clothes Jessi had brought

yesterday. His things were in my room, so he went there to get changed.

I stood in the living room, stuck in a daze for a minute. Bedding. That was what I needed. Trace needed pillows and blankets. And maybe one of my sleeping bags.

I went down the hall to my bedroom. The door was closed, but we'd spent most of last night naked together. Hadn't we? So I just twisted the knob and walked inside. "Sorry, I need to grab the extra bedding."

Trace had his jeans off and was tossing them onto the bed. He stared at me with an oddly wary expression.

Then I noticed his bare legs beneath his boxers.

The skin around his left knee was...mangled. That was the only word for it. It was thick with scar tissue, as if it had been taken apart and stitched back together. The scars stretched up to his thigh. How had I not seen it before? Or felt the skin last night when we were together? It wasn't like it made a difference to me. I'd noticed his limp and assumed he'd been injured before. But it was worse than I'd imagined.

"What happened?" I went closer, unable to take my eyes from the twisting scars. He'd avoided undressing in bright light around me. Maybe he'd kept me from touching that leg too, and I just hadn't noticed. The wounds looked healed, but did they cause him pain?"Does that hurt?"

"It is what it is. Doesn't change it to talk about it."

"But I didn't realize... You never have to talk about something if you don't want to. But you don't have to hide from me either."

Trace frowned. Glanced away.

All I could think to do was kiss him. I wrapped my arms around his neck and pulled him down. Moved my lips over his until he responded, his tongue licking mine in the way that made my toes curl. His grip was firm on my waist. Like he intended to remind me of his strength. As if I *ever* had doubts on that score.

I had to stop to take a breath. "I'm sorry I walked in on you. That was rude of me. And so unfair to my girl parts, because all I want right now is for you to throw me down on that bed and manhandle me."

The wariness left his eyes, replaced by heat. "Better go before I do it."

I started walking toward the closet to get the blankets, and he smacked my butt cheek. When I scowled at him over my shoulder, a small curve lifted his mouth.

After I'd made up the couch for him, Trace came out in his sweats and a tee. He gave me a soft kiss on the cheek. "Goodnight," he said.

"Thanks for staying with us."

"Thank you for being you." He lifted my hand to kiss the back of it. Such a chivalrous gesture. There was a strange, twisty sensation in my chest. "I'll see you in the morning."

I got ready for bed and slid beneath the covers. The mattress felt cold without Trace here. Lonelier.

I thought of the man on my couch, with all his secrets.

The girl in my guestroom who needed a home.

And me, twenty-eight years old and still struggling to face the traumas of my childhood.

All three of us in this house were broken in ways. We'd been through a lot. We had scars inside and out. That didn't mean we weren't strong.

But I had to believe we were stronger together.

CHAPTER TWENTY-ONE

Scarlett

A MONTH PASSED in the blink of an eye.

On a Tuesday afternoon, I pulled up outside Hartley High School. Students were streaming out of the building, which they shared with the middle school students on the other side. Virtue had tested well enough to join the ninth grade class, despite her lack of formal schooling.

I kept watch for Virtue, spotting her as she made a beeline toward my Jeep. She had her backpack on and her headphones slung around her neck, where they'd been permanently fixed since Trace had bought them for her a week ago. The boot was still on her injured foot, but it had been healing up fast.

She got in and tossed the pack at her feet.

"How was the second day of school?" I asked.

"About as crappy as the first. My English teacher despises me."

"Oh?" I doubted it, but I wasn't going to outright contradict Virtue's feelings either. I'd already learned *that* way led to her pouting in her room all evening.

I pulled away from the curb, steering us toward Main Street, and we talked about her day and her homework assignments. Virtue had been adjusting well to life in Hartley, or so I'd thought. School was a new challenge. I remembered how much I'd hated it when I'd first started. Public school had been a different world compared to what I'd been used to.

"Still want to go to Jessi's?" I asked.

A couple of times a week, I took Virtue to a therapist in a nearby town. She'd given mixed reviews to that. But today, Virtue was supposed to spend her afternoon at the diner doing homework and helping Jessi bake. She'd been excited about it.

"I guess," she said.

At least she brightened up when I asked about her friend. "How's Stephie?" She was Deputy Keira Marsh's younger sister.

"We had lunch together." Virtue chewed her lip, which was already chapped. "Stephie invited me and some other girls for a sleepover this weekend. Kiera's going to be there to supervise, and so will Stephie's parents. Can I go?"

"That sounds really fun, and it was sweet of her to invite you. But I'm not sure you're ready for that."

"What *am* I ready for?" Virtue rolled her eyes at me. "I'm not even allowed to talk to my brother without you giving permission!"

"Trace and I told you the reasons for that."

Toby had been writing us a few times a week. We let Virtue and Toby speak as much as they wanted. But while I'd bought Virtue a phone, I hadn't allowed the siblings to communicate directly. Trace had agreed with me that it was too risky. Someone at the compound could get hold of Toby's phone and use it to lure her. I wanted a buffer between them, so that Trace or I knew whenever they spoke.

"You and Trace aren't my parents," she said.

Ouch. That shut me right up.

Trace had stayed at my house with us most nights. He'd

continued to sleep on the couch. But for me, having him close had been a godsend. Even if we rarely got time alone. He was taking his Protector gig very seriously.

And whatever else was between Trace and me…it had been taking a back seat to our other responsibilities.

We pulled up to the diner. "Trace and I mean the best for you," I said.

"But you treat me like a little kid. Trace won't even sleep in the same room with you. I'm fifteen, not five. I know you and Trace have a thing."

My skin flushed. Oops. We'd tried to keep that quiet, but hadn't done as good a job as I'd assumed. "Trace and I aren't together. We're very close, but he's not my boyfriend."

"Then maybe you should figure that out. Focus on your own messy life instead of trying to control everything about mine."

"That's disrespectful. And uncalled for."

She pushed open the passenger door. "And I don't need you to drive me from school to the diner, or from the diner back home. I got all the way to that cabin in the woods by myself. I can go a mile down Main Street."

I hadn't realized she was so frustrated with me. *Anything else I'm doing wrong?* I wanted to ask. But instead I said, "I'll pick you up at five like we planned. Have fun with Jessi. Don't forget to say thank you."

Virtue got out with her backpack, slamming the door closed behind her.

I dropped my head against the seat rest. Tears burned in my eyes.

The drive back to my house took all of two minutes, and yes, that was a short distance. Virtue could've walked it from the diner even with her boot. But it was too much of a risk. I was still so worried for her. We hadn't caught my stalker. We had no idea what Dawson Witkins could be planning to get back at us.

There hadn't been any more scares since we'd returned with Virtue to Hartley. No creepy comments on Instagram. Yet I sometimes still felt unseen eyes on me. Every time I smelled cigarette smoke, it made me wonder. Of course, I had nothing specific to go on. Just gut instincts. And those same instincts were telling me to keep Virtue close. She wasn't out of danger yet, even though she was eager to spread her wings.

If something happened to her, I wouldn't have been able to take it.

I parked at my curb and got out. Trace's car was here, which I was happy to see. I started toward the front door. Stray dead leaves blew down the street. Fall color was peaking, and the aspen grove near my house was glowing with golden leaves.

Then the skin at the back of my neck prickled, making me turn. Nobody was around. But I felt it again. That sense of being watched. Of something coming.

I shook off the feeling. Trace was waiting for me, and we were safe.

As I approached the front porch, Trace opened the door. "Thought I heard the Jeep. How was your day?"

Ugh, I didn't want to get into that. "Not the best. But Virtue's at the diner with Aiden and Jessi for the next couple of hours."

"Is she?" He seemed to get a better look at me and realized something was up. "You look like a woman on a mission."

I put my palm in the center of his chest and walked forward, pushing him into the house. He walked backward. Once we'd cleared the threshold, I kicked the door shut with my foot and locked it behind us.

"Do you want to talk about it?"

That question coming from him? Really? "No, Trace. I don't wanna talk about it. Not right now."

Trace put his hand over mine on his chest, and he advanced on me, backing me up until I was up against the front door. "Then what can I do for you?"

"Anything you want. I just don't want to think."

"That can be arranged." He kissed my forehead. A gentle brush of his lips.

Then I gasped as he grabbed hold of me, tossing me upward and catching me under my thighs. Trace carried me into the living room and laid me on the fuzzy rug by my fireplace. The late afternoon light warmed the space in golden tones.

"Don't move," he commanded, and just like that, a little of my tension eased.

He quickly went around the room closing curtains. In seconds, he'd returned, crawling over me until his body was stretched out above mine. By now, I was well acquainted with how Trace kissed. Commanding, but treasuring too. I relaxed, little by little. His hands moved over me with equal confidence and care.

I had on a knit dress today, and his fingers slowly made their way beneath it. Teasing my inner thighs. Running along the seams of my panties. Finally, he pressed two fingertips to the center of the fabric, right over the most sensitive part of me, and I moaned.

"Should I taste you?" he asked. "Is that what you're in the mood for?"

"Told you. Don't wanna think."

He made a rumbly sound and moved down between my legs. I raised my arms over my head. Closed my eyes.

My panties tugged down over my hips. Trace hooked his hands beneath my knees, and his warm tongue slid over my core, working the tip inside me, and my brain really did stop stressing. All I could do was lie back and enjoy that ridiculously talented tongue. The brush of his beard between my thighs.

When he'd wrung every last drop of pleasure from my body, he unzipped his pants to free his cock. Trace lifted me up and carried me a few feet to the living room wall. There, he pushed inside of me, taking me roughly until he'd found his own climax.

So. Perfect. Exactly what I'd needed.

Somehow we ended up on the rug again, still half clothed. He was lying on his side, facing me with his elbow propped. "What prompted that?" he asked. "I'm far from complaining. But if I can help with whatever's bothering you, I will."

I sighed and dropped my arm over my eyes. "Virtue hates me."

"She doesn't hate you. You're her savior. Her hero."

"I think you're mistaking me with *you*."

"Last I checked, you and I were pretty distinct. I doubt many people would confuse us."

I pushed his shoulder. "Shush, you know what I mean. You keep us safe. I'm just...the person who's trying to control her and ruin all fun, apparently." I told him about our conversation after school, leaving out Virtue's remarks about my "messy life" and my relationship with Trace. "It's only been a few weeks. She's not out of danger yet. But she's also been deprived of independence for most of her life. Should I give her more freedom?"

"Not necessarily. She's scared for Toby, and afraid that any day, her parents could start legal proceedings to force her back to the compound. Plus regular teenager stuff like making friends and fitting in. But deep down, she's also heartbroken that her parents *don't* try to get her back. That's got to be hard. Knowing they didn't care enough to protect her before, and having that confirmed yet again. Now you're the closest thing to a parent she has. So you're bearing the brunt of all those emotions. She relies on you, but she's also afraid you might abandon her too."

"That makes sense." I'd felt something similar when I'd left the compound at Virtue's age. I'd been grateful that my mom loved me enough to let me go. But I *still* hadn't gotten over the fact that my mom had chosen to stay at Paradise Ranch instead of coming with me. I would never understand that.

Adopt me, Virtue had joked that day at the hospital. She hadn't mentioned it again, and neither had I. It seemed ridiculous. Me, adopting a teenage girl. And maybe her brother too, once we got Toby away from the compound. I hadn't even wanted kids.

But I wouldn't abandon Virtue or Toby either. In fact, I often loved having Virtue around. Until she'd started at school this week, Virtue and I had been inseparable. She'd helped me at the sweet shop, and we'd binge-watched a hundred nature documentaries on Netflix. She made me laugh every day… Except when she nearly made me cry.

"How do you know so much about teenagers?" I asked.

He stretched flat on his back beside me. "I'm just good at reading people. It's a skill. In my old work, it meant I could manipulate those I needed information from. Not exactly admirable."

"I admire you plenty," I said in a teasing tone. "I couldn't have gotten through the last few weeks without you."

"But it'll get easier. The danger will pass, and Virtue will adjust. So will you."

What did he mean by that?

I turned my head to study him. Really looking at Trace for the first time today. I'd been so caught up in my own head. But he looked tired too. Worn down by the last few weeks.

Since that one time that he'd fallen asleep in my bed, I hadn't seen him sleeping. Not once. Whenever I got up in the morning, he was already awake and dressed. During the day, when I worked at the sweet shop, he ran errands for Jessi and checked on the construction at Last Refuge. But he'd been vague about how exactly he spent the rest of his time.

He was always around for me and Virtue. But sometimes he still got that faraway look in his eyes. That tension in his spine. How could I be sure that Trace had what he needed, too, when he refused to ask for it? When he never talked to me about what was going on in his mind?

"Shower with me?" I said. "We've still got another hour until I need to pick Virtue up."

We went to my bedroom and stripped off the rest of our clothes. I was glad Trace wasn't self-conscious anymore about his scars. But this was the first chance we'd had in weeks to get all the way naked and take our time. I washed him and massaged his tight shoulder muscles for as long as he allowed me. Then he took over like he always did, washing us both. He gave me another orgasm with his fingers. But I stopped him when his fist closed around his erection.

"Let me?" I asked, dropping to my knees. "Please?"

Trace had never let me make him feel good like this. I wanted to show him how much I appreciated him. How much he deserved this.

Trace insisted on grabbing a hand towel to place beneath my knees. I kissed both of his thighs, and he tensed up when my lips touched his scars. But he didn't pull away.

When I finally took his hard length into my mouth and sucked, his head fell back against the shower wall. And he didn't seem to be feeling any worries at all.

I made us cups of coffee, extra sweet the way we both liked, and we cuddled up on the couch. "Feeling better?" Trace asked.

"So much better."

All my stress had melted away. I had ten more minutes until I had to leave, and I wanted to spend them right here, curled up with my man.

Well, not *my* man. A couple of hours ago, I'd insisted to Virtue that Trace wasn't my boyfriend. We weren't together.

But would it have been so bad?

For the first time, that idea wasn't off-putting. I'd never felt so attached to a lover as I did to Trace. He excited me, but he soothed me too. Helped me through the day. Not just the worst ones, like when we'd run from the compound, but days like this too. When I needed a sounding board and reassurance. Every time I needed him, he was there.

"Virtue knows about you and me," I said. "That we're…'a thing,' in her words."

"Yeah?"

His voice didn't betray a reaction. So I kept going. "She said you could sleep in my bed if we wanted. It wouldn't bother her."

He didn't say anything.

"What do you think? I know that I said we didn't have to define what this is. We could just be. And I said I wouldn't ask for more. But…"

"Do you want more?"

Oh my God. Did I?

I glanced over, and I couldn't understand the expression on his face. Wariness. But also longing.

"I don't know," I said. "I'm probably just floating on post-orgasmic endorphins."

His thumb drew a circle over my cheekbone. He opened his mouth to say something.

A knock at my door interrupted him.

He scowled. "Shit. Whoever that is, I'll get rid of them."

It wasn't Virtue, because she had a key. And she wasn't supposed to walk home on her own. "But it could be important," I said. Besides, I wasn't ready to have whatever conversation we'd been about to have.

I followed him to the front door. As soon as we got close enough to see through the window, Trace cursed again and threw the door open.

A tall guy with messy hair and black-framed glasses stood there. Trace's friend River, who'd been helping investigate my stalker and Dawson Witkins.

"What the hell are you doing here?" Trace thundered.

I was curious about that too. But River had done a lot for me, and I suspected he'd done far more for Trace. I squeezed past the grump looming in my doorway. "Hey, River. Good to see you." I gave him a quick hug.

"At least she's giving me a proper welcome. Hey, Scarlett. Nice to see you too. Hope I wasn't interrupting anything."

"You were, actually," Trace said. "How'd you even know where Scarlett lives? Or that I'd be here?"

River just gave him a *look*.

"It's fine," I assured River. "Come in. I have to leave in a minute anyway. I've got half a pot of coffee left, if you want some."

"I'd love it."

River grabbed his messenger bag, which looked like it held a computer inside. He had no other baggage. We went to the kitchen, where I poured a cup for him. "Sugar?" I asked.

"Black. I'm not like this one. You'd think he would be nicer with all the sweets he consumes." He pointed at Trace. "Did you know, our buddies back at Langley called him Sour Patch?"

"Don't," Trace muttered, unamused.

I held up a finger. "Please save the rest of that story, because I *definitely* want to hear it. But I have to get Virtue from the diner."

"I'll come with you," Trace said.

"No, you won't. You'll stay here with River. I'll be right back. If you really want to be weird about it, you can watch me on the cameras."

"That's what you're into, Novo?" River asked.

I left Trace's grumbling behind and jumped into my Jeep. A minute or so later, I pulled up to the diner. I would've walked, but I didn't want to tax Virtue's healing ankle. Maybe that made me overbearing. But I didn't care. It was my job to look out for that girl, and I wasn't going to let her down. No matter how much she yelled at me for it.

Virtue didn't come outside right away, so I got out. The bell on Jessi's door jingled as I walked inside. The diner was open for dinner tonight. They'd been opening for longer hours now that they'd hired more employees. Jessi was behind the counter.

But as I glanced around, I didn't see Virtue.

Jessi looked surprised to see me. "Hey, what's up?"

"I'm here to take Virtue home. Where is she?"

"Didn't you pick her up an hour ago?"

"I'm sorry, *what*? No, I didn't."

Jessi came around the counter. Aiden watched us from the kitchen, frowning. "But she told me you'd decided to come early. She left. We were busy right then, and I guess I didn't see her get in your Jeep, but..."

"She lied to you."

Virtue had been so angry with me earlier. *You treat me like a little kid. I can go a mile down Main Street.*

"Oh, Scarlett. I screwed up. I'm so sorry. But we'll find

her, okay?" Jessi waved at Aiden, and he pushed through the swinging door, taking off his apron.

"She must've wanted to walk home. To show me she could do it." I was shaking so hard my teeth chattered. "But she should've been there by now."

This couldn't be happening. An hour ago. Virtue had left an hour ago. She hadn't texted me or called.

Where was she?

CHAPTER TWENTY-TWO

Trace

SCARLETT CLOSED the front door on her way out. I returned my glare to River, who was happily guzzling black coffee from one of Scarlett's mugs.

"Don't worry," River said. "I'm not going to ask to stay here. I booked an AirBnB upstairs from the Hartley Saloon from a guy named Marco."

"I know him." Same apartment Aiden had rented month-to-month before moving in with Jessi. I'd taken over the lease until I'd moved to the cabin on Refuge Mountain. "But you still haven't explained what you're doing here."

"For one, I wanted to see the progress on Last Refuge. I'm a donor, in case you forgot."

"You're an anonymous donor. Did you forget what anonymous means?"

"Really, Novo? I figured you'd pull the grouch card when I showed up, but this is extreme. I told you I wanted to come to Hartley. You agreed. But your grumpy ass was never going to invite me, so I had to take matters into my own hands."

My pulse still hadn't lowered from that conversation Scarlett and I had started. She didn't know if she wanted more with me. A month ago, she'd been pretty clear that she *didn't* want that.

I was all up in my head right now, and I couldn't handle River on top of everything else.

"This isn't the best time," I said.

"Exactly why I came when I did. I wasn't going to call you out until after we had a beer or something, but you're giving me no choice. On our last video call, you looked like shit, and in person it's worse. Be honest, man. You're exhausted. You don't look like you've been sleeping."

I gripped the skin between my eyes. Why did River have to know me so well?

"I'm dealing," I said. "I promise."

He shook his head.

The past several weeks since we'd brought Virtue to Hartley, I'd been focused on the two women in this house. Scarlett and Virtue. Making sure they were safe and happy. It had been rocky, as Scarlett's argument with the girl earlier today showed. But that was to be expected.

What irked me? I should've done more. Should've made more progress on finding the stalker or nailing down Dawson Witkins. And yes, it was true that I hadn't been sleeping on any kind of regular schedule. At night, I kept watch. My nightmares had picked up in frequency, and I couldn't let Virtue or Scarlett see. I only slept when they were both safely elsewhere. Like at the diner or sweet shop. Or this week, at school.

And the feelings I had for Scarlett... I wasn't in the right mindset to think about that, much less discuss it with River.

"Do you have updates on our investigation?" I asked.

"Sure I do. I didn't come here empty-handed."

"Knew you wouldn't. You're a good friend."

"Ha. Right. Clunkiest change of subject ever." He swallowed the rest of his coffee, then went for his computer bag.

We sat at the kitchen table, and he talked me through the latest developments. "Bad news first. My lab contact finally uploaded the DNA sample from the cigarette butt to CODIS. We had to pretend it was from a missing person, so hopefully the FBI won't find out I lied and come knocking on my door."

"Worth the risk if you got a hit."

He pursed his mouth. "Sorry, man. This is the bad news, remember? We got no matches. Zero. No idea who that DNA belongs to."

"Dammit." That meant that Scarlett's stalker hadn't been in the military, hadn't been convicted of any crimes, and most likely hadn't even been arrested. There were exceptions depending on the laws of various states. But long story short, we'd come up empty, and that worsened my mood even further.

"Is there good news?" I asked.

"You doubt me?" He tapped at his computer. "Told you I wasn't empty-handed."

"You could've shared this in an email."

"Sure, but then I couldn't have staged my mini-intervention. Which is *not* finished, by the way. Because I'm your friend and I care about you, even if that sentiment isn't reciprocated."

I rolled my eyes. "Fine, I'm glad to see you. It's been too long."

"You need to brush up on your skills. Those lies were weak."

"I'm not lying." I gripped his shoulder. "Thank you for caring, okay? I know I don't make it easy. I will try to talk about…stuff."

"Stuff?" He snorted. "Very descriptive."

"Later. First, please tell me you found something I can work with to shut down this stalker. Or put Dawson Witkins behind bars. Either one would be great right now."

"I've made progress on both. Even though we didn't get a match on the DNA, the lab tech did confirm the brand of the cigarettes. Ashfair Menthols."

"It's something. What else?"

He pulled up a dossier. The info filled his computer screen. "Remember how the original comments the stalker left on Instagram were made using a VPN to hide his location? I finally had luck getting access to the VPN's servers overseas. Linked the IP address to a cell phone owned by Dawson Witkins of Creekview, Colorado. It was him. He left the comments himself."

"That cowardly fuck." I leaned forward, reading over the information. "Conforms to what we already suspected. He hired the person who was watching Scarlett outside her house. But that wasn't enough for Witkins. He wanted to harass her online, too."

It all came back to that guy. Scarlett and Virtue were never going to be safe while he walked free.

"Trust me, it gets worse. I've been digging into everything I can on the guy. He—"

The front door opened, and Scarlett burst in. "Trace!" she yelled. I jumped up and made it to her in the blink of an eye. She grabbed my arms. "It's Virtue. She left the diner an hour ago. We can't find her. Jessi and Aiden are looking. You've got that camera—"

"I'll check it." I pulled out my phone and opened the app for the surveillance camera I'd placed on Main Street. While she had access to the cameras on her own property, I'd kept this one separate because it wasn't entirely legal given its placement to surveil the public street. Scarlett trembled as she watched from beside me, and River had joined us, quietly taking in the situation without saying a word.

"Please hurry," she whispered.

"I know." I put my hand on the back of her neck. We both held our breaths.

I thumbed to the footage from an hour ago, then hit play at double speed. In the video, Virtue stepped out of the diner's glass entrance door, limping on her orthopedic boot. Then she rounded the block, starting down Scarlett's street. I slowed the playback. Virtue's dark blond hair was braided, and she wore her backpack as she slowly made her way down the block.

Scarlett's hand flew to her mouth. "*Oh, no*. Please no."

On the video, a black hatchback had just driven onto Scarlett's street. No plates. The make and model were common, nothing to make it distinct. It stopped next to the teenage girl.

A man in a heavy coat and hat jumped out of the passenger side.

"*No*," Scarlett moaned.

It felt like the air had gone cold around us. Nothing existed except for the terrible image on my screen.

The man tried to drag Virtue to the open door of the car. But then she fought back. She kicked him with her uninjured leg. Swung her backpack at him. She ran toward a neighbor's house, and the man in the heavy coat almost followed. But he changed his mind, jumping back into the car, which then sped away.

River moved first. He dashed for the front door, wrenched it open, and flew outside. I was right behind him. I heard Scarlett's footsteps and heavy breaths as she brought up the rear. We ran down the street in the direction of the neighbor's house, where Virtue had fled on the video.

At the same time, I hit Aiden's contact on my phone. He answered right away. "Aiden, I think we've found her." I rattled off the address, reading the numbers from the neighbor's mailbox. "If you haven't called Owen yet, *don't*."

A pause. "Copy that, boss." Aiden would want an explanation, but that had to wait.

I lowered my phone without bothering to end the call.

We rounded the neighbor's house. River stopped in the back and pointed at a thick cluster of fir trees. "In there."

We could just make out Virtue's blond hair and quiet hiccuping, as if she'd been crying for a while.

Scarlett walked cautiously forward. "Hey, sugar? It's me." She crouched at the base of the tree where Virtue was hiding. With a choked cry, the girl grabbed her and hugged her. Scarlett held on tight. I knelt on the ground beside them.

"Oh, honey," Scarlett said. "You had a scare, didn't you? I'm so sorry I wasn't there."

"No, I'm sorry. I'm so sorry. I didn't listen to you, and...."

"It's okay. You're safe now. I'm here, and so is Trace."

Virtue looked over, seeing me.

"Are you hurt?" I asked.

She shook her head. "My ankle aches. But I'm okay."

"Can I pick you up?"

I lifted her into my arms, cradling her. Scarlett kept a hand on Virtue's back. We walked to the house. I noticed Jessi and Aiden, but they stayed back, along with River. Giving us space.

I took Virtue into the house and set her on the living room couch. Scarlett sat beside her, while I knelt by her feet. "Tell us what happened?" I said. My voice was calm. Even. But inside? I was nowhere close to calm. My thoughts were dark. Vengeful. *Bloody.*

"I told Jessi that Scarlett was picking me up early. I just wanted to prove I could get home by myself. It was so stupid. Then that car drove up. The man got out. I fought him."

Scarlett rubbed her back. "We saw you on the camera. You were incredible. You did so well." She brushed tears from Virtue's face, and I reached for the girl's hand.

"Did you recognize him?" I asked. "Ever seen him before?"

"No. But I saw Elder Dawson. He was driving."

I locked eyes with Scarlett. I saw murderous rage, the same that I felt. But as I made my decision, everything within me quieted down.

I had my mission.

I couldn't let this stand. It had gone on long enough. No more waiting around. I had to protect the women in my charge. Dawson had made his move, so I was going to make mine.

Scarlett took Virtue to the girl's bedroom to rest. I found my sister in the kitchen, where Jessi had started cooking. The contents of Scarlett's fridge were spread over the counter, and something fragrant sizzled on the stove. "How's Virtue?" Jessi asked.

"Terrified." So was Scarlett, though when we'd found Virtue, she had instantly turned into a mama bear, projecting strength and focusing only on what Virtue needed. "But physically, she's fine."

Jessi's face fell. "I should've made sure Scarlett was really there to pick her up. I shouldn't have let her leave. It's my fault."

"It's nobody's fault except the pieces of human scum who tried to hurt her." Dawson Witkins and his accomplices. The elders and apologists of Paradise Ranch. The same people who'd hurt Scarlett before, and who'd do it again unless they were stopped.

If anybody deserved blame for not stopping them already, it was me. But feeling guilty wouldn't do Virtue or Scarlett any good. I'd save my self-castigation for later.

"Where's Aiden?" I asked.

"He's in the backyard with River."

"So you met my friend?"

Jessi's smile returned. "Yep, he introduced himself. So he's the anonymous donor who helped with our financing?"

I almost laughed. "Didn't take him long to share that info. Didn't realize he was so starved for attention."

"I'm glad he told me. Now I know who to thank. And as soon as this mess is over, I'll take him up to Last Refuge to see the progress on the construction. We've even got cell service up there now."

"At least *that's* going well."

Jessi shrugged. "It's not much given everything else that's happening, but I'll take good news where I can find it. Dinner will be ready in half an hour. I'll go check on Scarlett and Virtue in a minute."

"Thanks."

"You and Scarlett were there for me and Aiden before. Now it's our turn."

While Jessi returned to cooking enough food for the next week, I went out back to find Aiden and River. They were speaking quietly with serious faces, arms crossed. Night was falling, and the temperatures had dropped. Autumn was setting in. Any day now, it would snow. I was surprised it hadn't already.

River lifted his chin. "Hey, Trace. Aiden was just catching me up on everything I've missed. And vice versa."

"Good. That'll save some time." I gave them an update on how Virtue was doing. "She said it was Dawson Witkins driving the car."

River cursed, and Aiden shook his head. "Want me to call Owen now?" Aiden asked. "Or did you have something else in mind? Something that the sheriff won't want to know about?"

"The second." I glanced behind me at the house. The women inside were quiet, and nobody was out on the street. I was shocked that none of the neighbors had witnessed Virtue's near abduction. Nobody had come outside or said anything when I'd carried her back inside Scarlett's house. The people of Hartley could gossip with the best of them. But where were they when shit went down?

Like when Jessi had been harassed by thugs last winter. When Jessi had needed a hero, Aiden had stepped up, even though he'd just been passing through town. Owen had tried to help Jessi, but as sheriff, he'd been hampered by the laws he had vowed to uphold. Scarlett had tried too, the best that she could. But Jessi's neighbors? They'd been MIA.

Someone had to act. Who better than me?

"We need to leave the sheriff out of this one," I said. "When Scarlett and I first brought Virtue to Hartley, I argued we should wait before making a move on Dawson Witkins or Paradise Ranch. I'm done waiting. I'm going to do what's necessary so this scum doesn't bother Scarlett or Virtue ever again."

Aiden nodded. "Understood. I'm in. No question."

"So am I," River added. "Even before today, I would've been in. I didn't have a chance to tell you what else I dug up on Witkins. For a while, state and federal authorities have suspected Paradise Ranch of human trafficking. Moving underage girls between cult compounds that are similar to the ranch. They haven't been able to pin the elders with hard evidence. But from the hints and rumors I've found online, Dawson has personally escalated the activity of their trafficking operation. I'm talking girls even younger than fifteen. There's got to be a digital trail somewhere, probably linked to the dark web. If we can get access to the compound's computers, I'm sure I can find it."

I liked the sounds of that. But if I took out Dawson himself, I'd be cutting off the head of the snake.

"When do we leave?" Aiden asked.

I looked from Aiden to River. Two men I considered brothers. River wasn't a Protector like Aiden and me, but I had no doubt we could count on him.

Yet for all that, sometimes a man had to go it alone.

"You're not coming. Either of you." I crossed my arms, matching their stances. Feet wide. Shoulders back. "I'm going back to Paradise Ranch alone. You can give me a bug to upload to their computers while I'm there. It's best if no one except those of us at this house know I'm gone. What I need from both of you is your assurance that you'll keep Scarlett and Virtue safe. Whether or not I come back."

What I was planning could land me in prison for life if I were caught. And that was if I succeeded. Paradise Ranch was crawling with assholes who wouldn't hesitate to kill me if they caught me. I refused to put that risk on these men. Aiden had Jessi to think of. River had a bright future with the Agency.

Me? This was what I was good for. Where I'd always known I would end up.

Blood on my hands. Debts I could never repay.

Aiden listened thoughtfully, smoothing a hand over his bearded jaw. But River? My best friend, who'd had my back countless times and who refused to take my shit?

He wasn't having it.

"Are you fucking kidding me? *Whether or not you come back?* What kind of martyr bullshit is this?"

"I don't intend for this to be a suicide mission. Don't overreact. But there are risks."

"Of course there are. Risks that you and I have faced plenty of times together." River threw a hand in Aiden's direction. "And it sounds like Shelborne would gladly face them too. He told me about what you're starting here. The Last Refuge Protectors. Correct me if I'm wrong, but I got the impression the Protectors are a team."

"This is a mission I need to handle on my own."

River got in my face. "Like you've *handled* your other issues? You're a fucking mess, Novo."

I shook my head. "Don't," I warned, but he wasn't listening.

"You're not sleeping. You hid away from me for *two years*, and from what I've heard, you hide away from your friends here in Hartley too. Disappearing off into the woods. Refusing to talk about what happened to you. Does that sound like *handling it?*"

My hands balled into fists. Fury burned my insides.

"Admit it," River said. "You're not okay."

"Fine," I roared. My chest heaved as I breathed. "I can't sleep. When I do, the nightmares shock me awake not knowing where I am or what's going on. And during the day, it's getting harder to snap out of it when my brain starts to spiral. I don't know if I'm doing enough to protect the people I care about." I pointed an accusing finger at the house. "And I am *in love* with a woman who deserves everything that's pure and good, but all I can offer her is the washed-up remnants of who I used to be. No *shit* that's not okay."

River and Aiden both stared at me. But I wasn't done.

"I always knew that I couldn't stay forever in Hartley. At least if I take out Witkins before I leave, I'll know that I made Scarlett's life a little better. Even though she's better off without *me* in it."

Then the screen door to the house squeaked. I turned at the sound.

Scarlett stood there on the porch.

I hadn't heard the back door open. But River and Aiden

had to have seen her come outside. *Thanks, jerks,* I thought. *Really appreciate the heads up before I ran my mouth about her.*

"Scarlett," I said.

She pivoted and went back inside without a word. *Great*. I rubbed my forehead.

"Timing could've been better there," Aiden pointed out.

I glared at him. "You think?"

River sighed. "At least you can admit to us you're not okay. And that you're in love with her. Seems like progress."

"Doesn't feel like it," I muttered.

"Do you want a future with her?" River asked.

I sputtered. "Did you hear anything I just said?"

"I heard a lot of opening up. Good on you for that. But when you first open the floodgates, some crap is gonna come through before the water clears up."

"*What*?" I wasn't in the mood for creative metaphors.

"I think he means, you should take your time and not jump to any conclusions," Aiden said. "If you have feelings for Scarlett, don't assume it can't work. I did the same with Jessi at first. But denying what I felt just made it hurt more. For both of us."

"I'm not you. And Scarlett isn't Jessi. She doesn't want a future with me. She told me that herself." I'd even asked her today if she wanted more, and all she could say was, *I don't know*.

Aiden made a skeptical face. "If she didn't care about you, she wouldn't have looked so broken up just now to hear you were leaving."

Crap, I thought, glancing at the house.

River waved his hand. "What you need to do is *talk* to her. Tell Scarlett what's going on with you before you make big decisions that affect her too. But the same goes for this mission. You can't order me to let you charge into enemy territory alone. I'm going with you. That's final."

I was tired of arguing. More than anything, I wanted to follow Scarlett and explain what she'd just heard.

But River had made some valid points. I'd been keeping too much inside. I trusted him and Aiden with my life. It was time to act like it.

"I'm still leading the mission to the compound. But River, you're with me. Aiden, you'll stay in Hartley on protection detail."

They both nodded. River muttered something like, *Thank fuck he's finally seeing reason*.

"Give me an hour," I said. "Then we'll strategize. I want to be on our way by zero hundred tonight."

Now, I just had to talk to Scarlett and hope I hadn't destroyed everything between us before we'd had a chance to get started.

CHAPTER TWENTY-THREE

Scarlett

I WALKED in a daze to the kitchen, where Jessi was checking on a casserole dish in the oven. "Hope you're hungry." She stood up and got a look at me. "What's wrong? Is it Virtue?"

"No. She's all right." I'd left her resting and listening to music in her bedroom. Then I'd gone outside to find Trace, and I'd overheard his tense words with River. "Did you know that Trace never planned to stay in Hartley? He's going to leave."

"What? When? That's not what he's told me."

"I just heard him say it." He'd said, *I always knew I couldn't stay forever in Hartley*.

Which was right after he'd said that he's *in love with me*.

"He was talking about some mission," I said. "But it sounded like he doesn't know if he's coming back." I couldn't understand it. How he could say such different things in one breath. That he loved me, but I was better off without him. The second part, I'd heard before.

But he *loved me?*

Jessi put her hand on my shoulder. "My brother confuses

me even on a good day. There's got to be an explanation. He wouldn't just leave us that way. Leave *you*."

"I didn't think so. But I know what I heard."

"Scar, I know we haven't discussed the subject of you and Trace. You've had a lot going on, and so have I. But it's obvious that Trace cares about you. He's devoted to you and Virtue. Whatever else he's dealing with, I *know* that's true."

The back door opened. I knew who it was without looking. Jessi nodded at him, an uneasy look on her face.

"Scarlett? Can we talk a minute?" Trace said.

I shrugged. "I guess we should."

Jessi squeezed my arm. "I'll keep dinner warm."

We went to my bedroom. Trace shut the door. "I take it you overheard some of what I said?" he asked.

I sat on the edge of my bed. "I heard some things. Yeah."

"How much?"

Where to start? "You're planning some kind of mission?"

"Dawson Witkins has hurt you and Virtue too many times. River and I are going to Paradise Ranch to make sure he never does that again. Aiden will stay here to protect you and Virtue."

"You're going to kill Dawson?"

He blinked at me. "Most likely."

"You think I have a problem with that?" If we'd gone to Owen with the kidnapping attempt and everything else Virtue had been through, then Virtue would have to testify against Dawson. She'd have to relive time and again in a public courtroom what she'd experienced. All so that Dawson *might* be punished. So no, I didn't have a problem with taking a more definite route when it came to protecting that girl. And of course, stopping him from hurting any other girls or women. If I could, I would've done it myself.

But I had a big problem with the way Trace was handling

it. "Were you going to tell me at all?" I asked. "Or were you just going to take off and leave me wondering."

Trace sat on the bed beside me. "I planned to tell you. But honestly, I'm not sure I can back down on this issue even if you have reservations. This just needs to be done."

I jumped up, pacing across my room. I was a big jumble of misfiring nerves and racing thoughts. "Because that's what you do, isn't it? You decide things without asking me. Like avoiding me for all those months because you *decided* you shouldn't be in my life. Didn't matter what I might think. Then you changed your mind, and I thought it was because you were finally letting me past those boundaries of yours. But you're the same as you've always been. Holding yourself out of my reach."

He didn't defend himself, and somehow that pissed me off more.

I stopped pacing and turned to face him, head on. "You never meant to stay in Hartley? Well, that's news to me. You never thought to mention that?"

"I've been protecting you and Virtue. That was my priority. I wasn't going to leave that job unfinished."

"So you think if you get rid of Dawson Witkins, we won't need you anymore? You can just take off, like you've apparently been planning all along?"

"It wasn't a specific plan." He looked at his hands. "You told me before that you had no expectations. We didn't need to know what this was, or where it was going. I never would've let it go so far if I thought you'd get hurt."

"I know I said all those things. But that was before!" Tears pricked at my eyes and burned in my throat. My head was full of half-formed thoughts I'd only just now let up to the surface.

I'd thought I knew who I was. What I wanted out of life. And then everything had changed.

"I guess I do want more with you, and I realize that's not what we agreed. It's not what I thought would happen."

"I understand. I know exactly how that is. Because that's how I fell in love with you. It happened whether I wanted it to or not."

My hands flew to my mouth. Hearing him say that again hadn't lessened its effect.

He stood up and crossed the few feet that stood between us. Took my hands and gently held them at my sides. His dark blue eyes as deep and boundless as an ocean full of stars.

"Then why do you still want to leave?" I asked. "After everything?"

"Because I'm in love with you. Not much scares me. But that does."

"It scares me too, but not because I have doubts about you."

He pulled us back toward the bed and sat down. I stood between his spread knees, and he held my hands. Looking slightly up at me.

"There are things I haven't told you. About my past. Who I am. And what exactly I'm still struggling with."

I nodded. *Please tell me,* I begged silently. *Let me in.*

And finally, he did.

"I worked for the CIA. A lot of the time, I was helping make the world a safer place. I loved serving my country, both then and before, when I was a soldier. But I didn't know how much I'd have to compromise. There came a time that I couldn't compromise anymore."

He told me about the human trafficking ring. How he and a fellow officer had been assigned to gather intelligence, but keep the ring intact. Even though innocent women and girls were caught in its web.

"My friend and I decided to shut it down, but her cover

was blown. She was killed. And…" His Adam's apple bobbed. Trace's breaths came faster, shallower. "I found her body in a warehouse along with the victims we'd hoped to save. I hadn't reached them in time. They were all killed as a warning to me and anyone else who might try to interfere."

"My God, Trace. I'm so sorry." I couldn't fathom what it had been like to go through horror like that. I sank onto the mattress beside him. Our hands were still linked.

His eyes had gone glassy. Distant. "I suspected someone within our Agency had betrayed us. I trashed my cell. My laptop. Anything else they might've used to track me. And I hunted down the traffickers who'd given the kill order. They were all gathered together for a meeting in a foreign capital city. I went in. I killed them. *All* of them. The leaders, the bodyguards, the accountants. They were all responsible, and I made sure their deaths weren't quick or easy. But a lot of it is a blur. I don't remember being shot. I just remember… blood."

He was shivering. Staring into the distance. Gasping for air. I'd seen him before when he'd been triggered, but never this bad.

"Trace?" I said.

He didn't answer.

I straddled his lap, arms going around him, holding him as tightly as I could. Trying to surround him with my care and comfort. I wished I could take away what he was feeling. But I couldn't. All I could do was be here with him in this moment, be as strong as he was, so that he knew he wasn't alone.

"I'm here," I said. "I'm here."

Agonizing minutes later, his fingers shifted on my waist, and his breathing evened out.

"Somehow, I dragged myself out of there and made it to a doctor. Eventually, the Agency found me and relocated me to a secret hospital. Had to piece my knee back together. They covered up what I'd done because my secrets, my guilt, were theirs. Once I'd healed enough, they cut me loose. I came back to the states. About six months later, Jessi called. Asking for help."

"She doesn't know what happened?"

"No. You can't repeat any of what I've just told you. I shared a little with Aiden. River knows more. But not all."

I rested my forehead against his. "I won't. Thank you for telling me. I know it wasn't easy."

"Babe, you *don't* know," he said, not unkindly. "I've killed people in my past. That's being a soldier. But what I did that day wasn't authorized. As far as our government is concerned, I'm a murderer. And I'm ready to do it again."

I sat back, but only so I could cradle his face. Unshed tears shone in his eyes. I felt so deeply for this man. More than I'd ever imagined I could feel for another person.

"If going after Dawson will hurt *you,*" I said. "Then I don't want you to go. He's not worth your soul."

Trace blinked a few times. Clearly considering my words. "This is already who I am. My head is a very dark place sometimes. You've become a light in that darkness. But if you really understood the truth of who I am, what I've done, it would be too much for you. Because sometimes it's too much for *me*."

"You're right that I can't understand it at that level. But Trace, you're a light in my darkness too. Everything is so much better when I'm with you. You've shown me and Virtue the most incredible kindness. You've protected us and cared for us. Circumstances forced you into a terrible situation, but you didn't fold. You are steadfast. *That* is the truth of who you are."

"That's why I have to see this through." He said this firmly. No anger or hesitation. "Caring for you and Virtue is..." His voice went thick. Breaking. "It's the best part of me."

"But Trace, I want *all of* you. The dark and the light. More than anything in my life." I'd resisted those feelings. But the thought of him leaving forever had gutted me. I couldn't lose him.

He exhaled slowly. "I do want to be that for you. Not just a Protector. I would like more. It's just hard to believe it can happen. I have nightmares. Demons. I've had my coping mechanisms, but that's not enough anymore. I have a long way to go. And I...I don't know if I can do that in Hartley. Not because of anything you're lacking. There's just a lot I need to face."

"I can be patient," I said. "If I know you're coming back to us."

We were talking about our future. A possible future *together*. That was major enough. But I wasn't just responsible for myself anymore, and I had to make sure he realized what he could be getting into. "I never expected to be parenting a teenage girl. I told myself it would be temporary, but if Virtue wants to stay with me long term, I'm in. The same goes when Toby gets free of the compound. They need me. And I think they need you, too."

He didn't even blink. "You and Virtue belong together. I'm sure Toby will fit right in. I just want to deserve all of you."

"Then do what you have to and come home to us."

Whatever he needed to tackle his problems, I would do it. I couldn't fix him. But I could support him.

Maybe I could even love him.

"We could be a family," I whispered, and my tears overflowed. Streaming down my face. "Couldn't we?"

He kissed the wetness on my cheeks. "Yeah, babe. I think we could. Is that what you need?"

"Yes. So much."

"Then I'll go out and get it. Should've known I couldn't deny you."

"But you have to get better for yourself. Not for me."

"It's not just for you. It's for us."

We wrapped our arms around each other and held on tight. I hoped he wouldn't ever let go again.

CHAPTER TWENTY-FOUR

Trace

JESSI DID *NOT* LOOK happy when Scarlett and I came out of her bedroom, and my girl's eyes were red from crying. I was wrung out too. Exhausted. I needed rest, but that would happen later.

"What's going on?" Jessi asked.

"We talked some things out." I lifted Scarlett's hand to kiss it, then kissed her mouth.

"We're good," Scarlett assured Jessi.

"So we can acknowledge you two are together now? It's been making me crazy not to say anything."

Scarlett and I smiled softly at each other.

That had been one of the most difficult conversations I'd ever had. I hadn't wanted to share my history with Scarlett. Those events weren't anything that should touch her. But I hadn't meant to fall in love with her either. I blamed her for that. So damn irresistible. And I was only thinking of her generosity, sweetness, and bravery.

When you added those luscious curves? I was a goner.

For the past two years, I hadn't been able to imagine a future for myself. But now, I knew what I wanted. I was still scared that I'd screw this up. I'd hurt her. But at least now she knew the worst parts of me. She hadn't turned away.

We could be a family. I wanted so badly to give that to Scarlett and Virtue. Hopefully Toby as well. I had to figure out how to earn it. Get better so that I could give them *all* of me. Not just pieces.

That had to wait, though. My family was in danger. Scarlett had given me an out, if I'd wanted it. I could choose not to take this mission. But I believed this was the right choice. The legal one? No. But right. I loved her for standing by me either way.

But before even the mission, we had to eat.

"Need help with dinner?" I asked my sister.

Jessi huffed, hand on her hip. "Like you can cook. Scarlett, how about you tell Virtue that dinner's ready?"

"Will do." Scarlett kissed me on the cheek, then went down the hall toward Virtue's room.

Jessi fixed me with a glare. "Big brother, go find River and Aiden for dinner. But also? Know this. Scarlett likes to say she's got mama bear instincts when it comes to me, but the same goes in return. I've been giving you space to figure things out. But if you don't treat my best friend right, I'll be the first to rain hell down on you. And if you don't take care of *yourself*? I'll be such a pain in your ass, you'll wish we weren't related."

"I appreciate the talk. And I *really* appreciate that call asking me to come to Hartley. Changed my life." We'd never been very affectionate. But I pulled my sister into a full-out hug, and she was quick to return it.

I had no idea where I'd be right now if Jessi hadn't made that call. I wouldn't have met Scarlett.

I was Scarlett's Protector, a duty I took extremely seriously. But she was my savior, too. She'd given me comfort and understanding when I'd thought I didn't deserve either. I had blood on my hands, and soon there would be more. But I was finally ready to find my peace with that. To do my job, be a Protector, and still go home to my family and sleep without nightmares plaguing me. I was determined to figure out how.

Scarlett had given me the push I needed to change. She hadn't said she loved me yet, but I'd make that happen eventually. I'd earn it.

I had to go out there and get it.

We ate dinner together. Scarlett's kitchen table wasn't that big, but we squeezed together and pulled in chairs. Me, Scarlett, and Virtue. River, Aiden, and Jessi. People from my past and present. And hopefully, the future I hadn't believed I could have.

Afterward, River pulled me aside while Aiden handled the dishes. That man was so whupped for my sister. But Jessi was happy, wasn't she? Probably meant I should take some cues from him.

We went to the living room, and River opened his laptop. He had a fancy, souped-up model with an indestructible case. I'd rarely seen him without it. "Remember I told you I'd traced that Instagram stalker account to Dawson Witkins' cell phone? I accessed the data for the cell towers between here and Paradise Ranch. Confirmed that Witkins came to Hartley this afternoon, lurked around Main Street for a while, then returned home to the compound. I also believe I found the cell number of his associate, the one who tried to grab Virtue. It's a burner, no name. But that cell stuck close to Witkins. It's at Paradise Ranch now."

"Nice work." I would've preferred to know the name of whoever was helping Witkins. But this would do. I could take them both out once we'd reached the compound.

"My rental car is parked behind the Hartley Saloon," River said. "I walked over here. I figure we can take that car, remove the plates, drive it out to Creekview. Any cameras I need to know about?"

"None that aren't mine." We could easily avoid showing up on that one. We couldn't afford any documentation that we'd been at Paradise Ranch for this mission. That included registered cell phones. "Do you have comms for us to use?"

"I've got comms covered," Aiden said. He'd just appeared behind us. "I've been ordering gear we might need for the Protectors. After what happened last month when Trace and Scarlett visited Paradise Ranch, I thought I should get on that."

So that explained some cryptic questions Aiden had asked me in the last few weeks. But I was grateful he'd taken charge of supplying our equipment, because I'd had a lot to focus on already with Virtue and Scarlett.

"Weapons?" River asked.

Aiden nodded. "I've got some things to choose from. Unregistered, untraceable. Body armor and other tactical gear, too. We're a ways from the full arsenal we'll need once the Protectors are really off the ground, but it's a start."

That would make this a lot easier. Yep, Aiden was a keeper.

"I've done some prep work of my own," I said. "Promise I haven't been totally useless. Virtue's brother Toby is still at the compound, and he's been feeding me info." Using River's computer, I pulled up the map Toby and I had been working on. "They've got a computer room here, complete with their own server."

"That's where I'll be headed," River said.

"Toby's also kept track of Witkins' habits when he's at the compound. Obviously Toby didn't realize Witkins had come to Hartley, because he would've warned me otherwise. He's just one kid. But I know the areas Witkins frequents. He spends most of his time here." I pointed at the map. "This is the study in his personal home, a place that nobody else is allowed to go. His man cave, if you will. That's where I'll be paying him a visit."

"And I'll be here," Aiden said. "Ideally, we'd have another man to run the op from headquarters while I protect Virtue and Scarlett. But we have no headquarters yet, and there are only three of us. We'll make do."

I couldn't help thinking of Owen. I would've loved having him on our team. But I had a lot more groundwork to do if we wanted to get the sheriff on board. That was going to be a stretch, and it was a challenge for another time.

Taking care of Witkins and his helper? That couldn't wait.

"Hold up, I'm an official Protector?" River asked. "I get the title?"

"You helped us fund Last Refuge," Aiden said. "Far as I'm concerned, you can have whatever title you want."

River grinned.

I shook my head. "You shouldn't have said that. He'll have us calling him Royal Highness."

"Supreme Commander is fine," River said.

We talked through the mission again and possible contingencies, as well as our exit strategy. With that planning in place, Aiden and River left to gather the gear from Aiden's apartment.

I went to Virtue's room, where Scarlett was tucking her into bed. As a teenager, Virtue probably would've claimed she didn't need tucking in. But that was totally what was happening right now.

I hovered in the open doorway. "Can I come in?"

Scarlett was sitting on the bed beside Virtue, who'd changed into PJs and had her legs beneath the covers. Virtue nodded, and I stepped into the room.

"You're going somewhere, aren't you?" she asked.

Scarlett held up her hands. "I didn't say a word."

"You didn't have to," the girl quipped. "I have observational skills. Plus, that conference Trace, Aiden and River had going in the living room? Serious Dad energy. They were planning something." She turned to me. "Aren't you?"

Scarlett smiled, and I barked a laugh. Dad energy. I didn't mind that.

"I can't tell you what we're doing or where I might be going," I said. "It's important that no one outside this house suspects I was ever gone. But…whatever you're imagining, it's probably close to the truth."

Virtue nodded excitedly. "You can trust me. I won't tell a soul. You're taking the fight to Elder Dawson. Right? It's just like a movie."

"*Not* just like a movie. Aside from that, I can't confirm or deny."

"But you're getting Toby, right? You're bringing him back to Hartley so he'll be safe. We'll all be safe together. The four of us. You, Scarlett, me and my brother."

Scarlett's smile turned brittle, and a pang hit me in the chest. I went to the other side of Virtue's bed and sat on the edge. "I want that too. And I *will* make it happen. But this mission isn't to get Toby. If he disappears from Paradise Ranch in the next day or two, there will be difficult questions. He can't know anything else we're planning. That's for his safety as much as anything else."

Virtue's face fell. "I guess I understand. I don't like it though."

"Me neither." I held out my hand, and Virtue slotted hers into my grip. "But I will do everything in my power to make sure we're together at the end of this. The four of us. Scarlett and I will handle that part. We've got you."

She nodded slowly. Then she leaned forward, arms

opening for a hug. I returned it. I tried to put my promise into that embrace.

Scarlett and I left Virtue's room, closing the door. We took a few steps down the hall. Scarlett's hands moved over my chest, down to my stomach, then over my arms. Like she was memorizing the shape of me.

"Please be careful. I know you will, but I just have to say it."

I lifted her chin with my fingers. "That's my plan."

"If I could fall in love with anyone, it would be you. I want the chance to find out. So you have to promise me you'll come back. I'm demanding like that."

I leaned in to kiss her. She tilted her head, lips opening to me and inviting me in. My tongue stroked inside her mouth, and she sucked on it. With a quiet groan, I pulled her closer, regretting that we didn't have more time. *Later,* I thought. Once this was all over, we'd have time to enjoy one another.

Hopefully forever.

Reluctantly, I broke the kiss, my lips brushing over her cheek. Her hairline. "I already love you. And I have every intention of making you fall in love with me back. *I'm* demanding like that. I'm coming home to you, babe. Remember what I told you that day in the woods, after we'd run from the compound? I'll always come find you."

"Then get going. And hurry back."

CHAPTER TWENTY-FIVE

Trace

IT WAS MIDNIGHT, and we were on our way.

I drove River's rental car, while he tapped at a tablet, tracking our location and the cell locations of Witkins and his associate. Both were still at the compound, presumably asleep.

River and I had gotten a couple hours of sleep ourselves. It had done me a lot of good. I was feeling downright optimistic.

This mission wasn't going to be pleasant. Or easy. But I had more to look forward to now than I'd had in years.

"That little smile of yours is making me nervous." River hadn't looked up from his tablet. "Who are you, and where did you stash the real Trace Novo?"

"You're the one who always complains about my grumpiness. Don't you like this version better?"

"I've known you a long time, and you're usually still grumpy even when you're happy. But good point." He glanced up. "I take it the talk with Scarlett went well? Dug yourself out of that hole you were in?"

"It went well," I said gruffly. "But as for the hole I've been in. That's going to take some more work."

River seemed to notice the shift in my tone to seriousness. "You know I'm here for you. Whatever you need."

I nodded. "Thanks for coming out to Hartley."

"I'm glad I did. I've always loved Colorado. I ever tell you that I spent my summers here as a kid? Not too far from Hartley, in fact."

"No, never. Surprised that didn't come up. Thought I knew your life story, Riv. I'm disappointed."

"Gotta keep that spark going after all these years," he said with a wink. "I've still got some secrets. Like you've got yours?"

That was true. But I wasn't holding so tightly to my secrets now. "There's something I should've told you. It's about what happened when I left the Agency."

"Listening."

"Exactly how much do you know about it?"

He gave me a quick rundown, based on rumors. That I'd gone rogue after one of our fellow officers was killed. That I'd been injured, and the Agency had hushed up everything that happened and forced me out. "I know you went after the people responsible. I don't care if you crossed the line. Plenty of us have done it before."

"But you don't know what the Agency was hiding." I told him about the trafficking ring and the orders I'd received to leave it intact. "Someone from inside the Agency blew our cover. I'm sure of it."

I was driving, so I had to keep my eyes on the road. But I felt River's attention as he studied me in the near-darkness. "Names of possible suspects?"

"I don't have proof."

"Didn't ask for proof, Trace. I asked for names. *I* can find proof."

Did I want that? Would it make a difference? I couldn't go

back to my old life, and I didn't want to. I had so much more now.

I had people I loved. A purpose and a life worth defending.

"Don't forget," River said. "I'm on vacation right now. When I go back to DC, I'd like to know who I'm working for."

"Then I'll send you names. When we get back to Hartley." Once this mission was done.

The car climbed the mountain pass, then descended toward Creekview. We'd planned to park in a discreet location and hike the rest of the way to the compound. When we reached the designated coordinates, I stopped the car, and we geared up. River and I covered the vehicle with branches to make sure it wouldn't be seen from the road. We'd darkened our faces. Our earpieces were in place. We checked one another over, seeing that everything was secure.

I pulled my night vision goggles over my eyes. "Let's move."

It was nearing dawn when we reached the compound, but still dark. We'd approached from the woods. Lookouts patrolled the ranch perimeter by night, but we'd timed things so we'd be here for the shift change. It wouldn't be difficult to slip onto the property undetected and get to our destinations. We didn't expect any trouble.

River and I gripped arms when it was time to separate. "See you soon," he murmured.

The Witkins residence was on the edge of the row of houses, surrounded by its own fence like the others. I took off my NVGs and made my way inside, moving silently through doors in the wake of the women as they went about their morning chores.

I had the map of the home memorized. Within minutes, I was in Dawson's study, having picked the lock. I re-locked the door and positioned myself against the wall, out of sight from where he'd walk in.

Elsewhere in the house, I could hear breakfast being served.

This would be the longest part. Waiting for Dawson to come to his study. Toby had reported that the man visited the ranch operation with the elders in the morning, and that Dawson always returned to his own home for an early lunch. Then he'd spend the afternoon alone in his man cave.

Of course, yesterday Dawson had spent his afternoon in Hartley trying to kidnap Virtue.

Today, I would be the one waiting to pounce.

On the comm, Aiden confirmed everything was fine in Hartley. Jessi and Aiden had both stayed at Scarlett's overnight. Scarlett and Virtue were getting ready to spend their day as usual. We didn't want either of them to miss work or school and raise anyone's notice.

River checked in next, saying he'd finished in the server room. He'd uploaded his malware to the Paradise Ranch computers so that he could rifle through all their secrets. Now, he moved on to the building where the compound kept its supply deliveries. The next step in our plan.

"Just checked the location of Witkins' cell," River said in my earpiece. "Still at the compound, moving around the property. As expected."

"What about the other cell, the one belonging to his accomplice?" I asked quietly. "Can you confirm?"

"Negative. It dropped off the map. Looks like it's turned off."

I didn't like that, but my focus right now was Witkins. I'd track down his accomplice afterward.

The minutes ticked by. I had never minded waiting. It was essential in my line of work. Patience was a skill, and I'd gotten very good over the years at dulling my emotions. Bringing a strictly objective focus to the mission.

But when I'd sought vengeance against those human traffickers? Rage had boiled under my skin. And the same thing was happening to me now. Like flames licking at my insides. Yet instead of limping away from here with nothing, I would go back to Hartley to the people I loved. To the incredible woman who was waiting for me. I was lucky she had patience, too.

I didn't want the worst parts of me to touch Scarlett. But right now? I wasn't going to hold back that darkness.

I planned to make Dawson Witkins suffer for everything he'd done.

I heard voices in the hall. Dawson barked angrily at someone. Complaining that his lunch had been overcooked. I assumed he was berating one of his wives. A charmer, this one.

The door opened. I stilled in the shadows. Dawson came inside and closed the door behind him, muttering to himself. "Stupid woman can't even cook a damn pork—"

I stepped forward before he could notice me and placed him in a submission hold. His body tensed up. But he had no chance to put up a fight. Within moments, Dawson went limp in my arms.

I eased him to the ground. Made sure the door was locked. I didn't want to be disturbed.

Next, I took off my pack. From inside, I produced restraints and tape for his mouth. Once he was nicely trussed up like the pig he was, I pinched the insides of his nostrils until the man returned to consciousness, gasping.

"Hello, Dawson. Do you remember me?" I probably looked different in my tactical gear. But his eyes widened with fear. He grunted behind the tape. Yep. He remembered. "Good. That'll make this quicker. I'm sure you know why I'm here. But let me spell it out. You've threatened Scarlett. You've tried to hurt Virtue. You seem to believe both of them belong to you. But that's just not true, Dawson. It's *you* who belongs to *me*."

He screamed behind the tape and tried to wiggle away, but he wasn't going anywhere.

"I have some questions for you. I'll ask, and then I'll remove the tape from your mouth so you can speak. If you try to yell or alert others in the house, I will hurt you. Got it?"

He was glaring murder at me. But he nodded.

"What makes you believe you can force a fifteen-year-old girl into marrying you?"

I ripped the corner of the tape from his lips. He grimaced. "I don't have to abide by your narrow-minded ideas of morality." His eyes glittered with cruelty. "Besides, the younger they are, the sweeter the—"

I clamped my hand over his nose and mouth and squeezed.

Up until that moment, I'd allowed for the possibility that Dawson might survive this day. But not now. He was truly unrepentant. I wasn't going to enjoy ending the man, but some things just had to be done.

Still, I hoped I'd get something useful out of him first.

"Next question. How did you find out that Scarlett Weston was the same woman you once knew as Serenity?"

He gasped as I removed my hand, allowing him to breathe.

"Fuck you," he spit out. "Serenity is mine, not yours, and she always will be. You think you can disrespect me like this and walk free? You'll be caught and punished."

"I'm running out of patience." I decided to try my last question. "I know you've got an accomplice. I'm guessing he's the one who was watching outside Scarlett's house, smoking cigarettes. Maybe he's an outsider to Paradise Ranch. Or maybe he's one of your buddies who lives here. Either way, I want his name."

Dawson's mouth slid into a smile. "He's much closer to Serenity than you think."

"I know he came back here with you after you tried to snatch Virtue yesterday."

"He's someone who's loyal to me. If you believe you can turn him against me, you're wrong. I'm a king here. Your envy will never be able to touch me and my kind. The judgment of your small mind is meaningless to—"

I slapped my hand over his nose and mouth again to shut him up. I'd had enough. The guy wasn't going to tell me anything. He was too convinced of his own superiority. I could break him down, force the truth out of him, but that would require time I didn't have. This entire compound was full of guilty people, and River's computer bug would help reveal them eventually. Including Dawson's accomplice.

But that gap in my knowledge irked me. The smugness in Dawson's eyes, like he knew something crucial that I didn't.

Who the hell had been helping him?

CHAPTER TWENTY-SIX

Scarlett

IN THE MORNING, my house was busier than usual. Jessi and Aiden had stayed over, Jessi snuggling in with me while Aiden took the couch. Virtue seemed to love the commotion as we filled the kitchen, making eggs and bacon and coffee.

I was paying close attention to her, worried about how she was handling the ordeal she'd been through yesterday. But she was all smiles so far.

Once I was dressed, I knocked on Virtue's door. "Almost time to go."

Pop music played from her phone. She cracked open the door. "I'll be out in a sec. Just have to grab my backpack." She'd braided her dark blond hair, and she wore her new Hartley High sweatshirt.

"I wanted to check in with you. Are you sure you're okay for school? You can come to the sweet shop with me if you'd rather."

During the night, after Trace and River had left, I'd been up several times. I hadn't gone into Virtue's room because I hadn't wanted to scare her. But I'd hovered outside her door. I just hated to think of her being scared and me not knowing.

She wrinkled her nose at me. "But we're supposed to act

normal. Keep to our usual schedule. We can't draw any attention or let anyone know that Trace is gone."

"I know. But I also want to make sure you feel safe. I'm sure Trace would agree."

"I'm going to school," she insisted. "I already texted Stephie that I'm coming."

I chewed the inside of my cheek. I was helicoptering again. But I couldn't seem to stop.

The four of us piled into Aiden's truck. He dropped Jessi at the diner first, giving her a kiss goodbye, and then we headed for Virtue's school. She jumped out as soon as we pulled up to the curb, swinging her backpack onto her shoulder. "Later!"

"Hey, hold on," I said, leaning through the open window. "You need to wait inside after school until Aiden and I pick you up. Don't go anywhere else."

"I got it. I learned my lesson after yesterday."

I sighed as she thumped toward the entrance in her boot. Stephie Marsh was waiting for her, and the two girls walked in together, smiling and talking.

"Not easy to let her go, huh?" Aiden asked.

"Not at all." Between Virtue being away from me today, and Trace leaving for his mission to the compound, I was a bundle of stress.

"Virtue will be fine. She'll be surrounded by teachers and fellow students all day."

I nodded, trying to convince myself of the truth of his statement. But I was still nervous. "What about Trace? Have you heard from him yet?"

"I have. He and River have checked in. Trace wouldn't want you to worry about him. He's very good at what he does, and I have the feeling River is the same. If I could just get River to stay in Hartley and join the Protectors, then we'd really be cooking. We need a lot more guys than me and Trace. As today is proving."

I'd never had any doubts about Trace's level of courage. Whenever I was in danger, there was no one else I'd rather have with me. Yet it had taken even more than his usual strength for him to open up to me yesterday. To tell me the secret parts of his history that he'd been hiding. It was dark stuff. But his confession hadn't changed how I viewed him. If anything, it had only convinced me that I could fall for him. It felt inevitable, like the changing of the weather.

Because I had darkness inside me, too.

I was glad Dawson Witkins wouldn't get away with everything he'd done. Stealing the independence of more women than just me and Virtue. Killing his own brother, an innocent kid who'd only wanted to help me find a better life.

I'd never thought of myself as a vengeful, bloodthirsty person. Maybe I could've forgiven what Dawson had done to me. Chosen to forget. But after he'd tried to take Virtue away from us yesterday? Nope. I was all out of mercy. Dawson was the worst kind of predator. Someone who abused his position of power and trust.

And from what Trace had explained to me, Dawson wouldn't be the only one getting his comeuppance. River's computer handiwork would seal the fates of the other elders as well, even if they still had a chance of weaseling free in a court of law.

Trace was our guardian angel. But he was our avenging angel too.

And then, he would come home to us. Just like he'd promised.

I was hyperaware of everything as we drove to Main Street. The growing chill in the air now that it was October. The sunlight on the golden and red leaves.

Aiden stopped his truck in front of the sweet shop. "I'll

pick you up at closing time." That would be three p.m., the same time Virtue's school day ended. "I'll stay close. I've scoped out a spot halfway between here and the school where I can park discreetly and won't be noticed. I'll monitor the comms for Trace and River from there."

"I'd rather you stay near the school today," I said. "Like, close enough to watch the doors."

"That might be difficult. Owen's deputies are more likely to notice me if I'm watching the school. And I need to be able to get to Main Street if you need anything."

"Don't worry about me." I showed him what I'd hidden beneath my jacket.

Aiden whistled. "I hadn't realized you were packing."

"I didn't want Virtue to know."

I'd worn a concealed-carry holster with a Smith & Wesson CSX. I'd taken it from my gun safe this morning.

"When's the last time you brushed up at a range?"

"It was before Virtue lived with me. But I usually get in several times a year."

He nodded. "Don't get overconfident though. Stay vigilant. If there's anything suspicious, anything at all, text me. And then call the sheriff's office. Owen doesn't know what we're up to at the compound, but he'll help if you're in trouble."

"I know. I will. You'll let me know if anything goes wrong with the mission?"

Aiden pressed his lips together. I could tell he wanted to say no. "I'll try to keep you posted. *If* I can. Assume no news is good news."

"I'll try." I touched his arm. "Thanks, Aiden. I'm glad you stopped in Hartley back in January. Seems like that worked out well."

"I'm glad for it too. Every damn day."

I gave him a quick hug, then went inside.

As the day passed, I tried to distract myself with work. I whipped up a fresh batch of chocolate-covered marshmallows, Trace's favorite. Then some of the treats that Virtue favored. I'd have to find out what Toby liked. *Ugh, what if he was one of those people who preferred dinner to dessert?* That was a disturbing thought.

I'd lived by myself for years at this point. My little two-bedroom house had been plenty for me. But with Trace and two growing teenagers added to the mix? It wasn't going to be big enough. My whole *life* was growing. It was something I'd never thought I would want, yet now that it was in my reach, I couldn't imagine wanting anything else.

As soon as Trace's mission was over. As soon as Virtue was out of danger, and later, when Toby was safely in Hartley.

Then, I'd be able to relax.

Why were the hands on my wall clock moving so slowly?

A few customers stopped by. Someone must've been a smoker, because I started smelling stale cigarettes around the shop, which unnerved me. But it was probably just the reminder of those cigarette butts Trace had found outside my house.

Lunchtime came and went. I was too nervous to eat anything except a few nut clusters. I could've sworn that clock had stopped altogether. But finally, after agonizing hours of waiting, it was an hour from closing time.

Screw it, I thought. I was going to clean up and tell Aiden to get me. We'd pick up Virtue early.

In the kitchen, I finished up the dishes. The giant bowl for my standing mixer was always a pain. But I'd had it soaking for a while, so the sticky mess inside washed away quickly. Next was the trash. There was a dumpster in the alley behind the building, one that I shared with several other Main Street businesses.

I'd been out there countless times in the last few weeks.

But still, given my heightened anxiety today, I wasn't eager to go out there alone. Even with the gun concealed at my side. I'd refused Trace's offer to set up cameras here because my neighboring business owners would've asked nosy questions.

Then I realized I didn't have to be alone. Marco was a few doors down, behind the bar at the saloon. I texted him, asking him to meet me out back. We'd been friends long enough that he didn't ask me for an explanation. I appreciated that.

When I opened the rear exit and looked out, Marco was already striding toward me. He'd propped the saloon's door open. "Scarlett, hey. How have you been? We haven't caught up in a while."

"It's been busy." I walked over to the dumpster. Marco's shoes scraped the gravel behind me.

"I'm sure. With that girl who's living with you now? Virtue?"

"She's settling in." I'd told people she was my niece, and she was going through a rough time at home. People in Hartley were nosy, and I'd had to tell them something. I tossed the trash bag inside the dumpster and re-latched the lid.

"I hadn't even realized you had a niece." His voice was strangely muffled. "She came from the same place you did, right? That Paradise Ranch?"

Those two words made me shudder. When had I told him about Paradise Ranch?

Then I smelled it. Cigarette smoke. *Again.*

I spun around. Marco had a cigarette hanging from his mouth, hazy smoke around his head.

"I thought you quit." My voice was hollow in my ears.

He shrugged. "I did. Years ago. I must've bought enough of that nicotine gum to keep the maker's stock price propped up. But I slip sometimes. You know?"

A strange feeling spread to my fingers and toes.

He squinted at me, taking another drag. "Something wrong, Scarlett?"

"Just a long day." I was suddenly unsteady, and realized I'd placed my hand under my jacket. Brushing the butt of my gun.

I couldn't remember having told him about Paradise Ranch before.

Marco stepped forward. "I wasn't going to say anything, but you've been looking stressed lately whenever I've seen you pass by. Been meaning to check on you, and then you texted. Did you want to talk about something?"

I started backing away.

"I don't. No. Thanks, Marco. I'll see you later."

As quickly as I could, I went inside the sweet shop and locked the door behind me.

What the heck?

Marco had been my friend for over a decade. I'd known him since *high school,* for heaven's sake. He'd smoked back then, and off and on for years. And all those years ago, I must have mentioned something to him about where I'd come from. Paradise Ranch.

When Trace had found those cigarette butts outside my house, I hadn't thought of Marco for one second. But we suspected Dawson had hired someone to watch me. We also didn't know how Dawson had found out my new identity.

Was it possible?

I took out my phone and texted Aiden.

> Marco smokes. I thought he quit years ago, but I just saw him.

Aiden texted me back right away. He knew everything about my stalker that Trace or I did.

Are you saying you suspect him?

I don't know. But he also knew I came from Paradise Ranch. Maybe I told him a long time ago? When I first got to Hartley.

Did you check the brand of his cigs?

I didn't have a chance. I have no idea what to think.

Stay there. I'll come get you.

No, get Virtue first. Then me. Please Aiden. I need to know she's safe.

What *was* I even thinking? That Marco had waited around all these years and somehow got in touch with Dawson Witkins? Started working with Dawson against me? Why would Marco do something like that?

Unless it was money. That was a good enough motive for all kinds of things.

And Marco had just been asking about Virtue. Could he have been the man who tried to kidnap Virtue yesterday? She'd said she didn't recognize her attempted kidnapper. But as far as I knew, she'd never met Marco. I'd never taken Virtue to the saloon, for obvious reasons.

I breathed out slowly. Aiden would be here in a few minutes. Maybe I was wrong. But if Marco *was* my stalker, then Aiden and Trace would find a way to prove it. Maybe River could get a DNA sample and have it compared to the other sample from the Ashfair Menthol cigarettes we'd found.

I jumped when I heard a voice coming from the front of the shop.

"Anybody home? Scarlett?"

Crap, I had a customer. Because technically, the shop was still open.

I walked into the front area behind the counter. Skyler stood there, glancing over the fudge case. "There you are." He was smiling, oblivious to my inner turmoil.

"Sorry, didn't realize anyone had come in." I wondered how quickly I could get rid of him without being rude.

"I was worried I'd missed you. We wrapped up the electrical and plumbing work at Last Refuge today, and we're waiting for a big inspection before we can continue. Liam left Hartley yesterday morning, and I'm about to take off myself. This is my last chance for some of your peanut butter cup fudge until I'm back. Been too long since I had some."

I went to the fudge case and pulled out the container. "I've got plenty. How much do you want? It freezes well."

"Two pounds?"

I started cutting a piece to weigh it.

Skyler watched me from the other side of the counter. "To be honest, the fudge isn't the only reason I stopped by. I was thinking about that night we danced at the bar."

"Oh." This was the first time I'd spoken to Skyler since that night on the dance floor, over a month ago, when Trace had cut in. I'd thought about apologizing, but so much time had passed. And really? I wasn't in the mood to chitchat with the guy, nice as he was.

But he kept rambling. "I was going to ask you out that night. Then it seemed like you already had something going on with Trace Novo? I was surprised. Hadn't meant to get in the middle of it."

I set the piece of fudge on the scale. "Trace and I weren't together then. But we are now." *Not that it's your business,* I added silently as I wrapped up the fudge in wax paper. "I'll throw in some extra fudge. On the house. In fact, it's all on the house." Anything to get the guy out of here.

I glanced at my clock, but only a few minutes had passed since I'd texted Aiden.

Skyler's smile shifted. "Seems like you're trying to get rid of me."

"I guess I'm distracted today. I have other things going on. I need to get going."

And now, his smile vanished altogether. "No problem. But I'm going to pay. I wouldn't feel right about it otherwise."

"It's not necessary."

"Just tell me how much it is." He tugged a billfold out of his pocket and slapped it roughly onto the counter. Then I noticed the other item he had pulled out of his pocket.

It was a pack of Ashfair Menthols.

What. The. Hell?

I braced my hand against the counter, knees going weak. A moment ago, I'd been freaking out because of Marco smoking. Now, I couldn't take my eyes away from that pack of cigarettes. The same brand smoked by the stalker outside my house.

"Just take the fudge," I said. "I'm about to close. My ride will be here any minute."

"Scarlett, did I offend you somehow?"

I took a step back, surprised by the harshness of his tone.

"You're acting like you're afraid of me. Talk about mixed signals. One minute you're laying it on thick, calling me *sugar*, the next you can't get away from me fast enough. Like that night at the bar."

"You need to leave." I backed away from the counter. My hand edged toward my concealed weapon.

"And now you're looking at me like I'm going to attack you. Just because I said I wanted to ask you out? You're that uptight?"

I was so done with this. "You know what, *sugar*? I don't

need to justify myself. I asked you to leave. That means you leave."

Anger made his face draw up in a smirk. So much for Mr. Nice Guy. I had no idea if Skyler was my stalker. I just wanted him *out*. And he wasn't going.

"I'm serious. Get. Out." I took my Smith & Wesson from the holster, and Skyler gasped. I didn't thumb the safety yet, and I wasn't pointing it directly at him. But close enough to show him I meant business.

"You're *nuts*."

Skyler tripped over himself as he retreated, then full-out ran on his way to the door. Once he was outside, he continued down the sidewalk, casting shocked glances at me over his shoulder.

I followed and flipped the lock. *Jeez*. That had been too much.

The gun slid into its holster, and I rested a hand against the door frame, panting as I caught my breath. Skyler had left his wallet and the pack of cigarettes.

He was more of a jerk than I'd realized. Then again, that didn't have to mean he was working for Dawson Witkins. And even though he'd had that pack of menthols, he hadn't smelled at all like cigarettes... The whole thing was strange.

I was so tired of this. Constantly looking over my shoulder.

I searched my pockets for my phone, but it wasn't there. I must've left it in the back when I had been texting Aiden earlier. When I'd thought *Marco* could be the stalker. At least Aiden would be here any minute.

I went into the back room to find my phone. There it was on the ground. I must've dropped it there earlier when I'd heard Skyler's voice. I checked my messages and found Aiden had texted again. He'd picked up Virtue from school, and they'd be here soon. Thank goodness.

As I looked up from my phone, my skin crawled. But before I could turn around, a hand clamped over my mouth.

No.

Terror blanketed me. I started to struggle, and a gun muzzle pushed into my side. He'd just taken it from my holster.

"I need you to stay calm. Can you do that?"

I knew this voice. But it didn't make sense. Confusion and disbelief had shocked me into stillness.

"Not sure what that was all about with Skyler," he said. "But I can't blame you for wanting him away from you. The guy was desperate. Good, you're calm now."

He removed his hand from my mouth, and I gasped in a breath.

"*Liam?*" This was Skyler's boss. The foreman of the Last Refuge construction site. "What is…I don't…"

He was still holding me, gun pressed to my lower ribs. "I told Skyler I was leaving town yesterday because I had other things to do. But I wasn't going to leave without you." He smelled like stale cigarettes. The same scent that had hovered all afternoon.

Horror washed over me.

"You…You're the stalker."

"You need to relax, Serenity. I don't want to hurt you."

"*Relax?* You work for Dawson." My body shook uncontrollably. *He must've been hiding in my storage room,* I realized. *Watching me.* I should've been fighting him. Screaming. But I was frozen there in place, all too aware of that gun against my side.

"Dawson's paying you?" I choked out. "He wants you to take me back to Paradise Ranch? You realize *why*, don't you?"

Liam's arm tightened around my middle. "You still don't know who I am."

"You're the creepy asshole who's been watching me! Who tried to take Virtue yesterday!"

"I mean who I *really* am. I would never hurt you. I'll prove it." With a quick motion, he leaned us both over. He put the gun on the floor and shoved it. The weapon slid along the tile and underneath the oven, far out of reach. Then Liam stood us up again.

His lips touched the back of my ear. "You said you would wait for me in Creekview. But you didn't. I have never forgotten you though, Serenity. Not for a single day."

A terrible suspicion seeped through me, paralyzing me to my core.

"And now we're finally going to be together. Like we always should've been."

No. This wasn't possible. It couldn't be.

I pulled in a breath to scream. But he pressed a cold cloth to my face. A noxious smell hit me. Finally, my muscles responded. I fought. But I couldn't escape. The sweet shop got dimmer and dimmer in my vision. It felt like falling into a memory.

Into the darkest reaches of my past.

CHAPTER TWENTY-SEVEN

Trace

OUR EXIT STRATEGY went even better than I had anticipated.

I'd always been a fan of distractions. And I knew River could make it happen. A few minutes after I gave him the signal, he was waiting in a pickup he had borrowed from the compound garage. I assumed the keys had been in the cupholder, just as Toby had said they would be. This place operated by habits, and that was turning out to be their downfall.

We'd also chosen a block of time in the afternoon when few wives or kids would be about at the Witkins residence. So nobody saw us as I lifted Dawson out of the window and carried him over my shoulder to the gate in the fence.

River helped me haul the man into a delivery crate in the bed of the pickup. My friend was dressed like a ranch hand. If I'd seen him at a distance, even I wouldn't have recognized him. "Where'd you get the new outfit?"

"Somebody's dirty laundry. Hurry up so I can put on my own stuff again. These clothes stink."

In the distance, I heard a shout. And were those... squeals?

"Is that your diversion at work?"

"I let out the pigs. They're probably rampaging in the garden by now." He jumped into the driver's seat, while I lay in the bed of the truck beneath a tarp, where River had stowed his pack and gear. Unlike him, I didn't have a disguise.

The drive was bumpy. We weren't going through the main gate to the road. Far too likely we would be spotted and followed. I didn't want a repeat of last time. Instead, River drove us to the edge of the woods in a secluded spot, where we unloaded the crate.

We weren't headed out of town, anyway. We were headed for Paradise Lake.

"Say goodbye," I said to Dawson. "I can't imagine they'll miss you." He didn't answer, but I hadn't expected him to. He wasn't going to be saying anything ever again.

Dawson Witkins was about to disappear off the face of this earth, and the rest of us would be better for it.

A couple of hours later, we were hiking back to River's car. We made it to the vehicle by about three p.m. We'd already changed clothes, leaving anything incriminating behind. That evidence was now in a delivery crate at the bottom of Paradise Lake. Good riddance.

I contacted Aiden, letting him know we were on our way back. River drove this time. There was a charge in the air, but we were relaxed. Joking. Letting ourselves come down from the high of a successful mission.

Until Aiden came through on the comm.

"Repeat that?" I asked.

River's hands had tightened on the steering wheel. I forgot how to breathe.

Scarlett had texted Aiden that *Marco* was the stalker.

And now, she was gone.

The tires squealed as River turned onto Main Street. Trees and buildings flew past.

After Aiden had dropped the bomb that Scarlett was missing, he'd promised he was doing everything he could to find her. He'd also said he was taking Virtue to the diner, where she'd be safe with Jessi. He hadn't given us further updates. It had been almost an hour since we'd last heard from him. My adrenaline was jacked.

I spotted a crowd in front of the Hartley Saloon. Aiden, Owen, and Marco were on the sidewalk having a heated discussion, by the looks of it. I wanted to know why the bartender wasn't in handcuffs right now.

"Stop there," I told River. He pulled up to the curb, and I was out in an instant. My feet carried me straight to Marco, and my momentum didn't stop until I'd forced the man up against the brick wall of the building.

"Where is she?" I roared.

Aiden's palm landed on my shoulder. "That's what we're trying to figure out."

"I didn't do anything!" Marco protested.

The sheriff appeared on my other side, pulling me away from the bartender. "Trace, where have you been? I've been trying to call you."

Owen had probably been dialing my regular phone, which was back at Scarlett's house. I chose not to mention that. No way would I admit to the sheriff where we'd really been.

"My friend River and I were hiking. He's visiting from out of town. But that's irrelevant. I want to know what's going on."

Suddenly, everyone was talking over each other. Marco was babbling, Aiden and Owen were both asking angry questions. Skyler was here too, and he started up about something, waving his hands. River had gotten out of the car, computer bag on his shoulder, looking back and forth between all of us like he didn't know who to deal with first.

And of course, a crowd of Hartley residents were gathering to gawk, some adding in their own two cents.

This was not helping.

"*Enough*!" I shouted.

Everyone went silent, and every head turned to me. The sheriff's face flushed with indignation, but he held his tongue.

"We're going one at a time," I said. "Aiden, were you the last to hear from Scarlett?"

"Haven't determined that yet. She texted me after speaking to Marco. By the time I got there, she was gone. The back door to the sweet shop was wide open, and she'd left her purse and her phone behind. Owen got there right after me, but I hadn't called him."

"I saw Scarlett," Skyler chimed in. "I think she lost her mind. The woman pointed a gun at me!"

I glared at Skyler, and he went quiet.

"Sheriff Douglas," I said, figuring I should show Owen at least a little respect. We were on Main Street, and we had a crowd watching. "What do you say we head inside, so we can discuss this further in private?"

Owen nodded. "My thoughts exactly."

Marco led us into the saloon. He had a private space for events and parties with a large wooden table. The five of us piled around it. Me, Aiden, Owen, Marco and Skyler.

As quickly as I could, I picked up again with the questions. "Marco, where have you been this afternoon?"

"Here at the saloon. Been here the whole time, and my server can corroborate."

"Which I already confirmed," Owen muttered, crossing his arms.

Marco kept going. "I stepped out back into the alley when Scarlett asked me to. I think she was afraid to take out the trash by herself, which I can understand. I heard about the stalker thing. But *I* didn't do anything to her. I'm as worried about her as anyone else."

My fists clenched on the tabletop. I forced myself to stay calm. This was costing us precious minutes, but I had to reconstruct Scarlett's last steps.

From what I could tell, she'd already been missing for over an hour by now.

"Sheriff, why did you go to the sweet shop? How did you know Scarlett was in danger?"

"I didn't." Owen hooked a thumb at Skyler. "This guy came to the station, saying he'd been assaulted at the sweet shop and wanted to press charges."

Now, everyone turned to Skyler. He scratched his jaw sheepishly. "Look, I thought about letting it go. But she pointed a gun at me for no reason whatsoever. I hadn't done a damn thing."

"You sure about that?" Owen asked. "Scarlett Weston isn't the type to point guns at men without provocation."

I agreed wholeheartedly. If she'd been frightened enough to pull a weapon, Skyler had done something.

"All I did was try to buy fudge! I mean, what the hell?"

"All right." I lowered my hands, settling everyone down again. "Take us through what happened before she pulled the gun. Step-by-step."

He paused to think. "She was getting out the fudge. Everything seemed fine. We were just talking."

"Talking about what?" Owen challenged.

"Just catching up! It was totally innocent. Then I took out my wallet and set it by the register. She started flipping out."

"I found Skyler's wallet there on the counter when I

arrived to investigate," Owen added. "Along with a pack of cigarettes."

"Cigarettes?" I asked sharply.

Skyler shrugged. "Yeah, they're Liam's. He left them at the Last Refuge worksite. I was going to return them the next time I saw him."

My blood was rushing in my head, fast and hot. "What brand of cigarettes?"

"What does that have to do with anything?"

"What brand?"

Aiden stood up, bracing his hands on the tabletop. "Just tell him the damn brand already."

"Okay. Jeez. They're… I don't have it memorized." Skyler pulled the cigarette pack from his pocket. Set them on the table. We all looked, and the moment seemed to crystallize.

Ashfair Menthols.

Fuck. *Fuck.*

Aiden groaned, running his hands through his hair. He knew as well as I did what this meant.

Liam was the stalker. How many times had I greeted him on Refuge Mountain while he supervised the construction? And the fucker had been working for Dawson. I'd never suspected him. Not once.

"Does the brand mean something to you?" Owen asked me. "Does this have something to do with Scarlett's stalker?"

I couldn't deal with explaining things to the sheriff right now. "Aiden, could you see Marco and Skyler out? We need the room." Marco and Skyler shuffled out, and Aiden shut the door.

"Could somebody explain to me what the heck is going on?" Owen said. "Why does it feel like I'm ten steps behind the rest of you?"

"Because you are," Aiden murmured, clapping Owen on

the back. "No offense. I'll try to catch you up. As much as I'm able, anyway."

At the end of the table, River had already set up his computer. His fingers moved quickly over the keyboard. He had a look of intense focus, so whatever he was doing, I left him to it.

Instead, I logged onto the website that connected to my surveillance cameras. It wasn't as easy to navigate as the app, but that was on my other phone. I pulled up the footage from the camera on Main Street.

A little over an hour ago, a dark sedan had driven past. No plates. It was the same car that had tried to snatch Virtue yesterday. I couldn't see who was driving, and there were no passengers. Did that mean Scarlett was in the trunk? She had to be in that car. But where had Liam taken her?

Liam couldn't have known that Dawson was dead. If he'd been taking Scarlett back to Paradise Ranch, we would've passed his car on the road.

Please, I thought. *Please let her be all right.* I'd survived a lot. But losing her this way? I didn't think I'd make it through this one.

I'd promised I would come home to her.

I walked over to River, resting a hand on the back of his chair. "Tell me you've got something."

"I'm checking on that burner phone we lost track of earlier."

"The one that belongs to Dawson Witkins' accomplice?" I asked.

"Yep. And...it just turned on again and started pinging towers near Hartley. I'm pulling the live coordinates now."

My pulse ticked up another notch.

Owen and Aiden had joined us at River's end of the table, all of us focused on River's computer screen. "What exactly are we looking at?" Owen asked. "Is that *cell tower* data? *I* don't even have access to this, absent a warrant."

"Don't ask questions you don't want answers to," River said over his shoulder, still tapping away.

"Do you know what question I would love answered? Who even *are you*?"

"My friend River," I deadpanned.

"From out of town," Aiden finished.

Owen scowled. "You two think you're cute, don't you?" He shook his head. "You know what? I'm not asking any more questions until later. For now, let's find Scarlett and get her back safe. If you can help me do that, I don't care how you make it happen."

Those sounded like famous last words. But I would take it.

"Welcome to the team, Sheriff." Aiden grinned viciously. The guy looked downright scary when he smiled like that. "You're a Protector now."

Then River shouted, "I've got it! The burner phone is at Refuge Mountain. It pinged the new cell tower there."

I looked at the map. "Last Refuge. The construction site."

But why would Liam have taken her there?

What was he planning to do?

CHAPTER TWENTY-EIGHT

Scarlett

MY EYES BLINKED OPEN. I tried to sit up, but my head was killing me. Pounding like someone was hammering inside my skull. My mouth was dry. A chemical, noxious taste coated my tongue.

Pressing the heel of my hand to my forehead, I managed to get up to my knees. A voice spoke from somewhere nearby. But I couldn't place the source.

What had happened? Where was I?

The ceiling above was open rafters. Sunlight bled through the windows and painted long stretches of yellow across the wooden floor. Stacks of tools and a table saw sat nearby. And through a doorway, I saw stainless steel appliances with plastic over them. Everything was coated in dust.

This was Last Refuge Tavern. Jessi and Aiden's restaurant, still under construction.

"Hello?" I coughed. My mouth tasted awful. Maybe I could find water somewhere. If I could just understand what had happened. I felt around my pockets for my phone. I had to find a way to tell Trace where I was. But my phone wasn't here.

I tried to stand, but my head spun, and I had to sit down

again.

Suddenly, the memories flooded back. Trace leaving Hartley on a mission to Paradise Ranch. Liam grabbing me at the sweet shop after Skyler had run off. My gun sliding beneath the oven. And that cold, harsh cloth pressing to my face.

Holy crap. The man had kidnapped me.

Liam. That was whose voice I heard now in the nearby room. I couldn't see him, but he was close.

"Dawson, don't play games," Liam was saying. "Call me back."

He'd brought me here. But why?

No. My panic deepened as I remembered the rest. He wasn't Liam. That wasn't the name I'd known him by all those years ago.

I had to get the heck out of here.

The floor creaked as Liam walked back and forth in the next room and continued to speak. "I'm sure you're still pissed, but I don't care. I'm not afraid of you anymore. The sooner you accept that, the sooner we can sort this out. The old deal? It's off."

I had no idea what he was talking about, and I didn't want to know. Crawling forward, I spotted a door to the outside down a short hallway. But I'd have to go past the room with Liam to reach it.

"So you'd better call me back unless you want me to start making your life really damn hard."

Liam stopped talking. He was done with his call. I had seconds.

I pushed myself upright. Tried to reach the door. But my knees went weak. I stumbled.

"Serenity?" Liam ran into the entryway. He put his hands under my arms, scooping me off the floor. "You're going to get hurt."

"Get away from me. That's not my name. Don't touch me!"

I tried to fight him, but I was still weak. Liam took me back to the larger room with the tools and set me on the floor.

"Serenity is your name," he insisted. "And you know my real name, too."

I scrambled away, backing up on my hands and feet until I reached a wall. "No. You're not him."

Liam looked too old to be *him*. Lines framed Liam's eyes and mouth. His skin was tanned dark, and his face was too sharp.

"You're lying."

He shook his head. "Deep down, you remember me. You remember the nights we talked by Paradise Lake. Imagining how good it would feel to escape and see the world we'd read about. You remember that last night too, I bet. When I told you to run."

I stared at the man. Bile reared up in my stomach.

"Kenny," I whispered.

His face lit up. Transformed completely when he smiled. And for a split second, I did recognize him. The boy who'd helped me escape. Who had died helping me. Who I'd mourned and still felt guilty over.

My friend.

"What happened to you?"

"I guess I can't blame you for not recognizing me. Dawson didn't at first either. You might say I led a hard life. Too much sun, too little sleep. Wears on a man."

I was confused. Overwhelmed. This man had kidnapped me. But he was also the boy who'd been my best friend. It didn't make sense. "They said you were dead."

He sat down a few feet from me. "That night, after you ran off and the others were chasing you, Dawson took me to the lakeshore. He could always fly into a rage at the slightest thing, but that night, he was just...*cold.* And that scared me even more. He just glared at me with a gun in his hand. I thought he was going to kill me."

I shivered, imagining it. "What did he do?"

"He said that if I didn't want to live at the ranch, then I didn't deserve a place there. He said, *If you want to run, then run*. So I did. I ran as fast as I could. He started shooting at me."

I covered my hand with my mouth.

"He missed. I just kept running. As long and as far as I could. And that's what I've been doing ever since." He blinked, looking over at me. "I went to Creekview, you know. Where we were supposed to meet. You weren't there."

"A woman picked me up on the road and took me to Hartley. She knew the sheriff." It was like I had gone back in time. I was fifteen years old again, eaten alive by guilt over leaving my friend behind. "I wanted to go back and help you. But when we went to Paradise Ranch and the sheriff confronted the elders, they all lied. When I asked about you, my sisters said you were dead. And I believed them. I'd heard the shots that night. Kenny, I'm sorry."

He gazed across the room. Dust motes floated through the beams of sunlight. "In Creekview, I didn't tell anyone where I was from or what had happened to me. I was too scared. I thought if I went back, my brother would kill me for sure. So I just survived. I was seventeen, and it wasn't that hard to convince people that I was a year older. I got a job as a ranch hand over near Montrose. After that, I started working construction. I wound up at Mayfield, the company I work for now. Made my way up to being a foreman. Not bad for thirty years old, considering I'm a former runaway who started with absolutely nothing. Most people don't know those things about me, though."

"Do you have a family?"

"No, Serenity. I've never had anything like that. I've just worked. That's all people know about me. All they notice. I'm the guy who does what's asked of him, and otherwise, I'm not important. Admit it. You barely looked at me twice this summer. Even when you spoke to my face. When you danced with me the night of the ground-breaking ceremony. You had no clue."

"I never could've imagined."

"No. I guess not. But I imagined plenty. What might have been. What it would be like to find you. How happy we'd both be. I never meant for..." He trailed off, instead waking up his phone and glanced down at it, frowning at whatever he saw. Then he resumed his story.

"Earlier this summer, my bosses at Mayfield Construction got a call. An architect we knew was designing a renovation of a ranch in Hartley. We came out to inspect the site. Skyler was with me, and he kept talking up the sweet shop. Said he wanted to visit it again because there was a really pretty woman who worked there. So finally, I gave in and went with him on our way out of town. And there you were. Serenity. *My* Serenity."

I didn't remember that at all. But Skyler had mentioned coming into the shop before. Scores of tourists had been visiting Hartley over the spring and summer. So much had happened...

Like those threatening Instagram comments Dawson had left using the anonymous account. Because Dawson had finally figured out my new identity.

"You told him, didn't you? You told your brother you had found me. How could you do that?"

"At first, I was just shocked that I'd found you. *Finally* found you. I almost said something to you that day, but then you looked right through me." He shook his head. "That ate at me. The fact that I knew you in an instant, but to you, I was a stranger. Irrelevant. You barely even smiled at me. You didn't care."

"You could've told me who you were."

"But that wouldn't have been enough!" he shouted.

I flinched back from him.

His chest moved as he breathed. After a minute, he'd calmed down again. "I couldn't think of any other solution than to go to Dawson. Ask him for help."

"Help with what? Do you realize what he did once he found out my new identity? He started harassing me. Terrifying me. Why would you be a part of that?"

Had Kenny been the stalker who'd smoked outside my house? But it was Skyler who'd had the pack of Ashfair Menthols. Had both of them been in on it?

Skyler wasn't here, though. He hadn't kidnapped me.

Kenny opened his mouth, and I just knew he was going to make excuses. I didn't want to hear it. "Were you watching my house? Yes or no."

"Yes, because—"

I cut him off. "Someone helped Dawson try to kidnap Virtue yesterday. Was that you as well?"

"I didn't want to. But I had to."

"How the hell do you justify something like that? Virtue's a kid. Just like I was. The boy I knew would never have done that."

As I'd spoken, his face had turned redder and redder. And finally, he exploded.

"Because I wanted you! You should've been mine, and I had to do whatever was necessary to make that happen. Even back when we were kids and Dawson decided to take you away from me, I knew you should've been mine. I thought when we escaped the ranch, you'd eventually fall in love with me. You'd be grateful, and we could be together. Why else do you think I did it? Leaving everything, my family and my home and my security. I destroyed my whole life for you. Could've died for you. Don't you see that?"

I was going to be sick. No wonder I hadn't recognized him. This man was nothing like the boy who'd been my friend.

"It wasn't an easy decision," he went on. "When I contacted him again, I hadn't seen my brother for over a decade, and Dawson had tried to kill me before. But I did it because I knew you'd never want me back otherwise. You're interested in men like Trace. Not me. You didn't even notice me. This was the only way I could think of to have you."

I felt like I would shake apart with fury at what I was hearing. But sadness tore at my heart, too. Imagining Kenny so lonely and lost. His kindness twisting into something dark and ugly.

Or was I wrong? Had the seeds of this cruelty been inside Kenny from the start, because of the way he'd been raised? Growing up with a brother like Dawson and a Paradise Ranch elder as his father?

We'd both escaped from that place. But it had kept its hold over us. Kept its hold still.

"So you planned this for a while," I said. "You wanted to kidnap me, and for reasons that only make sense to you, you asked for Dawson's help. Where did Virtue come into it?"

Kenny looked away. We were still sitting beside one another. Close enough I could see the muscle in his jaw pulsing. "I didn't know about the girl. Not at first. It was only about you."

"What did your brother promise you?" I asked in a monotone.

"He said if I did whatever he asked, he would eventually give me a house at Paradise Ranch. He would welcome me back. I could go home."

So *that* was why Kenny had gone to his brother.

"I knew there'd be a price to pay. Dawson said..." Kenny grimaced. "He said he still owned you because you were betrothed to him. But he promised we could...share you."

My stomach churned again. "*Share* me? Are you kidding?"

"That was the old deal. I just left Dawson a voicemail. I'm changing the terms." Kenny stuck his phone in his pocket, and I heard a jingle of metal as he moved.

Keys.

I glanced down and saw a bulge in the side pocket of his coat. Those had to be his car keys. His car was up here somewhere. Of course it was. How would he have gotten us here otherwise?

If I could get to it...

"You're better than Dawson," I said, keeping my tone gentle. Like I wanted to reason with him, even though I suspected he was beyond that. "But you're acting just like him. You became exactly what you used to hate. If you listen to what you're saying, you would realize that."

My arm brushed against the pocket with the keys. The metal and plastic were hard beneath the fabric of his coat.

"No, my brother is greedy. And he's stupid. Obsessed with punishing you. Sending you those ridiculous comments online. Insisting that we wait until after his marriage to Virtue, as if he doesn't have enough wives already. That's why I didn't take you straight to him today. I'm renegotiating our deal. I know enough to cause all kinds of problems for him. I want my own place at the Ranch, and I want you as my wife. My only wife. And I'll be your only husband. I want you to be happy, Serenity. I could make you happy."

"How could taking my freedom ever make me happy?"

"Because you don't know what you really want. You think Trace can take care of you? He can barely take care of himself.

I've seen him up here, barely holding himself together. But I could take care of you. I'll always protect you."

He took my hand. The touch disgusted me, but I didn't pull away. Not yet.

"Don't you remember those nights by the lake when we were kids?" He paused, like he was truly waiting for a response.

"Yes. I do remember."

"We could have that again. We'll be happy together, the way we were supposed to be. If you just try. I wouldn't have to force anything if you give this a chance. Please."

An idea formed. If I could make it work. Make him believe me.

I pretended to hesitate. "And Virtue? What about her?"

Kenny blinked at me, as if he'd already forgotten about Virtue's fate. His wistful smile shifted to a frown. "Dawson still wants her back."

"But what if you refuse? If…if you guarantee her safety, I could…" I swallowed. "I'll go with you voluntarily to the compound. I'll be your wife. If it means Virtue's safety."

The desperate desire in his eyes made me want to gag. "Would you?" he asked. "You'd live with me there? You wouldn't try to escape?"

"Yes. But you have to promise Virtue would be left alone. And that Dawson wouldn't touch me. He threatened me that day when I went to Paradise Ranch looking for Virtue. You wouldn't let him hurt me? You'll protect me?"

Kenny stood up, pulling me to stand with him. "I promise. Whatever you want. What I've done has always been for you. I've been waiting so long for this." He still held my hand, and he lifted his other to caress my face. I forced myself not to cringe away.

"Would you kiss me, Serenity?" he asked. "Please?"

Holding my breath, I leaned in.

At the last second, I slammed my fist into his nose, then his throat. Kenny screamed, his hands flying to his face and letting me go. Pain spread through my hand. I was worried I'd broken it. But I ignored it.

I grabbed for the keys in his coat pocket. Once the ring was in my hand, I elbowed him as hard as I could. He didn't go down. Instead he took a few steps back, steadying himself, and bellowed in anger.

I turned and ran for the door. He was right behind me. I managed to open it and threw it backward. The wooden edge caught Kenny in the shoulder. I dashed outside into the dying afternoon sun. Distantly, I thought I heard sirens. But maybe that was just the loud rush of my pulse in my head.

The car. Where was the car?

I ran around the side of the building. Just trying to get away from him. Buy some time. I spotted the dumpster and went around it. Shadows slanted sideways through the trees.

I heard Kenny's footsteps. "Serenity!" His voice sounded thick and hoarse. He was so close. But maybe he hadn't seen where I'd gone. I crouched beside the dumpster, scanning for a better place to hide.

Then I saw the car. Parked out of sight of the road and behind some trees. If I could get inside the car, I could lock the doors. Kenny wouldn't be able to get me.

But now, I couldn't hear him. Where was he?

My heartbeat shook me. I couldn't wait here any longer. I had to move. He could find me at any moment. My lungs filled as I took a deep breath.

I ran toward the car.

Kenny lunged out to my left. I screamed and sprinted toward the vehicle, pressing the key fob frantically.

I wasn't fast enough.

Kenny tackled me from behind, and I went sprawling in the dirt a foot away from the car.

CHAPTER TWENTY-NINE

Trace

WE GRABBED our tactical gear and weapons from the back of River's car, where we'd left them. Owen pointed at us in turn. "Aiden, ride with River. Trace, you're with me."

I followed him to his sheriff's department SUV, which was parked just down the block.

We zoomed down Main Street with the siren blaring. Last Refuge was about twenty-five minutes away. Less at this speed. But it was still a long time. Anything could happen during those minutes.

Owen radioed his deputies for backup, then glared at me sideways. "I'm assuming our suspect is armed and dangerous, since Scarlett had a gun with her earlier. Tell me what else I need to know. Off the record."

I recounted what I could about Scarlett's stalker, who was apparently Liam. The Last Refuge construction foreman. "We believe he was with Dawson Witkins in Hartley yesterday. They tried to kidnap Virtue."

"*What*? You didn't mention this to, I don't know, *me*?"

"We chose to keep that intel to ourselves. We can get a positive ID from Virtue later. Confirm that Liam is the guy who tried to grab her on her way home."

"Shit. Okay. So we're not a hundred percent sure Liam is the accomplice?"

"No, I'm sure. I'm going to shoot on sight." So long as Scarlett was out of the line of fire, I wasn't going to mess around anymore. "He's mine." I'd already said the same to River and Aiden on our way out of the saloon.

Owen exhaled slowly. Didn't say anything for a good five minutes. "I don't intend to lie in my official report. Make sure I don't have to."

We made it first to Last Refuge, with River and Aiden right behind. There was a gravel lot just off the road for parking. No sign of any cars.

But the door to the main building was wide open.

I jumped out, rifle at the ready. Immediately, I signaled the other men into position to begin a search.

Then we heard footsteps. A scream. A thud and a muffled cry. I raced in the direction of the noise.

Liam had Scarlett on the ground. He grabbed her around the middle and hauled her upright. She struggled. Elbowed him and kicked at his knee. My finger hovered at the trigger guard. I didn't have a clear shot.

Scarlett broke free of Liam, but she stumbled. Went to her knees. And at that same moment, she turned and spotted me. "Trace!" she screamed.

Liam had terrorized Scarlett and Virtue, and he was just as guilty as Dawson had been. I wanted the man dead. So much I could taste it, hot and metallic. The taste of blood. Vengeance. For Scarlett. For Virtue. For the other women who'd been robbed of their freedom. Who I'd failed to save.

I had my shot lined up. I started to squeeze the trigger.

But something in Scarlett's face made me pause for that split second. I wasn't even looking directly at her. It was more like I *felt* her. Her lips moved. *No*.

I almost shot him anyway.

But just in time, my trigger finger lifted, the blood lust ebbing.

Liam had frozen, staring at me in fear. I crossed the distance and shoved him backward. My rifle lifted. Aimed at his face. "Don't fucking move."

"Okay! Don't shoot!" The guy raised his hands, giving up instantly.

"You're under arrest." Owen rolled Liam onto his stomach, cuffing the guy while he recited his Miranda rights. Aiden and River closed in, flanking Owen.

I flicked the safety on my rifle and shoved it on its strap to my back. Scarlett had gotten up and retreated toward the building. I went over to her. Opened my arms. She rushed into my embrace. I slid my fingers into her hair, holding her to my chest.

"Hey, babe. You okay?"

"He's not Liam. He's Kenny."

"He's what?"

"Kenny. Dawson's younger brother. I thought he was dead. But he wasn't, and…I knew you were going to kill him. He's done a lot that's wrong, and he should answer for all of it. But he did save me once. I didn't want to see him dead. I just couldn't. I couldn't."

"I understand." I didn't, really. There was a whole lot that had to be explained. But more than anything, I wanted to give Scarlett whatever she needed. "You didn't tell me yet if you're okay."

"Hurt my hand. And I've got a killer headache. But yeah, I'm okay. You found me. You came back."

I kissed her hair, her forehead, her nose. Whatever I could reach. "I told you. I'll always find you. And now, I'm going to take you home."

Except we couldn't go home just yet.

Owen and a couple of his deputies took Liam to the station to book him. Scarlett did her interview, recounting everything that Liam—or rather, Kenny Witkins—had told her. How he'd escaped from the compound. How he'd seen Scarlett at the sweet shop by chance. Stalked her by night while he worked as the Last Refuge construction foreman by day.

When I heard about his sick plans for Scarlett, I was glad the guy was behind bars and not within my reach. Because I would've enjoyed strangling him.

But Owen had searched Kenny at the scene, and the man had been unarmed. Probably for the best I hadn't shot the guy. Aside from upsetting Scarlett, Owen wouldn't have appreciated writing that up in his official report.

For certain tasks, unofficial was a much better way to go. Not that Kenny would be finding that out. For Scarlett's sake, I would let the police handle him.

We swung by the hospital to get Scarlett checked out, since she'd been drugged. She'd also banged up her hand by punching Kenny. She needed a splint and icing for the swelling. Then finally, River drove us back to Scarlett's house. Aiden was already there with Jessi, who'd stayed with Virtue the whole time. Deputy Marsh and her little sister Stephie, Virtue's friend, were here too. The moment we pulled up to the house, Virtue ran out to meet us.

There were tears. So many hugs.

Virtue wanted to know everything. Scarlett and I both had to censor our stories a bit, but Virtue got the gist. She was safe now. Both Dawson and his accomplice weren't going to bother her again.

That night, the three of us didn't let go of each other for more than five minutes at a time. Bathroom breaks. That was about it. Our friends stayed for dinner, but eventually everyone else left. Scarlett, Virtue and I spread out every available blanket and sleeping bag in the living room and we bedded down right there, the girl in the middle. After Virtue had drifted off, Scarlett and I watched each other over her head.

"I love you," I whispered.

Scarlett didn't say it back, but her expression said plenty. "Thank you for everything. And especially for coming home."

I reached across Virtue to take Scarlett's hand. "I'm going to get Toby next. As soon as I'm able. But after the kids are settled…there's more I need to do. For myself."

"I know. I will support you in any way you need. Just let me know."

The next day, River had to head back to the East Coast. But a couple of days later, I got word from Owen. Every law enforcement agency and media outlet in Colorado had received anonymous documents linking Paradise Ranch to the trafficking of underage girls.

The news created a firestorm. Soon, authorities and social services had descended on the compound. The elders who hadn't fled gave themselves up peacefully. Multiple other adults, including Mercy—who'd been Scarlett's sort-of step-mother—were arrested as well for their involvement in covering up child exploitation.

But Dawson Witkins? He had disappeared. Nobody at the compound had any clue where he'd gone. Not even his wives. There was speculation that Dawson had advance notice of the police raid. Maybe even that he'd been involved in that anonymous tipoff himself.

Those of us who knew the truth certainly weren't telling.

Finally, I got a text from Toby, asking for us to pick him up. Exactly what we'd been waiting for.

The three of us drove out to Creekview. Toby was waiting there in town with a social worker. Owen had put in a good word for us and helped pull some strings. It had made all the difference that Virtue was already staying with us. There would be court hearings and other legal stuff at some point, but that wasn't my expertise.

There were more hugs. More tears. Toby was thrilled to finally meet Scarlett in person. Then he turned to me.

"Thank you. Thank you for taking care of my sister."

"Happy to," I murmured. "You helped a lot. Couldn't have done it without you."

I wished I could tell him exactly how much he'd helped. Toby's intel had made it possible for us to stop Dawson and for River to plant the malware that revealed the compound's secrets. I held out my hand to shake, but the kid turned that into another hug.

"Now it's your turn to be smothered, Toby," Virtue said. "Get ready for some helicoptering."

Scarlett laughed and put a hand on Toby's back. "We're all going to take care of each other."

The season's first snow fell in early November.

And then it snowed again. And again.

Scarlett was all about getting Virtue and Toby into a routine. Toby started at the middle school, and I took over driving him and his sister to school in the mornings. It took some convincing, but Scarlett finally agreed to let them walk home afterward. Sometimes they stopped by Jessi's Diner to hang out with friends and do homework.

Today, after dropping off the kids at school, I drove up to Last Refuge to check on the latest construction. They were wrapping up the first phase of work on the restaurant. Just in time too, since Jessi wanted to open before the end of the year.

Skyler was there, now working as the project foreman. An improvement over the previous foreman at least. He and Scarlett had smoothed things over. He understood why she'd freaked out on him when he'd pulled out those Ashfair Menthols. Skyler was as horrified as anyone that Liam had turned out to be a crazed stalker and cult member who wanted to force Scarlett to be his wife.

Still, Skyler hadn't visited the sweet shop again. That was fine with me. I'd never liked the guy much anyway.

When I got back to the house, Scarlett's Jeep was already parked outside. She had one of her employees handling the sweet shop today.

"I'm home," I said, sliding off my boots by the front door.

I passed through the living room, which was doing double-duty as Toby's bedroom. He'd been sleeping on the couch, and I'd been with Scarlett in her bed. The nightmare thing still made me nervous, though it had only been an issue a couple of times. Scarlett had done as I'd asked, not waking me. We'd been getting through it.

Some days, everything in my head got to be too much for me. When that happened, I went up to my cabin at Last Refuge. I always came back as soon as I could. There wasn't some magic solution. But I knew I could do more to meet my own needs. And I would. Very soon.

Aside from that, the four of us had been getting along great, despite the serious lack of space. Every day was different. Especially with two teenagers in the mix. The strangest part to me was how much I loved it. This fledgling family of ours.

It was a big commitment. Jessi was still shocked that we were doing this, even though she heartily approved. But Scarlett and I had talked it through. She was going to try to adopt the kids, depending on how difficult the legal process was. And

I was going to be right there by her side. I'd adopt them too, if that needed to happen. Hell, I would marry her if that was what she wanted. The legal details would figure themselves out. I didn't care so much about whether we were "official."

I just knew I cared about Scarlett and the kids. They needed me. And I needed them.

Scarlett was singing in the kitchen. She had ear buds in, back to me, hips swaying as she sang along with the music. I had to stop and watch her for a minute. And listen, too. I loved her voice. Scarlett was still shy about singing in front of others. She indulged me on occasion. But I liked moments like this one, too. Just getting to watch her. Because she was mine, and I was hers, and that meant I was entitled to a *tiny* bit of spying.

I walked up behind her. "Hi," I said, not wanting to scare her.

She pulled an ear bud free, smiling over her shoulder. "Hi."

I wrapped my arms around her waist. Then I noticed what was on the counter. Two slices of chocolate cake. "I thought you wanted us to have lunch together," I said.

"This is it. Don't tell Virtue and Toby." She handed me a plate. "We can have real food later. But this is one of those days I need dessert for lunch."

"Hey, it's good by me. You know I love my sweets. What prompted such a dire need for cake?"

She shrugged, scooping icing onto her fork. "Dealing with teenagers. This too-small house. Running a small business. The usual."

Neither of us brought up the fact that I was leaving tomorrow.

We fed each other cake. Scarlett had made it, so it was amazing. And better yet, when I kissed her, she tasted like chocolate. "We'll have the house to ourselves for a few hours," I said.

"I've been counting on it." Her gaze turned heated.

I took Scarlett to her room. *Our* room. She reached for her shirt, but I covered her hands with mine. "Let me."

I undressed her. Laid her on the bed and kissed all her curves. Her breasts, hips. Hills and valleys. Scarlett's body was my favorite place to explore. Always something new to learn.

How could I ever get enough of this? Her moans as I spread her legs and worked my tongue into the center of her. The way she quivered and threaded her fingers into my hair.

And then, when I stripped down and slid my cock inside of her. Every time was like coming home. Where I belonged.

Our tongues danced and our bodies moved together. Drawing out the pleasure at first, and then hard and rough and fast. We were wild for each other. Loud enough, it was possible the neighbors heard. *Good*. I was laying my claim. So there was no mistake, even while I was gone. *This one's mine*.

We curled up on the mattress afterward. Scarlett smiled languidly. It was her blissful post-orgasm face. Looked damn good on her.

We had the afternoon to ourselves, so we stayed naked in bed and talked about nothing for a while. The heater ran, keeping us toasty warm beneath the blankets. I wasn't moving. Not even for real food. The cake would have to do.

"We really need a bigger place," she said.

My fingers brushed up and down her collarbone. "We can look for one when I'm back."

Her eyes tightened at the mention of my trip. "I could rent this one out, if I can find someone who's interested. I've always loved this house. My adoptive parents left it to me. One year we repainted it, and they let me pick out the yellow for the siding myself."

"We could stay here and build an addition instead. If you don't want to leave."

She made a face. "No construction workers. It's an honorable profession, but after my experience lately? No thank you. I need some time."

I chuckled with her. But that reminded me of something I'd been wondering.

"Why do you think Kenny took you to Last Refuge that day?" We'd spoken many times now about Kenny and what had happened. I knew it didn't bother her to ask about it.

She snuggled into me. "At some point he must've heard me and Jessi mention her real purpose for Last Refuge. Not just the hotel or restaurant, but a safe place for people who need it. As messed up as Kenny was, he must've longed for that, deep down. A refuge. It's why he was willing to go so far to get his old life back at the compound. His fantasy version, anyway. He felt abandoned. It makes me want to shelter Virtue and Toby all the more. So they always know they're loved."

My sweet, wonderful Scarlett. "I'm sure they know. They couldn't ask for a better parent than you."

"And you." Her eyes went damp as they searched mine. "The kids are going to miss you while you're gone. So will I."

Tomorrow, I'd head back to Virginia. I'd been in touch with a former commanding officer of mine. A man I hadn't spoken to in years, but I respected him. I'd called him up, asking for his advice. Begging, really. He'd told me to come stay with him for a while so we could talk. I planned to visit River as well. Maybe see some of our old friends.

I was going to face things I'd been avoiding for way too long.

Getting myself where I wanted to be was a process. It would take more than a weeks-long trip. But this would be the start I needed. A *real* clean slate. Not just running to a new place, like I'd done when I'd arrived in Hartley. But grappling with my past.

"I'm sorry to leave you," I said.

"Don't be. Trace, I love you. I believe in you. And I'll be waiting for you. We all will, as long as it takes. Even if I *really* hope you'll be home by Christmas."

"That's the plan. Christmas in Hartley. I need to bring the Dad energy. But can we go back to the part where you said you love me? I'd like to enjoy that for a sec."

She rolled on top of me. Kissed me. "I love you. I really do."

"Oh, babe. I love you too." My hands slid down to squeeze her ass cheeks. "And I really love all this T and A you've got going." I grunted.

She snorted a laugh. "Just when I thought you were civilized."

"Never."

Our mouths slotted together. A few more kisses. Memories to take with me. But not the last. So far from the last. We had a lifetime of memories ahead of us. And I couldn't wait to get started.

Epilogue

Scarlett
Christmas Day

"Do you guys want marshmallows with your cocoa?" I asked.

They looked at me like I'd lost my mind.

"You're right, foolish question."

I finished up our mugs with piles of mini-marshmallows, adding a candy cane to each before I tucked the mugs onto my tray. I was about to carry them into the living room, but Toby appeared and picked up the tray. He looked festive in his plaid flannel pajamas. "C'mon, Scarlett," he said. "We're about to start the movie."

In the living room, Trace lounged on the couch as Virtue fiddled with the TV remote. Toby handed out cocoa mugs. Then the kids stretched out on the floor, while I snuggled into Trace's side.

"What're we watching?" I asked.

"Miracle on 34th Street," Virtue announced. "The original black-and-white, of course."

Trace arched his eyebrows at me. "Of *course*."

The title credits appeared. Remnants of wrapping paper

were strewn over the rug, and colored lights blinked on the tree. A fire crackled in my fireplace. My house smelled like evergreen, chocolate, and spices.

Best Christmas morning ever, I decided.

The very best part was that we were here together. All four of us.

Virtue hadn't decided on her new name yet, but she had settled into school. As it turned out, she'd discovered classic films lately, and already had a long list assembled to educate me on the history of cinema. She had very strong opinions on the subject. Toby's start in school had been as rocky as his older sister's, but he'd made friends and joined the Nordic skiing club.

And Trace was here. *Home*.

While the kids were focused on the movie, he trailed soft kisses over my neck. He was wearing a Santa hat with the white puff-ball hanging over one eyebrow. "Hi," he whispered. "Think they'll notice if we sneak away?"

I turned and smiled. "Yes. You know they will."

Trace had returned to Hartley after a month of visiting friends on the East Coast. He had regular Zoom appointments with a therapist skilled in treating veterans, and he'd said that he felt solid about his progress. His energy and demeanor seemed lighter now than ever before. Smiles coming more easily. Not as many nightmares.

And since arriving at home, his sex drive had been *insatiable*. Stamina indeed.

We'd been getting naked at every available opportunity. With two teenagers who loved hanging around this house during their winter break, those opportunities had been too rare.

But I just loved having him around. His kisses and sweet words. The way he welcomed my touch and the comfort we gave each other.

Trace shifted on the couch, pulling a small box from his jeans pocket. "One more delivery from Santa. Sorry about the bow."

The red ribbon was crushed, but it was still the sweetest thing I'd ever seen. "We weren't supposed to get each other gifts."

He shrugged. "Since when do I follow the rules?"

I pulled the ribbon free and opened the lid. What I saw inside made my chest squeeze and my breath skip. "Trace. It's beautiful."

He picked up the chain and worked the clasp, placing it around my neck. I lifted my hair. It was a necklace with four silver hearts in a row, each linked to the next. He hooked the clasp, fingers brushing up and down my neck after he was finished. "You like it?"

"I love it." Tears burned my eyes and nose. I turned my head to kiss him, brushing that ridiculous puff-ball out of the way. "I love you so much."

"*Ew,*" Virtue said without looking back. "Stop disrespecting the cinematic experience."

"I'm glad she doesn't know what teenagers used to do in the backs of movie theaters," Trace whispered in my ear.

Laughing, I snuggled my face into his neck.

"Merry Christmas, babe."

I smiled against his skin. "Merry Christmas."

After the movie, a brunch of pumpkin-spice French toast, and far more candy than could be advisable before noon, we got dressed and headed up to Last Refuge.

Snow dusted the evergreens with white, and smoke curled from the chimneys of the tavern. We parked, and Toby and

Virtue dashed out. Virtue had on a hideous sweater with bells all over it, so she jingled with every step.

Inside, mellow Christmas music played. The restaurant was draped in greenery. I inhaled the warm air, soaking in the aromas of roasting turkey and cinnamon as happy voices met my ears. Virtue and Toby carried our dishes for the potluck into the main dining room, while Trace lingered with me in the entryway.

"You good?" he asked.

I knew what he was thinking. That I might have reservations about having Christmas dinner at Last Refuge given what had happened here with Kenny. But I'd been up here several times since then, including a week ago for the restaurant's soft opening.

No place was entirely free of bad memories. We carried those with us whether we liked it or not. But they got easier when we were surrounded by people we loved.

I went onto my toes to kiss my handsome man. "I'm very happy. Promise."

"Me too." Trace touched my neck to adjust my new necklace, making sure the hearts were symmetrical. "Want to meet me in a cabin in ten minutes? I'll strip you down and get you all toasty warm..."

I groaned quietly. Trace had moved his belongings out of his cabin and into my house now that we were officially living together. But I guessed he still knew where Jessi kept the keys. "Don't tempt me. You have a one-track mind."

"Guilty."

"Come on. Let's go be social."

Trace pretended to frown, but he let me drag him into the dining room, where our friends had gathered for today's private event. Keira and Stephie Marsh were here with their parents. Owen and Marco chatted by the punch bowl, and others sat at the tables. I spied Aiden in the kitchen.

Trace gave me a peck on the cheek. "I'll go see if Aiden needs help with…something."

"Go for it." It was no surprise that he wanted to hide out in the kitchen with the other resident grump. Those two men could happily hang out for hours and barely say three words to one another. Even though Trace was healthier and happier these days, those aspects of him hadn't changed.

I found Jessi arranging the food on the buffet table. She was decked-out in a poinsettia apron and elf hat. "Merry Christmas," I said. "Need anything?"

"A drink." She hooked her arm through mine and dragged me behind the bar. Jessi poured us each a glass of red wine, and we clinked them together. "Well, here we are," she said. "We really did it."

"*You* did it."

"No, it took everyone here." She sighed as she looked around the dining room. At the tables, the decorations. Our smiling friends and found family. The tavern was simple, but the whole place sparkled today.

Construction wasn't finished yet. Now that the restaurant was open, the next stage would be an addition for the inn. A few of the cabins with wood stoves were available to vacationers now—or to Trace and me, if I agreed to be bad with him and sneak away later—and the rest would be fixed up in time for spring.

And of course, if anyone needed housing for more dire reasons, they'd find help at Last Refuge too. We hadn't had any new cases yet. For a while, I'd thought others from Paradise Ranch might end up needing our help. But it hadn't happened that way.

Kenny was awaiting trial in the county lockup, along with the Paradise Ranch elders and their accomplices who hadn't made bail. But many of the residents had decided to stay at the compound, including my sisters and most of my brothers at the bachelor house. As it had turned out, plenty of people at the compound had wanted change, but they'd been afraid to speak up. Now, they had the chance to make Paradise Ranch into a better place for all who still lived there.

After the new year, I planned to take Virtue and Toby back to the compound for a visit with their family and friends. I had mixed feelings about it, but I knew the trip was important for them. Trace would definitely come with us. That was nonnegotiable.

But most importantly, the four of us felt secure in our new family. Virtue and Toby's parents had agreed to relinquish their rights. The kids wanted to be with me and Trace permanently. Our four hearts, linked together into a single unit.

I touched the chain of my necklace and smiled.

"Trace looks good since he got back," Jessi said. "Better rested. More smiles."

"I think so too. He misses River, though. River promised to come visit again when he can."

"Obviously he's welcome any time. After he solved my financing hitch? He's going to eat and drink free here for life. Both here and the diner."

"I'm sure he'll appreciate that." From what I'd seen of River, the man could eat.

But I wouldn't be the one serving up meals at the diner. After considering Jessi's offer to take co-ownership, I'd decided to turn her down. I had more than enough going on with two teenagers at home.

Jessi gave me a side-hug, her gaze studying me. "I'm glad you're comfortable being here at Last Refuge after what happened."

"I am. More than anything, this place makes me think of how Trace found me that day. Aiden, Owen, River. They all came to help me. And you were there for Virtue. We started out talking about Last Refuge like it would be a safe oasis, away from the rest of the world. But it's not. Nothing can be."

"That's why we need our Protectors. They're the real Last Refuge." Jessi winked. "Just don't tell them that. Those men have confidence enough as it is."

We both laughed and clinked our glasses again.

Aiden and Trace were our Protectors, but we fiercely protected them too. Their hearts and happiness and wellbeing. That didn't mean a perfect absence of danger or heartache. It meant we defended and cared for each other. No matter how messy and imperfect it might get.

But when we made it to the other side, this was our reward. Love and laughter and holiday sparkle. Our family. Our joy.

Trace

Owen lifted his chin, looking past my shoulder. "You have a visitor," he said.

"Me?"

We'd finished dinner, and Aiden had pulled out a bottle of 18-year, double cask Macallan. He, Owen and I had gathered around the far corner of the bar, sipping scotch and reflecting on a year nearly past. Almost a full year since Aiden and I had separately arrived in Hartley. Almost a year since I'd met Scarlett, though it had taken me way too long to get my head out of my ass.

My trip east had gone as well as I could've hoped. Talking through what had happened to me, both with my mentor and with River, had been tough. I'd hated every second of it. Yet I'd made it through, and the experience had been freeing. Like I'd let go of some small pieces of those jagged, broken parts of me. The cuts didn't go so deep anymore. It was day by day. Night by night. But I had support now. I had strategies, more than just disappearing into the woods. The key one being the acceptance of Scarlett's love and support.

I was healing. I was proud of my progress, but I gave Scarlett most of the credit. Simply because she hadn't given up on me, and she'd given me all the reasons not to give up on myself.

On this Christmas Day, I had everything I could need right here around me. So the last thing I had expected was a visitor. But when I turned around, I found my best friend shaking snow off his jacket in the restaurant's entryway.

"Holy shit. *River*? What're you doing in Hartley?" I strode over and gave him a back-slapping hug. I didn't have to ask how River had known we were at Last Refuge. I had my phone with me. For River, that was enough.

"Had to bring your Christmas present. This one's best delivered in person."

I brought River to the bar, where Aiden poured him a glass of scotch. "Have you eaten?" Aiden asked.

"No, man. I'm starved. Drove straight here after I landed in Grand Junction."

"I'll make you a plate." Aiden went to the kitchen, while River toasted me and Owen. Merry Christmases all around.

"It's great to see you," I said.

"This is a much better reception than my last arrival in Hartley."

I shrugged. "You did say you'd brought me a gift."

"You know me. I never arrive empty-handed." He took out his phone, unlocked the screen, and handed it to me with a press release already pulled up. It described the imminent retirement of two government officials after their *long, distinguished careers of service*.

I recognized these names.

These were two of my Agency superiors I'd suspected of betraying me. The names I had given to River the last time he was in Hartley.

"Is this what I think it is?" I asked.

He leaned in, dropping his voice to a whisper. "I told you I'd find the proof. I would've preferred making the truth public. But you know how these things go. At least they're done within the Agency. Forced into retirement. Pensions cancelled."

Not quite justice. But more than I'd ever expected. "Thank you. This was a big risk for you."

He took a generous sip of Macallan. "Doesn't matter. I'm done with the Agency, too. I've had enough. I'm out. In fact, I'm done with DC."

I held my friend's gaze.

Owen leaned his elbows on the bar top. He'd overheard some of our conversation, not that River or I minded. "What're you planning to do next?" Owen asked.

Aiden returned with a plate, piled high with prime rib, turkey, dressing, and green beans. River thanked him, then looked from Aiden to Owen to me. "I heard there might be a gig available here. Are the Last Refuge Protectors still looking to add to the team?"

"It doesn't pay well," Aiden said. "In fact, it pays nothing."

"I'll survive. But I get to be Supreme Commander, right?"

Aiden lifted an eyebrow in my direction. I enjoyed a swallow of scotch. "Sorry Riv, that job's already taken," I said. "You can be head computer nerd."

He laughed, scooping dressing onto his fork. "I'll take it." Then he pointed his fork at Owen. "What about you, Sheriff? Have you officially joined the Protectors yet?"

Owen frowned around the lip of his glass. "Let's keep it off the books. There are some things I can't know. Like what really happened to Dawson Witkins. Very mysterious, how he suddenly disappeared from Paradise Ranch without word to any of his family or friends, never to be heard from again."

The rest of us did our best to look innocent. Probably wasn't too convincing, because Owen shook his head, covering up a smirk. "There's some investigative journalist out of Denver who's been on my ass lately, asking questions about Witkins and Paradise Ranch. And also the other controversies we've had in Hartley the past year. She claims some of the reports out of the sheriff's department leave out key details. That they don't make sense."

Aiden rested his hands on the bar. "Is this the same journalist who wrote those articles about Hartley already, accusing your department of wrongdoing?"

Owen nodded. "The same. Genevieve Blake." He spit out the name in disgust. "She's the type who has it out for law enforcement. I'm handling it to the extent my office legally allows me, but just wanted to give you all a heads up. If Blake has her way, the Protectors' activities might not stay quiet for long. Which would obviously be a problem for all of us."

"Maybe you should ask her out," River suggested. "Sweet talk her. Lay on some of that hometown Hartley charm."

"That's not going to work. I couldn't find a picture online, but from her voice on the phone, she seems like a battle axe out for blood. She's vicious." He shivered.

Aiden reached across the bar to put a hand on Owen's shoulder. "No matter what happens, Sheriff, we've got your back."

Owen sighed. "And I've got yours. Not because you're my friends, but because I believe in what you're doing."

"To Last Refuge." River lifted his glass. "And to finding a place to call home."

We all drank to that.

After a while, the rest of my family wandered over. Jessi and Scarlett were thrilled to see River, and even more thrilled when they learned he was moving permanently to Hartley. Virtue remembered him from his last trip here, and she was excited to introduce Toby, who hadn't met him yet.

"River is a computer wizard," Virtue told her brother, and Toby's eyes lit up. "And like, a super spy."

River grinned. "I'll show you all my tricks."

"Don't teach them anything that'll get them arrested," I warned my friend.

"So I should make sure they know how to cover their tracks. Got it."

Aiden poured scotch for the adults, spiced cider for the kids. More of our friends gravitated to the bar to join us. We talked and laughed while Christmas music played. Then Virtue clanged a spoon against her mug of cider.

"Everyone, I have an announcement. I've decided on my new name. It's going to be Vivian."

There were lots of congratulations, but Virtue—Vivian—came to Scarlett and me for a hug first. Toby joined in. My chest puffed up with pride.

Scarlett and the kids meant everything to me. When this year had begun, I never could've imagined I'd end up here. Living this rich life with a family of my own. A family I'd defend and love with every fiber of my being.

I had something to defend. But more than that, I had people to *live* for, in every sense of that word.

Eventually, Scarlett and I were able to sneak away. But we didn't go far. Just to a secluded corner of the restaurant. I pulled Scarlett into my arms, and we swayed to "Have Yourself a Merry Little Christmas." She sang along in a low, sultry voice. Man, it turned me on when she sang like that. Just for me.

"Guess what," Scarlett whispered. "Jessi offered to take the kids tonight. They're going to have a sleepover here at Last Refuge. She sent Aiden to get a bunch of sleeping bags."

I hummed, anticipating having Scarlett to myself tonight. In *our* bed. One of my favorite places to have my way with her. "I want you wearing the necklace I gave you. And nothing else."

"Sounds just right to me. I want you in nothing but that Santa hat."

I growled and twirled her around as a new song came on. Then pulled her even closer.

"I've been thinking," I said. "I don't want to move out of your house. The kids love it, and you love it. We should stay there. But I'm going to build an addition myself."

"You?"

"I'm a fast learner, and I've always been good with my hands. For anything I can't handle, I'll hire someone. But I will manage every aspect of it. As long as you're comfortable with that. And if it goes well, I can do what I need to get licensed as a contractor and make it my day job."

She bit her lower lip, looking up at me. "I trust you. And I'm sure you can do anything if you set your mind to it. But what about the Protectors?"

"That'll come first. But my job as a Protector doesn't pay. I know you're killing it with the sweet shop and your online orders, but I'm going to contribute to our family."

"I do like the idea of you waiting at home for me, though." Her hands trailed down to my butt and squeezed. "My very own sexy, rugged mountain man."

"I'm more than a piece of meat, Scarlett."

She snickered. "Sorry, you're right. You're an independent man. I don't own you."

"No, that's where you're wrong." I bent to brush my lips over hers. "You own every part of me. This is all yours if you want it. Especially my heart."

"You own my heart, too." She threaded her fingers into my hair as we kissed, and the music played, and just for a little while, the world was nothing more than this. Last Refuge. Our friends and our beautiful family. Warm and safe and ours.

Owen's story is next in HOME TOWN KNIGHT, coming in 2024.

A Note from Hannah

Thank you so much for reading Trace and Scarlett's story! This one took me in some directions I wasn't expecting. It turned out that Trace and Scarlett needed more than just each other for their happily ever after. They needed Virtue and Toby too. (And vice versa). They've experienced dark times, which I did feel was necessary to be authentic to these characters and their histories, but their little family has many years of goodness and happiness ahead of them.

Now that Trace has fully accepted his role as the leader of the Protectors, and they've added River into the mix, what's next? It's Owen's turn. He's a hometown knight who's done his best to protect his citizens. But Owen meets his match when Genevieve, a fierce investigative reporter, comes to Hartley and needs a Protector of her own.

Until next time!

-Hannah

Also by Hannah Shield

Last Refuge Protectors

Hard Knock Hero (Aiden & Jessi)

Bent Winged Angel (Trace & Scarlett)

Home Town Knight (Owen & Genevieve)

- And more coming soon -

West Oaks Heroes

The Six Night Truce (Janie & Sean)

The Five Minute Mistake (Madison & Nash)

The Four Day Fakeout (Jake & Harper)

The Three Week Deal (Matteo & Angela)

The Two Last Moments (Danny & Lark)

The One for Forever (Rex & Quinn) - Coming soon

Bennett Security

Hands Off (Aurora & Devon)

Head First (Lana & Max)

Hard Wired (Sylvie & Dominic)

Hold Tight (Faith & Tanner)

Hung Up (Danica & Noah)

Have Mercy (Ruby & Chase)

About the Author

Hannah Shield writes steamy, suspenseful romance with pulse-pounding action, fun & flirty banter, and tons of heart. She lives in the Colorado mountains with her family.

Visit her website at www.hannahshield.com.

Made in United States
North Haven, CT
31 December 2023

46872138R00190